FARAWAY RIVERS

Patricia Kelly Polewski

ATHENA PRESS
LONDON

FARAWAY RIVERS
Copyright © Patricia Kelly Polewski 2003

All Rights Reserved

No part of this book may be reproduced in any form
by photocopying or by any electronic or mechanical means,
including information storage or retrieval systems,
without permission in writing from both the copyright
owner and the publisher of this book.

ISBN 1 932077 63 4

First Published 2003 by
ATHENA PRESS
Queen's House, 2 Holly Road
Twickenham TW1 4EG
United Kingdom

Printed for Athena Press

FARAWAY RIVERS

Contents

Prologue	7
Étienne's Question	9
Paris to New France	19
Visit to the Montagnais	34
Scurvy	42
Iroquois War – 1609	48
Ochateguin's Hurons	54
Champlain's Request – July 1615	73
Huronia to Carantouan	80
Captured	99
Seneca Village	112
Alone to Huronia	117
Huron Romance	128
Huron Wedding	138
Wedding Feast	152
Nipissings	155
Manitoulin	172
Trois Rivières – 1618	183
Le Grand Lac – 1623	196

Peace Mission	234
Fall of Québec	258
His Death	282
Marsolet's Letter	291

Prologue

In the spring of 1608, the Hundred Years War between France and England had been over for a century and a half. England's James I reigned with a firm hand, the strength of the royal treasury, and the support of most of the nobility. France had an empty treasury and so many internal problems over religion that it was in a poor position to contest England for anything, and certainly not Spain.

The French King, Henry IV, sometimes ate in other people's homes because there was no food in his own, and he always had to be on guard against uprisings of both Huguenots and Catholics. The French peasants suffered serious want.

Frenchmen had been going to the New World since before Cartier visited in 1525 and found fishermen from Normandy already at the Newfoundland Banks. Along with the Normans were Basques, many of whom spoke both Spanish and French. They told stories of the wonders seen by the Spanish conquistadors in Mexico and South America. Some French sailors had already sailed on Spanish vessels, among them Samuel Champlain, later called The Father of Canada.

The stories of Spanish conquests and exploration were soon recounted in every village in France. These tales kindled hopes and desires in men who found no

Prologue

opportunities at home. But France did not have the navies of England and Spain, and there wasn't money in the French treasury to encourage exploration and trade.

Into this bleak picture came the French fur trade. Wealthy nobles were outfitting ships and hiring captains and crews to go to New France to barter for the beaver pelts that were so much in demand in Europe to make men's hats. Great wealth was possible in the fur trade, and it didn't depend on armies and navies.

In France there were people like Champlain who were eager to explore and longed to find a route through the continent to the Far East. Neither France nor England had Spain's intense desire to convert the natives, but the desire to spread Christianity was certainly a factor in France, too. It was always important to Champlain.

Peasants and laborers, who had scarcely dreamed of farms of their own, heard of empty lands to be settled. Étienne Brulé, a sixteen-year-old peasant heard these tales of adventure and of possibilities for great wealth. He would become the first white man to learn Algonquin and Huron–Iroquois. It was his strength and daring that paved the way for the fur trade as far west as the Upper Peninsula of Michigan. His ability to live among both Algonquins and Hurons made possible the extraordinary feat of being the first white man to explore each of the five Great Lakes – and he did it all in a birchbark canoe.

Étienne's Question

The last notes of the evening Angelus were fading across the fields as the farmers returned to the little French village of Champigny. It was early spring in 1608, the ground was too wet for planting, but they had cleared the fields and prepared the soil for a new season. Smoke was rising from the chimneys and women were preparing to serve the evening soup.

All was as it should be, and yet Étienne Brulé felt ill at ease, dissatisfied, confused. The recent death of his parents made him wonder whether a young man of sixteen should still be taking time from the ever-present work on the farm to study history, geography and mathematics. But here he was, ready for another lesson from the village pastor.

The mud lay heavy on his wooden shoes, so he knocked off most of it and left the sabots at the door of the rectory that was also the only school he had ever known. Because the shutters had not been closed for the day, Étienne could easily see Father Treguer straightening up papers on his desk and carrying pens and ink over to the table where he gave lessons.

"Bonsoir, mon père."

"Come in, come in, my son! How are you and your dear sister doing on the farm?"

Étienne shrugged his still boyish shoulders and said, "Things are improving, Father. My sister is learning to

Étienne's Question

cook better and I seem to be able to do the chores more like my father. My Uncle Paul moved in to help us now that our parents are gone. I can hardly believe they are dead. It seems that they were well, then they were sick, and a day later, they were dead."

"This year's sickness took many of our parishioners. A very bad year." The old priest sighed as he finished clearing a space at the rectory table for the lesson.

"When you go home tonight, stop in the kitchen and take the white and green bundle on the table with you. It is full of asparagus; it can be boiled and eaten with salt and butter. Henry IV may be a Huguenot now and then, but he is the first king I have ever heard of who encourages farmers to grow and sell vegetables! He does as much as he can without the support he needs from the great lords. The French crown, Étienne, is more a crown of thorns than anything else. They tell me that Henry is once again without funds and the nobility won't help because they distrust him. Reasonable, I suppose. Many of them remember starving in Paris when he lay siege to it. Ah well, we must hope for the best."

"Well, if the great Catholic lords won't help, perhaps the Huguenots will," Étienne suggested hopefully.

"No, the rich Huguenots do not care what the peasants eat, or don't eat. For them, all must be profit. They find it hard to trust Henry because he is a Catholic once again. Meanwhile, the poor peasant has help from neither Catholic nobility nor Huguenot merchants. Still, we all have our troubles, and this life is always a vale of tears." He changed the subject

Étienne's Question

abruptly to one they could deal with, and asked, "Are you able to make cheese yet, my boy?"

"Oui, mon père, I haven't ruined any in weeks, and Catherine hasn't served burned eggs for days. Even the horse has stopped trying to kick me! Thank you for the asparagus. I sampled some once before. Very good! Easy to remember the name, just like the beginning of mass when the priest sprinkles the people with holy water, the Asperges."

"Perhaps we could all ask to be blessed and forgiven when we eat the vegetable! Now where were we when you had to stop your lessons after your mother and father were called to be with our Lord?"

I was studying New World geography and French history, Father. We were using those two books that the Bishop lent you. You were teaching me mathematics, so that I can chart a course at sea, or gauge distance. I have forgotten some things that I really need to know well."

"We'll get out the maps and globe and go back to working with them. I cannot go much farther with mathematics. You would need to go to Paris or Salamanca, Spain to have good mathematics teachers, but the basics of arithmetic we can still work on. I was sorry at first that you do not have a vocation for the priesthood. But I understand now that your inquiring mind will be used by God in other ways."

"I sometimes wonder what that could possibly be, since I have no interest in farming and that is the only work available. Unless you count that I make cheese."

"Certainly, I count that!"

Étienne's Question

"What I really want to do is so out of the question, I can hardly speak of it."

"Oh, speak of it anyway. Sometimes, when we talk about things, we understand ourselves better."

"Don't laugh, mon père, but what I really would like to do is go exploring with le Sieur de Champlain. He is in Paris now and is recruiting young men he thinks will be able to learn the languages of the people there and help in the fur trade. Without knowing the languages of those people, it is not possible to convert them either."

"No, it certainly is not. But how do you know that Champlain is in Paris?"

"Uncle Paul and I took a barge load of cheese over there and we talked to some sailors who were going to Honfleur with Champlain. They will sail soon for New France. They told us that he has already recruited some boys of my age. One is Nicholas Marsolet, he's from Rouen. I don't know why I remember his name, but I keep thinking that if Nicholas Marsolet can go, why can't Étienne Brulé?"

"Why not indeed?" said the priest with a slight chuckle.

"I have not mentioned this to anyone before, Father. Champlain is expected to be gone for a year. The sailors say that if any of the young men want to return then, they can. But the hope is that they will learn languages, live with the savages, and then be able to explain their way of life to the French already there. So the boys might be gone longer than a year if they are the help that Champlain hopes they will be. He is looking for boys who are orphans, and I certainly am

Étienne's Question

an orphan." Étienne paused and looked hesitantly at the priest.

The priest sputtered indignantly, "Looking for orphans, is he? You may be an orphan, but you are important to Catherine and Paul, and to tell the truth, you are very dear to me, too. I suppose he feels he can do whatever he wishes with you if you have no parents to complain."

Étienne laughed and tried to be reassuring, "I don't think that means he plans to feed us to the bears! After all, it costs a great deal to ship anything or anyone to New France. It probably means that he wants boys who really want to go, and not someone whose father wants him to go."

"Hmph, wants him to stay home, more likely. What would Catherine and Paul say if you told them all this?"

"I fear they would be against it. I can hardly blame them. There is too much work for the three of us as it is. Some days the cheese-making alone is a full-time job.

"Étienne, if that is their only problem, I know an experienced cheese maker who has no children and whose wife died last year. He is good-natured, easy to be around and he is lonely now. He would probably be glad to live out at your farm and help out. The priest paused a moment and reflected as he pushed his lower lip over his upper lip and back again. You told me once that Catherine does not have much of a dowry. Certainly le Sieur de Champlain expects to pay the young men he brings to New France! Perhaps you could save a large part of your wages for a dowry for

13

Étienne's Question

Catherine. That would make it easier for her to let you go, do you agree?"

"I don't know, mon père, but it is worth a try. Do you think you could come to Paris with me and tell Champlain that I really have had some studies and that I come from a decent family?" Étienne paused, smiled self-consciously at the priest and added, "And that I really am an orphan."

"I am not pleased with that requirement. But I will certainly tell him that you have studied history, geography and mathematics, and more important than anything else, I can tell him that I have instructed you for years in the truths of our holy religion. It can't hurt to tell him that you studied Latin, since he wants you to learn languages. Le Sieur de Champlain is said to be a fine Catholic in spite of being born into that hotbed of Huguenots at Brouage. I wonder why he was named Samuel? Even that sounds Huguenot to me. But then, he certainly must work for Huguenots if he expects to do any exploring at all in New France."

"So then, you will come with me!"

"Yes, if Catherine and Paul are willing to let you leave the farm for a year or two. I know you have always wanted to see the places we studied about, and you would be able to experience a sea voyage and learn what the natives in New France are like. I can go over with you on Monday after mass. We will return by Tuesday night. I need a new cassock. I should buy vestments with the money the widow Fontaner left for that purpose in her will. No one in the parish is sick unto death, so there is no reason why I couldn't be gone two days. I even have a friend from seminary

Étienne's Question

days who is at Saint Sulpice parish and I am sure we could spend the night at the rectory."

"That is far more than I hoped for, mon père. Thank you! I want to go home now and talk to Uncle Paul and Catherine. I can't concentrate on lessons now. I will come in tomorrow after we are through work for the day. You must make your plans, too."

"Yes, go and ask your family. God bless you, Étienne. If I am not here, leave a note with the housekeeper."

"Bonsoir! Mille remerciements!" Étienne picked up the bundle of asparagus in the kitchen, hurried out the door, shoved his feet into his wooden shoes and went off down the rutted and muddy lane toward his family farm. He thought it was important that Father Treguer had not acted as though his dream of going away for a year or two was strange. Perhaps Catherine and Paul wouldn't be as hard to convince as he had feared.

He ran much of the way back to the farm, not easy to do with the heavy mud making the already clumsy shoes even heavier. The excitement of telling his family what he planned was almost more than he could stand. The feeling that he longed to go, and the sense that perhaps he should not leave Catherine and the farm, made him anxious to get his question asked and answered.

The dog ran out to meet him barking excitedly, just as if he hadn't seen him a couple of hours before. Étienne scratched its head, patted him and had another gulp of emotion. He couldn't take the dog to New France either. He kicked off mud from his sabots and left them at the door of the farmhouse made of timbers and fieldstone.

Étienne's Question

Catherine was sitting at the table mending a sock and talking quietly with Paul as he repaired a harness. The light from the two fat candles on the table was hardly enough to work by, but their light softened the scene. The room was so familiar and so dear; his mother had made those candles, his father had traded cheese for the table and chairs. The crucifix on the wall had been on his grandfather's coffin before he was buried. Étienne took a deep breath.

"I have something I want to talk about to you." He recognized that his voice was trembling slightly, and he saw Paul and his sister exchange worried glances.

"No, it isn't anything to make either of you ashamed of me. I believe it is a great opportunity. It is something I truly want to do, but I suppose I won't if you are opposed."

He paused, and then added, "Our pastor will go to Paris with me to look into it more closely. Perhaps I could bring some of the cheese we have ready for sale?"

"I never object to anyone selling our cheese. But what great opportunity is that?" Paul looked perplexed and shook his head. "Have a good barge ride down to Paris and enjoy yourself!"

"Well, it isn't cheese so much. What I want to do is see le Sieur de Champlain. He is recruiting young men to go to New France with him. They are expected to learn native languages and help out in the fur trade. He wants only literate boys of about my age who are in good health and get along easily with people." That part was true enough, but he decided to skip the orphan requirement since that had not pleased the priest.

Étienne's Question

He could see that his enthusiasm had spilled over onto Paul, at least a little bit, but Catherine looked very sad and wiped her eyes with her apron.

"Oh Catherine, don't cry! In this village when boys leave home it is to go to sea as sailors or fishermen, or worse, they have to go off with one captain or another to a war. I'm not going to be on the sea long. Probably about a month. And no one is taking me off to battle. I would be exploring with the great le Sieur de Champlain! I would see places and learn things …and yes, I will be paid. I don't know how much, but I certainly want most of it to provide your dowry. That is something we have all worried about. What could I spend money on in New France? Perhaps a bear rug?"

"Bears! The woods are said to be full of them, and who knows what other wild animals all looking for food." With this doleful picture in her mind, Catherine began sobbing in earnest. "I want you here more than I want a fine dowry."

"Du calme, ma chère Catherine! I want to go, but if you believe that I am absolutely needed here, I won't leave."

"Oh, I suppose I can struggle along without you for a year," she said rather reluctantly. "I think by then you will want to come home." She put her arms around his neck, kissed him on the cheeks and held him in a tight embrace. "I'll even help you find the things you will need over there."

Paul, Catherine and Étienne talked and somehow it began to seem like a reasonable undertaking to all three of them. Paul went out to the cellar dug into the side of the hill next to the house and returned with a

Étienne's Question

pitcher of cold cider. "Every year we think we will have enough until cider making time again. And every year we are wrong. This is the last of it, but it is a great occasion. Étienne, go out to the dairy and bring us a round of cheese to go with it." Paul got out three glasses and poured the cider. He and Catherine talked excitedly while waiting for him to come back with the cheese.

Étienne put a sharp knife next to the cheese he had brought in. "We are all thinking that Champlain will take me with him, and we don't know that. Perhaps he will already have all the young men he needs. I will feel better about having the cheese to sell, it will make me feel less foolish. Father Treguer says he wants to buy vestments there too, so no one else need ever know why we really went to Paris. Oh, but I hope Champlain will choose me!"

Paris to New France

The cheese sold as soon as their barge landed at Paris; there was never a problem selling it there because it was something the sailors could have that wouldn't so easily go bad during the long voyages. With a few questions to the men on the dock, Champlain's ship was located. They walked over to it and Étienne almost held his breath as they asked to go up the gangplank to see the captain. A sailor went to ask if a priest and a young man might talk to him. Champlain came out on the deck and greeted the priest with great respect and Étienne with a pleasant, "I would guess this is a young man who wants to go to New France?"

"Oh yes, mon Sieur, I really do." Étienne almost had to swallow in the middle of those few words. Now, he thought to himself, Champlain will think I am tongue-tied. A great start for a would-be translator.

Father Treguer made things easier by talking about the studies Étienne had done, about his good Catholic family, and his desire to learn languages and see foreign places.

Champlain asked if the boy's family were agreeable to his leaving France. The priest stiffened somewhat but said, "Yes, they are willing since it is a great opportunity."

On their return to Champigny, Étienne was so excited that he talked more than he had in months.

Finally Father Treguer suggested an hour of meditation to calm him down.

★

Catherine and Paul were not surprised to learn he had been chosen. Uncle Paul bought several pairs of thick wool socks from a widow in town who sold knitted goods, and Catherine went to the fruit cellar and brought out the last of the fruit preserves their mother had made, wrapping the stoneware jars well in their father's heavy winter underwear.

"Grand Merci, Catherine! I never expected you to help me get ready! I was worried that you wouldn't want me to go."

"Well, that part is true. I don't want you to go, but I know how you feel. This is your chance, and I won't ruin it. If I were a boy, I'd want to go, too."

"I'll ask Champlain to bring my wages back with him if he returns before I do. He can leave the money with the priest friend of Father Treguer at San Sulpice rectory in Paris."

"Étienne, I'm not concerned about the money. I know I need a dowry, but we do have this farm and there are good men who would be glad to work the farm with me without my having anything more. I can get by with our mother's linens for quite some time. I have clothing and can use hers, too, if I can get someone to help me make dresses smaller. I want you to have the Agnus Dei medal that she always wore. Father Treguer took it from her neck before we buried her, and gave it to me. It must be yours now. Wear it

Paris to New France

always to remind you of your good home and family and of le bon Dieu who is with you always, although we cannot be." Catherine spoke firmly and enthusiastically, but Étienne heard the sadness in her voice as she took the medal on its black silk cord and draped it over his head. His hand instinctively went to the medal that now rested on his own chest. He caught his sister to him and stroked her hair.

"Ah, ma soeur, you will not be sorry you let me go. I will send you enough for a fine dowry! Do not choose anyone till I have been gone a year. By then, you will have more than we thought possible just last month."

"And if my heart tells me to choose earlier than that?" she asked coquettishly.

"Go right ahead and marry him! The money, when you get it, will help make the marriage last!"

Catherine laughed, "Spoken like a good peasant! Did Uncle Paul tell you that we are going with you to Paris? We will take our horse and cart and go straight to the house where Champlain said you should go when you saw him."

"I am glad you are both coming. We were lucky to get the cheesemaker, too. Without him, you and Paul couldn't come with me, not to mention that it will make things easier around here when I am gone. Now I'm going into town to say farewell to all my friends. I won't be home at midday, but I will be here for the evening soup." With that he left the kitchen, merrily singing, "A la Claire Fontaine." He knew he couldn't fool Catharine about his state of mind by singing, but singing always made things easier for him.

Paris to New France

In later years, in Huronia and in Québec, Étienne always said he couldn't remember a word that was said on the trip from home to Paris, but insisted that he could remember every tree, every cow in every field, and every friendly face that they passed on their journey.

★

After a last farewell to his sister and uncle, Étienne walked into the building where Champlain was to meet him. There was a servant at the door who informed him that le Sieur de Champlain was meeting with several important men and to please wait outside. It seemed like a bad start to Étienne, but taking his bag of clothing, he went outdoors again and looked for a likely spot to rest and wait.

He found a huge chestnut tree with soft grass all around it, put down his bundle of belongings and heard a voice from the other side of the tree asking courteously, "So, how are you? One of the translators, I would guess?"

"Yes, I am. And are you Nicholas Marsolet by any chance?"

The young man moved around the tree so they were facing each other. He gestured that Étienne should sit beside him and both sat with their backs against the tree trunk. "No, I am not Nicholas Marsolet. I'm Jean Girodet and I come from a farm near Paris. What is your name and where are you from, translator?"

"I am Étienne Brulé from Champigny, and it's

useless to consider me a translator because I know only French and some Latin, so far. It's a pleasure to meet you. I was getting uneasy, and I feel better having someone more or less my age who is going on the same ship."

"You are too kind! As for me, I am a common seaman who wants to sail with Champlain. Not that he has good ships. No, indeed. They are never much because he isn't rich. I doubt that this house belongs to him; probably lent to him by one of the merchants who pay for his voyages."

"So why sail with him?"

"I like an intelligent man with common sense better than a stupid one with a great ship at his command. I had that experience once and I didn't enjoy it. Champlain waits for the weather, always is on watch for pirates, and he is an experienced seaman himself."

"Does he know you are here, Jean?"

"He probably expects all of us to be here. Not Nicholas Marsolet. He is going straight to Honfleur and will meet us on board. He's from Rouen, no point in coming this way just to go back again. Do you know him?"

"No. I've only heard his name. Has he been in New France?"

"No, I think there are several who have never set foot on a ship before, about eight, I believe. There are twenty-eight of us in all, including Champlain. You will have a little bunk in the Captain's quarters."

"But why?" Étienne asked, feeling quite upset about being so close to his employer so much of the time.

"I suppose because he thinks he will like you well

Paris to New France

enough to tolerate your company day and night, and also because you are going to be sort of a servant to him as well."

"Well, that part's fine. Just so I know what to do. I really am not much of a servant, unless he requires me to make cheese, and even the cheese I make doesn't always turn out well."

"If he does ask you to make cheese, it will be a miracle if you can. After the milk is gone, two days from Honfleur, there will be no milk again until we return to France. No butter, no cheese, no eggs, but we will have fish off and on, dried biscuit, dried peas dried beans. Hope for a quick trip and that they have had a good year on the Newfoundland Banks. There are always Basques and Normans there who have brought huge amounts of provisions. Once you see a Basque eating a meal, you will understand why they bring ample food along."

"Do they have food for sale, Jean?"

"Not intentionally, but we can often buy some of it if they are about to sail home to Bilbao. It's easy to understand how happy we all are to see Basques and Normans. They may be simple fishermen, but they are never without food. They understand Newfoundland, and they never underestimate the cold. The Basques return to their mountains between France and Spain before the ice and cold set in here, and the Normans are back in Normandy drinking Calvados when the first snow falls. Did you know that Basques and Normans were here when Cartier arrived in 1525? Imagine how surprised that great captain was! Fishermen and sailors never get enough credit for anything," Jean said resentfully.

Paris to New France

"I'm sure you are right. How long will we be on the Newfoundland Banks?"

"Just long enough to stretch our muscles and get the latest news from the Normans and Basques. Perhaps buy some food. After the Newfoundland Banks, we will go farther up the River of Canada to Tadoussac. Men were left there from former voyages with orders to cultivate a couple acres of land. Maybe they will have dried peas or something, it won't be much."

"This doesn't sound too promising. Won't the natives give or sell us supplies?"

Jean laughed ruefully, "The Montagnais make a full-time business of starving! I have never seen them with enough food to share. To think of it, I have never seen them with enough food for themselves."

"Is the soil so poor?" Étienne sounded shocked.

"What strange questions you ask. No, the soil is fine. They don't want to plant crops."

Étienne was about to ask why, when the front door of the house opened and they saw the Parisian businessmen leaving the imposing looking mansion. Carriage after carriage drove up for the elegantly attired men, all of whom wore high beaver hats, a reminder that the fur trade had an effect in Paris. Most had portfolios under their arm, although some were attended by other men who carried their papers, opened the carriage doors and generally seemed obsequious. When they had all hurried off, the servant who told Étienne to stay outside when he first arrived, came to the door and motioned for them to come in.

A table had been set in the dining room for any of

Paris to New France

the crew who might have arrived. It all looked good to Étienne who had been too nervous to eat breakfast. Now it was well after noon and he eyed the meats and bread hungrily. Champlain came out and greeted Jean and Étienne by name. He urged them to sit down and he would give a blessing, and anyone who came in later could join them.

Jean and Étienne both noticed that Champlain ate very little. He was a small man and wiry, not much interested in what he ate. He seemed distracted as though his mind were elsewhere. But he did tell them that the next day they would begin the trip to Honfleur by barge on the Seine, others joining them from time to time along the way. The boys slept in the house that night and went to the dock next morning where the barges plied the River Seine. A barge would be their home till they reached La Manche, the body of water that separates England and France. The Seine, like a giant serpent, twists back on itself in a series of loops, making the trip far longer than it would be by land. But it was safer, no highwaymen on the Seine, and the journey was more comfortable than in a carriage bumping over the poor trails that passed for roads. Champlain and his men had the barge to themselves, they told stories, played games and sometimes stopped to buy produce or fresh bread and meat. It was a pleasure for Étienne to see France spread out on both sides of the river as they glided through the countryside. Champlain gave a running commentary on the history of the area they were passing through. This was like a dream come true to a boy starved for knowledge and adventure.

Paris to New France

Two weeks later they reached Honfleur. Champlain told them to accommodate the goods on board ship as best they could, and he left with one of the seamen to get supplies in Honfleur. It was Étienne's first chance to explore the ship. He looked out over the water and looked again at the ship. Finally he said to Jean, "This looks like a child's toy. It will be exciting when we get into the Atlantic, won't it?"

"I hope not, but I'll wager that it will."

The wooden planks all seemed to creak and groan and the sails made enough noise to make him concerned about their stability.

"I always thought ships would be quiet and move through the water like swans. This one makes as much noise as an animal in pain," Étienne complained to Jean.

"Ships are alive until they sink, Étienne, and they always make noise. Have you noticed that ships are called "she" by sailors? They are lively companions, not dead pieces of furniture. This one is called *Le Don de Dieu*, isn't that a nice name? *The Gift of God*. Certainly sounds lots better than *Le Levrier* – *The Greyhound*. And there is one other, I don't know the name. All three of these have been fitted out by le Sieur de Monts. *Le Levrier* is commanded by Pont Gravé and it has left already. The third one must have gone earlier too. It's going to Acadia. And then there is this one."

"Why is le Sieur de Monts spending so much money on ships and sailors?"

"He and Champlain have talked Henry IV into giving them another year of monopoly of the fur trade."

Paris to New France

"Just a year?"

"Oh, I suppose Henry will renew it. The King's idea isn't to enrich de Monts but to encourage the trade, and besides, Champlain keeps talking about discovering a route to the East. Without a monopoly for de Monts, there would be no hope of making enough to defray the expense of simply going to New France, to say nothing of discoveries."

"That explains de Monts, but why do you go to sea, Jean?"

"I suppose I just like the adventure."

"Do you have a wife?"

"Almost. My father and her father have our marriage arranged for next year. I'm very pleased with the plan. Their farm is next to ours, she has no brothers and her only sister is in the convent. My fiancée is willing for me to go to sea from time to time and I am glad of that because I couldn't stand always being on the farm, though I like farming well enough. I have promised only to go to New France because there are so many pirates nowadays in the Mediterranean and farther south in the Atlantic. I have nightmares about being captured and brought in chains to Morocco." Jean shuddered.

"Have you known anyone who was?"

"Yes! Every seaman has either known someone taken by pirates, or has himself been captured and ransomed. They pay ransom more readily in Spain because they have religious charities there that raise money for that purpose. But it is harder for French sailors. If their own families aren't rich, there is often no help."

"Jean, don't think about that now! We have the Captain's quarters as neat as we can manage, so let's go out on deck and see if we can meet the others. I particularly want to see Nicholas Marsolet."

It wasn't hard to find Marsolet. The sailors called him "Rouennais" because he was from Rouen and most of them were from Saint Malo, Champlain's part of the country. Étienne smiled. He could almost see himself in Marsolet who seemed to run all over the deck, asking questions and trying to help the sailors. Étienne felt sure that they would be friends. At that moment, the other boy looked up at him, and a smile spread across his face as he walked over to embrace Étienne. "Ah, I have been waiting to meet you, Étienne Brulé from Champigny! Do you know any language other than French?"

"A bit of Latin," Étienne said and shrugged his shoulders helplessly.

"The same. We will be busy, won't we? Did you know that Champlain had a translator before he hired us? A Micmac native who learned some French and was a great help to Champlain in 1604. I don't know what happened to him. I've been afraid to ask."

Marsolet took him down to see the dark, crowded quarters where the men would live on their way to New France. Étienne felt grateful for his narrow cot in Champlain's tiny quarters.

It turned out to be easy to share the little room with Champlain because he was seldom there and when he was, he was studying maps or writing. Champlain was a skilled artist, and effortlessly illustrated his letters and his log. Étienne learned early that his employer was a

Paris to New France

born teacher and happy to answer questions and show any of his young men how to plot a course at sea, gauge distances on land or water, and use the astrolabe and compass.

★

The ship had just left the channel between England and the continent of Europe when a lookout yelled, "Forbans, sous le vent!" Étienne was with Champlain when he heard that cry of "Pirates, leeward!" He turned to look at his Captain but Champlain was already running toward the bridge. The other boys hurried up on deck to see what was happening and joined Étienne who was right behind Champlain.

"Will it try to board us?" Marsolet asked one of the sailors.

"Oui! I don't think they do these things for sport. What I wonder is what we can do to prevent it."

Étienne and some of the others were looking around for weapons of any kind, and saw nothing useful. Some of the men seemed paralyzed with fear and had gone completely motionless.

The ship had already been turned sharply to starboard and sail was set which would either take them into the English port of Plymouth or to the bottom of the sea because the ship was never intended to be that heavily laden with sail, nor to fly before the wind that fast, but the alternative was Moroccan captivity and Champlain didn't hesitate.

"Will we be safe from pirates if we reach Plymouth?" Étienne asked Champlain.

"Yes, it is a major English seaport; they will have several ships there eager to take on pirates. If we can reach Plymouth, or armed vessels coming from Plymouth, we will be safe because the pirates will turn back to sea."

Champlain could see how nervous his young men were and instructed them to sing "Ave Maris Stella" an old hymn to the Blessed Virgin as Star of the Sea. It gave them the sense that they were at least doing something. Meanwhile, the ship tumbled through the waves like a piece of flotsam as it headed steadily for Plymouth. Prayers for deliverance were many and fervent. For a time, the pirate ship was so close that they could see privateers with cutlasses in their belts and knives in their teeth hanging onto the ropes that they would swing out from if they got close enough to board.

"Ah, bon Dieu, I think I can smell them!" Étienne said.

"Just so we don't have to feel their cutlasses. I don't know what we could fight them with, maybe the cook has something?" asked Marsolet almost hopelessly.

After it became obvious to the pirates that the little ship was headed for Plymouth and might well make it before it could be boarded, the pirates changed course and headed back out into the Atlantic. The whole deck rang with shouts of joy. Champlain had them all kneel and thank le bon Dieu and Notre Mère for their deliverance from harm. It was very easy to be thankful.

"We won't have to go all the way to Plymouth, just close enough to make contact with an English ship." Champlain acted as if it were all in a day's work.

Étienne sought out Jean Girodet after the prayers were over and the ship was heading lazily into English waters. Jean greeted him with, "Didn't I tell you that Champlain was a great captain?"

"Yes. But what would we have done if Plymouth weren't close?"

"Well, there's that." He shrugged his shoulders and grinned.

★

Le Don de Dieu had sailed from Honfleur on April 13 1608 and on May 26 it arrived in Newfoundland. The crossing had been relatively easy and they expected to find Pont Gravé and his ship there, but it had already gone on upriver to Tadoussac loaded with the tools and the workmen that Champlain would need for building the Habitation. The Habitation was to serve as both a dwelling and a fortress overlooking the narrowing of the river at that the natives called Kebec – meaning the narrowing of the waters.

On June 3, Champlain's ship arrived at Tadoussac where it turned out that Pont Gravé had become a prisoner of the Basques. That tough old sea Captain had announced imperiously that the King of France had given de Monts a monopoly on the fur trade, and that the Basques would have to limit themselves to fishing the Newfoundland Banks and do no more fur trading. The Basques found Pont Gravé and his ultimatum both funny and annoying. So annoying that they wounded him seriously, and killed one of his men.

It struck the Basques as humorous that a French king, who had never been to the New World, would have the audacity to tell Basques and Normans that only de Monts could buy furs, since both groups had regularly fished in Newfoundland for almost one hundred years and often bought furs to sell.

Pont Gravé was in considerable pain with his wound; and the Basques had control of his ship and saw no reason to return it. Champlain dressed himself as elegantly as possible, plumed hat and all, and had one of the sailors and Étienne take him to shore in a lifeboat to reason with Pont Gravé's captors.

Some of the Basques knew French, and Champlain managed to talk them out of keeping Pont Gravé and his ship. He said, "Oh, continue to trade with the natives and sell the furs in Europe if you like. You know, and I know, that we can't stop you. But it is to your advantage for us to have a settlement here where civilization can flourish and we can Christianize the natives. Pont Gravé and his ship will do you little good. The Spaniards don't care if the French are up here, they have their hands full with other colonies and the Spanish Basques would only annoy the crown of Spain by keeping Pont Gravé and his ship. You don't want the French king accusing you of piracy! Why have both Spain and France angry with you?" Whatever Champlain's exact words were, they worked. And the ship and men were returned to the command of Pont Gravé and the two French ships continued on together up the river.

Visit to the Montagnais

In 1525 Cartier found the place we now know as Québec City; the natives called it Stadacona. By the time of Champlain's first visit in 1603, there was a much less advanced group in the general area than those of Cartier's time, and Stadacona had disappeared.

The constant movement of the various tribes was much like the ebb and flow of the sea. In 1608 when Étienne arrived, the natives were always on the edge of starvation. Even so, they didn't change their ways to conform to the realities of the harsh climate. The French called them "Montagnais" since they seemed like rustics. They were one of many groups who spoke an Algonquin language. Some of the tribes raised corn, beans and squash, and others, like the Montagnais, lived as best they could on fish, roots and berries, with the occasional addition of game.

The fortress at the narrowing of the waters on the River of Canada was to serve as protection from any marauders, and be a sheltering home for the little band of Frenchmen. Champlain was a practical man, and knew that shelter had to be built before they could give much thought to the fur trade. The cold is unforgiving.

Always uppermost in his mind were his main goals of establishing a strong foothold for France in the New World, and finding the long-sought Northwest

Visit to the Montagnais

Passage that he believed must exist; near to his heart was the hope of converting the natives. In order to do any of these things, he would have to engage seriously in the fur trade. That required Frenchmen skilled in languages and accustomed to the ways of the various tribes. Champlain had no way to support anything without the fur trade and that was impossible without native hunters.

Everyone worked at building the fortress. Étienne was quite contented as a carpenter's helper because he was learning something useful, and knew that the building of the fortress would not be his permanent work.

When he was called into Champlain's makeshift office, he was pleased to hear employer say, "Étienne, I would like you to learn Montagnais. Do you think you can live with them for a little while?"

"I can try, mon Sieur! Certainly they can't complain that I have bad habits." He smiled at Champlain who laughed aloud.

It was impossible to leave anything untended outside the Habitation since there was nothing the Montagnais didn't need, and therefore nothing they wouldn't take. When it was possible to share food with them, they did, although those who had been there a season or two said that it was a losing proposition because the Montagnais seemed unable to change their ways, and would always need food.

"Just one favor, mon Sieur. I don't think I can eat rotted dog. Can I take my own food with me? And will they steal it from me?"

"Yes, to both questions. Don't stay for more than a

Visit to the Montagnais

month, and you can come back earlier if you need to do so for any reason. I know you can't possibly learn a language in one month, but you will get a feel for their customs and learn at least a few useful words. Then when you come back here, we will be ready to go down the river to Tadoussac to meet the Huron who come to the fur trade. I want you with me then, because it is those people who we need to understand most."

"Of all these people, which group is most important to us, mon Sieur?"

"The Huron. They are the great traders. They have furs of their own to sell, and also furs from the nomadic tribes who live around them. The people who live along the River of the Ottawa have magnificent pelts to sell."

"How can we know who is coming and when?" Étienne asked.

"Traders come when the ice floes go off the rivers. They know that the French ships can't get into Tadoussac until spring. There are Frenchmen who go up the Great River to where another river empties into it. That place is called Trois Rivières because the river has three mouths and seems like three separate rivers. Sometimes the harbor there is clogged with canoes all heavily laden with furs."

"I will set out tomorrow for the Montagnais camp with my own bag of dried and pounded corn and some dried eel. Maybe I can catch fish or do some hunting."

"Perhaps. But you cannot take a musket. Only bow and arrows. It would be dangerous for you to have firearms. Well, perhaps not for you personally, but

Visit to the Montagnais

they would take the musket as soon as you fell asleep, and then what?"

"That's fine. I can use the bow and arrow a little now. Marsolet and I practice. Do you think the Montagnais will take me in?"

"Certainly. They have seen you with me many times. They may be savages, but they aren't stupid. When you try to learn Montagnais, it will be obvious why you are there. We often don't know what group people belong to, what we do know is that they can't read or write, have a primitive set of superstitions and rarely engage in anything as advanced as simple agriculture. This doesn't mean that they are savage in the sense that they are vicious."

"Yes, they simply seem like destitute, primitive people who live in a cold climate. This land is so huge."

It was fortunate for Étienne that the natives all seemed to understand that he was an emissary of the white captain, the great Champlain. They were glad to find a place for him in a rude shelter with several other young men. They helped him cut spruce boughs for a bed and even gave him a few filthy skins to spread out over the spruce boughs and a few more to use as blankets.

It was a good thing for Étienne that he liked games of skill and foot races. He organized relay races, and the Montagnais placed obstacles in the path. They liked his company, and he realized how important that was. He even managed to enjoy the long days of hunting for apparently non-existent game. Without guns, there was no way they could get any healthy

37

Visit to the Montagnais

animal unless it was trapped in heavy snow, and it was too early for snow. The Montagnais didn't object to Étienne cooking his portion of meat or fish, but by the time he had a fire going well enough to cook it, he was beginning to understand how a truly hungry man might well dispense with the cooking part.

He judiciously used the two bags of sagamite he'd brought. This pounded and dried corn was obtained in trade with the Huron or more advanced Algonquin tribes. Étienne set aside some of it to use as prizes for games, and for evening story-telling sessions. He didn't know many words in the language, but the most skilled storytellers kept the audience enthralled, so the winners were easy to identify. Perhaps because all the people knew that the sagamite was being used for prizes, no one took any of it.

The young men were great at running, but Étienne often won. He smiled inwardly, thinking of the times he had been told as a little boy not to waste his time playing games. He determined to tell several people back in Champigny how helpful it was that he liked games of all kinds. He made rough balls for boules out of leather and sinew-covered packed earth. The Montagnais taught him useful words and phrases, and daily his vocabulary grew. The month went faster than he had expected, but he was glad to be returning to the little band of Frenchmen at the Habitation.

"Il arrive!" called one of the workers who was on the upper story of the building, which was a serviceable fortress. Some of the men had wagers on how long Étienne would stay with the Montagnais. Those who knew him best, like Marsolet, had been

Visit to the Montagnais

sure he would make the full month. The others lost their bets.

"Bonjour, mon Sieur," Étienne called out as he waved happily to his employer who was standing on the almost completed upper walkway where he could see him and his companions as they approached the Habitation. Étienne bade farewell to the two young men who had accompanied him on his way from the Montagnais encampment. They were laughing and Champlain congratulated himself on having found an ideal helper because not all young men could adjust that well to primitive conditions, manage to make friends and come back laughing.

Nicholas Marsolet found Étienne some clean clothes because his were so caked with dirt that his companions respectfully requested that he wash them a good distance from the fortress. Marsolet brought in a large tin basin with water so that Étienne could finally bathe, and one of the others brought him soap.

"Where did you get the soap?" he asked in amazement.

"Do you think we have all gone native? No indeed. My wife used to make soap in France and I just used beaver fat and ashes and voilà! we have soap, too." The carpenter who answered him was proud of his effort at soap-making and pointed out that the soap didn't smell as bad as Étienne, so it was an improvement.

"What did you eat there?" asked a Frenchman.

"Anything that didn't try to get me first."

"Were you afraid of them?" asked another.

"No, they were friendly."

"Who is their chief?" asked a third.

Visit to the Montagnais

"I ate things you don't want to learn about, I wasn't afraid of them, and no one really seems to be in charge of anything, certainly no one you would call a chief. Now I must bathe, wash and detangle my hair and go and see Champlain. I'll tell you more later."

★

"So, Étienne, it looks very much like you have had a successful month! Tell me everything. For example, tell me what you think is the most important thing that you learned." Champlain was always curious.

"Mon Sieur, I think it is that the Montagnais are not unhappy! I don't know why they are not, but they seem to be quite content. And believe me, they have nothing. Absolutely nothing at all. They have no treatment at all for any sickness or wound. They suffer, they die. Sometimes they have food. Often not. But they are always eager for any diversion, and I have them playing boules like Frenchmen on their way to Sunday mass," Étienne chuckled. "I am going to write down every word that I can remember, every expression, every idea."

"Tell me, Étienne, do they have any religion?"

"Not that I can see. They do worship various objects or trees, but those things change from day to day, and aren't ever venerated by everyone. It is strange, mon Sieur. And so are they. But they were pleasant, good companions."

"Well done. Write me a list of the words and phrases you have learned. I don't have a gift for languages, but it is good to have copies of important

Visit to the Montagnais

work, and I consider this important." Étienne left to write down every word he had learned and every custom; it would help him or someone else to know such things.

Scurvy

The months of June, July and August of 1608 passed pleasantly at the place the Algonquins called Kebec or the narrowing of the waters. The tiny settlement of a few huts had the beginnings of a serious fortress as all hands worked to have part of it finished before the winter set in again.

On his return from the Montagnais encampment, Étienne taught Nicholas Marsolet all the vocabulary and phrases he knew. Marsolet was a quick learner and the two boys practiced their little bit of the Montagnais version of Algonquin. Champlain kept the written information Étienne gave him, and the words and their translation, but didn't attempt to learn Montagnais himself. He had given up on languages during his time on Spanish ships, reasoning that if he couldn't learn Spanish in five years from men who also knew French and had books to help him, then his chances with Algonquin didn't look good. It was for that reason that he brought along the young men to learn languages, and to be extra eyes and ears. New France had many tribes and many dialects of Algonquin alone, so interpreters were necessary.

There was plenty of time to go fishing, to look for berries in the surrounding forests, and to learn every scrap of information available concerning this huge land so much larger than France, but on the same latitude. Because of the similar latitude, the French persisted in thinking it must be like their homeland. Berries were scarce and they didn't have enough to dry and store, but since they had dried peas and beans brought from France and the Saint Lawrence River on their doorstep was well stocked with fish, they didn't worry about food.

In September the temperature dropped daily and the leaden skies drowned the greens of the hardwoods. The shortened days left the trees flaming red, bright orange, and the yellow of lamplight. Some places looked as if lit from below. The trees glowed with color, but that didn't last long. The winds picked up, the leaves fell from the hardwoods, leaving only the green of the spruce and cedar. Then the snow began to fall. At first it was amusing to play in the snow and to attempt to use snowshoes. The boys were soon racing around the area near the Habitation and the men were doggedly plodding along trying to get used to snowshoes.

Étienne asked Michel if the snow would melt before spring. He had been in New France with le Sieur de Monts in the dreadful winter of 1604 when so many men died. The pull of the wilderness had drawn Michel back to Canada as a workman on the Habitation.

Michel thought for a moment and said, "I don't think so. I dread winter but not the cold as much as I fear scurvy. I think we will be warm enough in the huts, or in the finished part of the Habitation, or on the ship. We have wood cut aplenty and we have warm clothing, although we don't have any way to keep our

Scurvy

hands warm enough to work on the fortress. Our feet will soon tell us that we can't stay outside long. But what can anyone do about scurvy." It wasn't a question, and Michel merely shrugged his thick shoulders and sighed.

"How do the Montagnais survive?"

"Many of them don't. It sometimes gets too cold. But they don't get scurvy. I suppose you heard about the great cure that one of the savages showed Cartier?"

"No, what is it? Do we have it?"

"When so many of Cartier's men died of scurvy seventy-five years ago, one of the natives who lived near them and worked with them, got the bark of white cedar and made a tea of it, which stopped the scurvy in its tracks. It's all in Cartier's log and has long been known, but..."

"Why didn't le Sieur de Monts use bark of white cedar in 1604?"

"We tried everything. I suppose we didn't have the right kind of tree, perhaps it wasn't really white cedar?" Michel looked at Étienne as if he might have an answer.

"Did you ask the Montagnais, even in sign language?"

"Certainly. We tried everything. They didn't seem familiar with the ailment and wanted to get away from us as fast as possible; we were a miserable looking crew and our sickness frightened them. Champlain thinks scurvy comes from living in areas that have never been plowed, and that the dampness of the newly cleared land, never before exposed to sunlight, makes the people who work the land sick."

Scurvy

"Do you think that is the reason?"

"It may be one reason. I don't know. I do know that sailors suffer from it and they aren't even on land! I have bits and pieces of every kind of bark I could find in the forests here, hoping that perhaps one of them will be the right one – if we need it."

Michel had reason to fear the disease. Although he had been spared in 1604, he was the first to fall ill in 1608. His legs and face swelled, his lips had huge sores, he could scarcely breathe and when he did draw a good breath, it was lost in fits of coughing.

Naturally, the other men made teas of Michel's pieces of various kinds of bark, and someone would hold him in a sitting position so that he could swallow a little. It was terrifying to see. Étienne realized he could never be a physician when one of Michel's best friends asked him to hold the patient so that he could cut away part of the rotting gums that were making swallowing so difficult. The sufferer didn't even cry out, but Étienne felt himself becoming dizzy and nauseated. A few days later, it was apparent that Michel would never have to struggle to breathe again.

The snow was deep around the Habitation. Both the Saint Lawrence and the ground were frozen for several feet down. Champlain ordered the men to wrap their comrade decently and bury him in a snowbank. This they did. Then they returned to the ship and Champlain read services for the deceased – the first of many such services. This one shocked Étienne the most. After it became almost commonplace to find another man dead, he began to feel numb. With the second funeral, everyone realized

45

Scurvy

without so much as discussing it, that they had better bury their comrades at night. It would not be prudent to have any of the native people know how weak they had become, because the little they had would seem like a treasure-house to the natives.

Work on the ship had to be done on a continuing basis, and Champlain had the men do lots of pounding and yelling back and forth especially whenever they had visitors. Bands of starving Montagnais began to come almost daily in the hope of getting something to eat. They needed everything, and it seemed to them that the French had good supplies. But there wasn't much to spare since the settlement was only provisioned for one year. Champlain understood well that they had to provide for themselves first, but he always wanted to do something. Usually he could at least give frozen fish to the ragged and hungry natives.

Étienne had saved his sweet preserves for some kind of celebration, but it was becoming hard to believe he or anyone else would see spring. After one of the funerals, he went to the tiny cabin he still shared with Champlain, took out a jar of preserves and carried it with him over the few feet of frozen river to where there was a good fire going on the shore because they were melting pitch for ship repair. Two of the men were also using the fire to boil a pot of dried peas. Étienne filled a kettle with water from the river and put in several big gobs of preserves.

"We are going to have some sweet tea, it will remind us of home and maybe it will do our bodies good. None of us looks very lively and I feel so tired." Everyone including Étienne recognized exhaustion as

Scurvy

an early sign of the disease. The hot fruit tea tasted good to the eight remaining men. No one fell sick that day, and every day Étienne made the same hot drink. He didn't think it was medicine and neither did they, but no one wanted to stop taking it. There was no jam left in the last jar when they all agreed that they did seem stronger and two weeks had passed since the last death.

The winter of 1608–1609 was waning. Little signs of spring appeared even though the ice had not gone off the river. Bits of green showed through the snow. They saw a scrawny mother bear lead her cubs across the clearing in front of the Habitation.

Spring was here. Only eight of the twenty-eight men had survived.

Iroquois War – 1609

Spring had come to New France. The increasingly long days were speeding the recovery of the survivors of scurvy who were back at work on the Habitation. On the fifth of June, a ship from France arrived at Tadoussac. Its captain was Champlain's trusty friend, the indomitable old Pont Gravé who remained at that tiny settlement and sent his son-in-law, le Sieur des Marais, upriver to Québec in a shallop loaded with supplies.

Leaving Des Marais in charge in Québec, Champlain set out in a small barque to confer with Pont Gravé about the advisability of an expedition into Iroquoia. To no one's surprise, a voyage of exploration sounded like a good idea to the old man. Champlain told him about the frequent Algonquin requests for help in a war against the Iroquois, and wondered if the two functions could be combined – discovery and war. Pont Gravé thought that they could.

On arriving in Québec, Champlain found a delegation of Montagnais who hoped to go to war against the Iroquois with the help of larger bands of Algonquins, Hurons and, they hoped, with the help of the French at the Habitation. Since Champlain had already decided he would assist them in the war, he took with him Des Marais, La Routte, and Étienne, plus four other men. Des Marais and La Routte were experienced with the arquebus, a heavy, but portable matchlock gun. The others were provided with muskets.

About twenty-four leagues from Québec, the flotilla of native canoes and Champlain's shallop encountered a large assembly of what he reckoned were two or three hundred warriors, both Huron and Algonquin. Their chiefs were Ochateguin and Iroquets who were already on their way to the Habitation to seek out Champlain. But rather than continue on to Iroquoia, they wanted to go to Québec first, although it would mean going back over the same twenty-four leagues (about fifty miles) for both the French and the Montagnais.

Some of the natives had seen French houses and Frenchmen earlier, most had not, and they wanted to satisfy their curiosity before setting out on the warpath. Champlain agreed. They all returned to Québec where the tribes feasted and held dances for the next five or six days – considered a necessary preparation for war. Finally they set out in their canoes. Champlain and his men in the shallop were as well provisioned as possible. They would not have to rely on native cooking if all went well.

When they reached the falls of the River of the Iroquois, they began to operate as a Huron–Algonquin army. One third of the fighting force went ahead as scouts, and one third fell behind the others to hunt, fish and gather food. They no longer cooked food so as not to light fires and give away their presence. The natives had a supply of baked sagamite which they put into cold water to make a sort of liquid food and drink. Everything else was eaten raw.

With the little army was the usual pilotois, or

Iroquois War – 1609

soothsayer. He built a small tepee just big enough for one man, and according to long-observed custom, he would enter it and begin to speak in gibberish, sometimes in low guttural tones or a high falsetto. Then the whole tepee would rock back and forth violently. The natives squatted on their haunches around the tepee, marveling at the works of the shaman and his ability to converse with the oki, or manitou, or devil.

Étienne asked, "Mais certainement, mon Sieur, they can see that it is the pilotois who is shaking the tepee?"

Champlain laughed and said, "I suppose they can, but they want to believe. Even if they couldn't see, they could hear that it is the same man both questioning and answering. People are very strange."

After exhausting himself, the pilotois emerged from the tepee with the news that the oki had told him they would have success in the war and that they would bring back many prisoners to torture. Great rejoicing followed.

When the army encountered a large body of Iroquois, they sent out two men to formally announce their intention to do battle and to say that they were ready to begin immediately. The Iroquois chiefs said it was too late, but they would be happy to begin at dawn. The rest of the day and all of the night were spent yelling insults back and forth, and in laying out a plan of attack.

Champlain tried in vain to have the men get some rest before the battle, but finally gave up. At dawn the two armies were eager to engage each other, and Champlain ordered his two arquebusiers deployed in

Iroquois War – 1609

the woods, one on the left and one on the right of the Iroquois forces. He himself was attired in armor and wore a metal helmet with a huge white plume, much like the one he had seen on Henry IV at the siege of Paris. The natives were impressed. Two chiefs of the Iroquois were in the forefront of their troops; Champlain loaded his arquebus with four shots, and fired at one of the chiefs. Two of them fell dead. Apparently the shot went through first one and then the other. Now the Iroquois were really impressed. The arquebusiers fired from left and right; Iroquois warriors panicked and fled into the nearby woods where Champlain followed and killed a few more.

Joy reigned in the Algonquin–Huron forces. Many of the enemy were beheaded and the heads became souvenirs. Others were scalped, and still others were saved to bring back to torture. No show of disgust by Champlain and his men had any effect on the happy warriors. They wanted to please Champlain, however, and one of them kindly brought him the head of a large fish, a garpike, which had rows of sharp teeth. It was considered useful for headache, the teeth being placed over the part of the head that ached, and when blood was drawn, the cure was complete. The French thought that might well be possible since letting of blood was a popular cure in Europe.

One prisoner was burned gradually. Sometimes they stopped and tore out his nails or applied fire to his private parts. The top of his head was scalped and hot gum poured upon it, his arms pierced near the wrists and sinews pulled out with sticks. And on and on it went. Champlain begged to be allowed to shoot the poor wretch. The natives refused. Then, as a show of respect, they relented, and Champlain dispatched the sufferer with a musket-shot. Étienne went off into the woods and vomited. The severed arms of another were given as a gift for Henry IV. Champlain promised to present them to the king, but without any intention of doing so.

The return to the Algonquin villages and Huronia began as the Huron and major Algonquin tribes departed together, the Frenchmen left with the Montagnais, and continued on with them to Tadoussac. Champlain wanted to discuss what he had seen of the Iroquois country with Pont Gravé and to witness the Montagnais victory celebrations.

The warriors strung the heads of enemy Iroquois on poles and held them out from the canoes. The women on shore undressed completely and swam out to gather up the heads which they managed to hang around their necks like jewelry.

Étienne looked at Champlain and sighed. It was sad and too savage to even hope to understand. His employer shrugged and said, "The siege of Paris was not uplifting either, Étienne. Though I grant you, it wasn't this bad."

"Will this be the end of Iroquois wars, mon Sieur?"

"For this year. They were enemies of everyone when Cartier arrived in 1525 and they still are. They want to eliminate the Hurons. We are Huron allies because they make the fur trade profitable. The Iroquois will hate the French even more now. But they would try to kill us whether or not we actually went to war against them. I wish I knew a way to stop the wars, but I don't even know how to stop raiding parties." Étienne fell silent but continued to consider the matter. This was a senseless war and dangerous because the dozen Hurons and Algonquins who were wounded all survived, and no one had been killed during the battle. Too many of them would think fighting Iroquois was heroic sport. Nothing had been solved. Would there be French arquebusiers next time? Could they count on Champlain? These questions didn't seem to trouble the victorious warriors.

Ochateguin's Hurons

The thawing ice on the rivers was the signal to the natives that French ships could now come up the Saint Lawrence and would be at Trois Rivières soon. They organized flotillas of canoes to go down the river with furs to trade, and to meet old friends, enjoy dances and feasts and hear the news of the latest Iroquois raids. Among the early arrivals at Québec were Chief Ochateguin and some of his band. Champlain took Étienne aside and said, "Now you remember my instructions?" "Oui, mon Sieur, I certainly do. I must try to learn Huron and the ways of Ochateguin's people. I should try to be wherever the men are discussing hunting or raiding trips they have made so that I can learn if there are ways to the Pacific Ocean that we can use."

"I feel sure you will do all of that even without my instructions! It is even more important that they like you. They could easily turn against the French because of the actions of one man, so be very careful of their feelings. They will have some customs that you will fail to observe, and you will know from their expressions that you have made a mistake. They will forgive you many things at first because they know you are French. Don't insist they do anything just because you do – like cooking meat."

"Oui, mon Sieur. I should just ignore it if they

Ochateguin's Hurons

forget to say the Angelus?" Étienne smiled sweetly at Champlain who closed his eyes and shook his head in resignation. He had instituted regular prayer schedules at Québec, but had failed to get Étienne to observe the Angelus; this was always a sore point between them.

"You can do penance for your laxity in regard to scheduled prayers by keenly observing the religious customs of the people. Then you can inform the missionaries who will be going there later. Now, gather up your things and we are on our way to Trois Rivières. The trip will be easy because we have several good river guides and the barque is well provisioned and loaded with trade goods."

Every year something new was added to the usual trade goods of knives, kettles and axes. In the last year, French shirts, and blankets sold well. The natives used blankets as shawls in the cold weather and as covering from the mosquitoes when they couldn't stand any more of the little pests. Some medicines, too, were sent to New France, but they were not found suitable for use in the fur trade since their main ingredient was alcohol. Still, the bottles were greatly admired. In France, most bottles were round; those sent to New France were often square in order to get more goods on ships with less breakage.

A treat for Étienne was finding Jean Girodet, a friend from his voyage to New France. Jean was going to be one of the crew. That sturdy, sea-going French peasant was standing on deck and grinning, waiting to see the surprise on Étienne's face.

"Is that really you, Jean?" I missed you this year and was afraid there was no way to get news to Catherine.

Ochateguin's Hurons

Do you have anything for me from Champigny?"

"Oui! I have letters from your sister and from Paul and I saw them both with my own eyes only six weeks ago. They are well and prosperous. The letters will tell you more. Father Treguer writes you with news of the parish – he is not well. He never really recovered from this winter's sickness. I will take word of you to him, if he is still alive when I return."

Étienne took his precious packet of letters to read and re-read later. He shook his head sadly about the priest who had helped him so much, and then asked, "And you, mon ami, did you marry the girl with the farm?"

"I did, and now our family farm and hers are joined and we are able to hire enough workers so I can go to sea for three months every year." Jean paused and his face reddened slightly as he said, "She's the delight of my heart, I think you should get married."

"Mais oui! I'll ask Chief Ochateguin if he has any likely prospects for me. Of course, none of them will have farms."

"Don't you intend to come back to France?" Jean looked at him with pity and something like horror showing on his face.

"I intend to go back very soon. Probably next year. I will go home when the ships leave at the end of summer and I may be gone until they return the next spring. But I know I will come back here. I call Champigny my home, and yet I feel perfectly comfortable here where there is so much to do and none of it involves plowing, milking or making cheese."

"Then you will marry in France?"

"No. It would be almost impossible to find a French girl who would be willing to live like I do. Especially if she really understood what that means. I'll find my wife here."

Jean paused to digest this bit of information and then said, "Well, I've seen some beautiful girls in New France. I suppose if they weren't worked so hard they would look as good when they are older as women do in other places."

"I think so. They have to work constantly here. Children have a good time of it and are rarely even spoken to harshly. But 'Honor Thy Mother and Father' is not practiced much; if children want to obey their parents they do, but no one insists on it."

★

The short voyage to Trois Rivières was a pleasure for everyone, even for the sailors because it seemed so different, so safe. The Saint Lawrence could be tricky to navigate at points, but with experienced pilots and a good vessel it was a welcome relief after the rigors of the open sea on the Atlantic. The thick woods on both sides of the river extended right down to the water. The hardwoods had bright green leaves and the evergreens were full, graceful, and sweet smelling in the warm summer sunlight. The smell of the forest was both exhilarating and restful. The native men and women enjoyed fishing, and liked to put canoes on the water on a summer's day. The children were playing on the shore and their mothers were carrying

Ochateguin's Hurons

primitive, leaky wooden buckets of water up to their dwellings, or washing themselves, children, or clothing in the river. Everything seemed peaceful and easy. The swift flowing Saint Lawrence was full of fish, its water was fit to drink, there was plenty of wood in the forest for fuel.

"This must be the way it was in the Garden of Eden," sighed Jean as he looked toward the shore.

"I hope not! These people have just gone through a terrible winter of cold and hunger. You went back to France after we landed here, you can hardly imagine the cold. I'm sure you've heard about the scurvy. These people are always in fear of the Iroquois; some warrior is usually dying of arrow wounds that have become infected. And, not to sound like Champlain, but they live in fear of crazy things – they don't really believe in anything, so they will easily believe in almost anything, at least for a day or two.

"Dreams are a real curse for these people. I have long suspected that the more intelligent among them simply don't repeat dreams that could be misinterpreted, and that is just about any dream at all." Étienne shrugged his shoulders. "No, it isn't like The Garden of Eden."

"And you plan to marry a native woman?"

"Some of them are not so superstitious. It's the foolish ones who seem to be heard the most. But that is often true in France, don't you think?"

"D'accord! The less people know, the more excited they get."

There were now so many canoes it was hard to find space to sail. The natives greeted the Frenchmen with shouts of pleasure. The activity on the shore was like a French village on market day, except that there were shelters put up here and there with no particular regard to any plan. Even a cursory glance showed that this wasn't a real town, but just a trading post which would be empty after the fair ended in a couple of weeks. Étienne put the letters from France that Jean brought him into the sack of clothing he would take with him to the Huron village. He had a few hours to spend talking to his friend and walking through the grounds. One of the Frenchmen broke away from the native he was bargaining with, hailed Étienne, and told him Champlain was waiting with Chief Ochateguin on board ship.

"Au revoir, Jean! I must go and meet Ochateguin. I am glad it is only for a year. I can't imagine staying any longer. At the same time, I do want to go."

"Succès, mon vieux!"

The natives had assembled aboard and seemed to be enjoying the experience of something new and different – a French ship. Their host had set out various dishes of food, which he'd bought from the women in the trading area. The Huron were familiar with all the foods and were eating heartily when he arrived.

"Ah, Étienne, I am glad you were so easily found!" Champlain said.

Étienne's glance swept over the small band of Hurons and he recognized the one called Ochateguin. There was no law saying the chief had to be bigger than the other men, but the tallest, most heavily painted and most colorfully adorned man in the group was the one the others seemed to defer to.

Ochateguin's Hurons

Some of the Hurons were wearing only breechclouts and furs draped across one shoulder, which they belted at the waist with cord. Ochateguin wore fine skins made into a shirt and pants, both pieces of clothing were heavily decorated around the borders with dyed porcupine quills. Some of the others wore assorted furs cleverly sewn together, or leather treated to make it as soft as wool. All wore moccasins that extended up past the ankle and folded over at the top. Most wore footwear decorated with quills, bone, or paint.

Trying not to stare at their elaborate hair arrangements, Étienne smiled and looked instead at his employer. Champlain had no trouble understanding the young man's effort not to be amused. Some of the band had one side of the head shaved and on the other side the hair was worn very long. Most had their hair dressed with bear grease to stand straight up on top. Since the Huron were larger to start with than the Frenchmen, it made them seem like giants. On seeing them, some of the French said, "Quelles hures!" (what boars) because their hair looked like that of wild boars. So they called the people "Huron". All were wearing face paint. Some had half their face in black and half in blue. But there seemed to be no particular favored design. It was obvious that they had gone to a great deal of trouble getting dressed and painted for the meeting with Champlain.

The food that had been set out for the visitors was now gone and the men sat cross-legged on the deck waiting for the meeting to begin. It was going to be a difficult one because they would have to rely on Brulé

Ochateguin's Hurons

to translate Algonquin into French. The Algonquin-speaking Huron warrior who Ochateguin had with him would have to trust Brulé's knowledge of Algonquin. Although Étienne had been expanding his knowledge in the two years since he arrived in 1608, he felt uneasy as a translator.

Étienne's heart was racing. He said quietly to Champlain, "Ah mon Sieur, I will do the best I can. I hope I don't end up selling you all into slavery by mistake."

Like so many men who do not have much luck with languages, Champlain thought his servant was just being his usual jocular self. He doffed his plumed hat to the natives and Ochateguin accepted the gesture with a solemn nod. The chief spoke in Huron and motioned to one of his men to rise from his seated position on the deck. The man arose in one smooth movement and began speaking slowly. He addressed Étienne rather loudly, as people are wont to do when they hope to make foreigners aware of their meaning.

In his turn Étienne translated, "Mon Sieur, he says that Ochateguin is grateful for our help in the war last year and would like you to help them fight the Iroquois again this year."

"Tell him I can't go this year as I must return to France, but I will be happy to go to war with them when I can."

Étienne paused a moment and then relayed Champlain's message in Algonquin. This was turned into Huron for Ochateguin. The latter showed by his facial expression that he was not happy to hear the news.

Ochateguin's Hurons

Then Champlain said, "Tell him I want to send you back with him to learn Huron language and customs."

Étienne had been practicing that line for some time and delivered it easily. It was relayed to Ochateguin who didn't seem particularly surprised and readily agreed. "Alors, mon fils, ask our worthy friend when he plans to leave Trois Rivières. I need to get some writing tools ready for you."

No problem with this message either. Ochateguin said he was leaving in two days. Champlain then bowed deeply, the chief inclined his head graciously and the visitors left the small barque by a rope ladder and used their canoes for the few feet between the shallop and the shore.

"Did you see the one with his face painted neatly in four colors?"

"Hard to miss him, Étienne. I am glad you are having this opportunity to be the first white man to learn Huron and the first to travel to Huronia, but I am going to miss having you around. One can get used to things like corns, bunions, well, you know."

"Oui, mon Sieur. Merci!"

"Come with me and we will get an oilskin packet ready with pencils and paper. You will be gone for a year, and it isn't going to be enough, but all the natives are so fussy about what people take in canoes. They won't tolerate anything extra. Even the oilskin pouch has to be carried inside your shirt. We will make a pocket inside it to hold paper and pencils. Most of the sailors have needle and thread and I have a piece of cloth for the pocket. Remember, try to find out anything you can about a passage to the Pacific, learn

Ochateguin's Hurons

Huron and Huron ways and don't annoy anyone."

"Shall I convert the whole nation, mon Sieur?" Étienne looked quizzically at Champlain.

"It wouldn't hurt to make an effort I suppose. Start by giving good example."

★

There was great noise and calling back and forth as the flotilla of canoes were loaded up to return to Huronia. Champlain was smiling broadly. Étienne supposed that meant he wasn't particularly worried about a snag that had come up in the plans when Ochateguin told the other Hurons that he was bringing back the young Frenchman. They were not at all pleased. What if he dies? What if he comes back telling lies about us? What good can come of taking him? The fur trade was important to the Hurons and they didn't want to risk it.

Champlain was determined to have a Huron-speaking Frenchman. A French-speaking Huron would also be useful. A compromise was reached when Champlain agreed to take a young Huron called Savignon back to France with him in exchange for Étienne. Savignon stood next to Champlain, towering over the smaller Frenchman, and looking mournfully at his companions as they prepared to leave him behind.

The flotilla departed immediately after a morning meal. The men were wedged into the canoes with French trade goods filling every available space. There were no seats in canoes and the only two positions possible for the men were sitting back on their haunches or kneeling.

Finally it was dusk, and nothing was heard but the dip of the paddles. Étienne was restless and bored, his shoulders ached and his knees and legs were numb. For the first time he wondered if he could stand the voyage. Now, when his pain was almost too much to bear, the paddlers turned toward the shore and nimbly jumped into the water. They beached the canoe with Étienne still in it because his muscles had cramped up so much he couldn't move. Some thought it was funny; most of them totally ignored him. With the others out of the canoe, he had room to stretch his legs and little by little he worked his muscles so that he could move enough to go ashore.

Their arrival at Toanché had been expected and many of the villagers were down at the water making a great din when the flotilla arrived. None of the women had ever seen a Frenchman and many of the older men hadn't either.

The canoes had barely been beached when two women approached Étienne. One of them pulled up his shirt, yanked on his beard, ran her fingers through his hair and seemed to be in the process of pulling down his pants as well.

"Tiens-toi bien!" (Behave yourself!) he yelled angrily at her. No one understood the words, but all understood the meaning and this caused great merriment, but it gave him a chance to get away from the pesky women, take his bundle of clothing, and follow Ochateguin up to the village.

In the past two years he'd seen several Algonquin

Ochateguin's Hurons

villages. This was something far different; completely enclosed by a stockade, with huge longhouses arranged in a somewhat orderly fashion. Ochateguin led him into and out of several of them, probably to let the people who hadn't seen him when they arrived get a good look at him. The longhouses were about thirty-five feet high and between fifty and seventy-five feet long. The only inhabitants during this warm summer day seemed to be children and old people. There were fire pits down the middle of the longhouses, but no fires. The dwellings were semi-dark, lit only by the foot or so of space at the top of the buildings which were left uncovered so the smoke of the fires could escape.

Ochateguin took him to the much smaller cabin of Aenons, one of the Huron captains who Étienne already knew by sight because Aenons had taken part in the Huron–Iroquois war the year before. He looked pleased to have him as his guest, and Aenons's wife was beaming with satisfaction. Étienne put his belongings under the sleeping bench that his host motioned him toward, and hoped he wouldn't do anything to annoy either of them.

He rested a few minutes and then went outdoors again to see this Huron town where he would live for a year. He went no more than twenty yards when he heard a pack of snarling dogs. There was no time to return to the cabin, no stick to defend himself with, and at least fifteen dogs were snarling and barking in undisguised menace. Their fangs were bared and their tails swung between their legs. Their growls seemed to him to come up from the ground itself. He felt sweat pouring off his brow and running clammily down his back. There was no retreat and he was unarmed. In France they always said to stare down growling dogs. How can you stare down dogs on all sides of you? Or did they say not to look straight at attacking dogs? Just as he thought of the horror of being killed so far from home by an animal he usually considered a pet, several young men came running toward him, all yelling at the dogs and throwing stones at them. The men kept getting closer and hitting more of the dogs with their stones. One of them carefully put an arrow in his bow and let it fly. It killed the dog nearest him. The rest of the pack went yelping off, out of range of the men and their stones and arrows.

He tried to look nonchalant, but did allow himself the right to wipe the sweat off his forehead. His hand was shaking. A well-built, sharp-featured Huron came up to him and said, "Ahouyoche," and pointed at his own chest. Étienne repeated the name aloud so he would remember it. The others were calling Étienne "Aderestouy", the name the Hurons gave all Frenchmen, meaning "man of iron" because of the tools they sold the natives. He looked at the men and said as gratefully as he could, "Not Aderestouy, but Étienne." He pointed at his own chest and said his name again. They all said his name, and no one seemed surprised to see him. They acted as shocked as he was about the behavior of the dogs.

He asked in Algonquin, "How can you live with dogs like that?"

The one called Ahouyoche answered in passable Algonquin, "Oh, those were mainly wild dogs, mostly

Ochateguin's Hurons

wolf. I'm going to skin the one I shot and we will roast him tonight. Why don't you come to my fire and help us eat him?" He pointed to the longhouse where he lived. Étienne willingly agreed to go to the dinner. He had not eaten dog before, but thought he probably could choke down part of this one.

★

Later that day when the women were back from the fields, and the men from fishing, the unmistakable sounds of dinner about to be served got Étienne up from his sleeping bench. He had been reading and re-reading the letters from France. He was just beginning to wonder how you said to your host and hostess that you would not be joining them for dinner because you planned to eat roast dog elsewhere, when Aenons picked up his own dinner bowl and motioned Étienne to come along. Apparently he had been invited too. They walked along companionably toward the longhouse Ahouyoche had pointed out earlier. Aenons had two heavy sticks in his hand, and gave Étienne one of them. Obviously, he had heard about the attack by wild dogs.

"Merci, oncle." He had decided to call his host uncle, the Huron sign of respect for older men. The other guests were already gathered around the fire. Above it a large iron kettle was set on a tripod. But where was the dog, the pièce de résistance for the meal? The men all dipped their bowls into the large kettle and took the amount of boiled cornmeal they wanted and then sat down again to eat it with a wooden spoon if they had one, otherwise they drank the hot sagamite in loud sips.

A woman came out of the longhouse and brought with her several bark platters which she set in front of the diners. She took a long, forked stick and brushed the coals aside at the fire pit, and with the stick she extricated what turned out to be clay covered portions of the dog. She prodded each piece to the edge of the fire and onto a hollow log. Then she gave each piece a smart blow with a large stick and the meat inside was exposed so that the men could choose what they wanted. This was accompanied by the men's approving comments. Ahouyoche pointed at the woman and said to Étienne, "Eatenonha." The woman grinned at Ahouyoche and said in turn, "Eatenonha," as she pointed at him.

Étienne realized he had learned how to say husband and wife, and that it was the same word. The sagamite tasted like watery, salt-free cornmeal always does, but since water was never taken with a meal, the sagamite also served as drink. The dog turned out to be quite tasty. Thinking of it as wolf helped Étienne considerably. At the end of the meal the bones were gathered up and buried near the fire. With the aid of a lot of gestures and play-acting which caused considerable merriment around the fire, Ahouyoche explained that people who drowned or were burned at the stake also had their flesh cut off and their bones buried near the fire rather than being buried with the rest of the dead in a separate place. Étienne tried not to look astonished and asked why. But no one knew. It was just what ought to be done, and that was that.

Ochateguin's Hurons

When Aenons stood up to leave, Étienne did the same, but before leaving he went over to where Ahouyoche's wife was clearing up after the meal. He thanked her in French, licked his lips and burped pleasantly as the Huron did, and she smiled her appreciation.

The next day some of the young men invited him to go fishing. He learned that Ahouyoche meant trout, so he asked his new friend why he was named after a fish, and Ahouyoche said modestly that he had always been an excellent fisherman. When he was fourteen he went off alone to fast and meditate and had a vision of a trout. Étienne was mildly suspicious and it showed.

"Well, of course I was extremely hungry. Nothing to eat at all for three days. I was waiting for a vision and there it was, a nice plump trout."

"What did the trout have to say?"

"It said, "Eat me", so I went fishing, caught a trout and ate it."

"Hard to argue with that. Does everyone get a new name during the vision fast?"

"Some do. Usually you get one name as a child, one when you become a man or woman, and then you might get a new name if you do something important, or if your life changes – if someone is dying and then gets well, naturally, they need a new name."

"Do women get new names when they marry?"

"No, why should they? Men don't either."

"Can you refuse a new name?" Étienne asked thinking that he himself would not like to be called Trout.

"The Huron is always free. He is free to refuse the

Ochateguin's Hurons

name, but his friends are free to ignore his wishes if they want to."

Since Ahouyoche seemed so willing to teach him, Étienne continued his questioning and asked, "Where did you learn Algonquin? I am grateful you did."

"I was trading for furs up among the Nipissings to take to Trois Rivières and suddenly winter closed in on me, so I made the best of it. I had to go with them to their winter camp even farther north. I never was so cold. I was hungry too. The Huron isn't used to such hard living, Étienne. But I did learn Algonquin and over the years I've learned more. I have a big Algonquin who works for me. You will meet him one of these days. He comes here now and then. He's a great artist."

"Artist? Does he paint?"

"Oh yes. He paints designs on canoes and on clothes here in Huronia and on the outside of Algonquin tepees. He gathers clay from here and there and makes pots that the women all want. The pots look fine to me too, very decorative. But they don't last like a French kettle, you know. He makes flutes and plays them and he tells wonderful stories. He sings well and makes up songs that I like. We will all go trading together sometime."

"I would like that."

"Tomorrow there is a feast for the father of my wife. He is very sick. So it is an eat-all feast. You must come, but you must also eat all the food you are served. We want her father to live, and it would be bad for him if anyone left any food."

That evening the men came out of the longhouses

Ochateguin's Hurons

at the same time, almost as if they had an internal clock. Each carried a bowl.

Ahouyoche's father-in-law was far too sick to know what was going on. A medicine man was screaming at demons and making frightful faces at the invalid. This feast was indoors, and not at all the informal affair of the roast dog. This was solemn, and the men seemed to be there as a duty. At least a dozen women went among the crowd carrying kettles of sagamite and each bowl was filled. No one said he wanted only a little. They set to work eating the watery porridge. This course was followed by an equally large serving of beans. Étienne wanted to leave, but it was obvious the he couldn't do that and be socially acceptable. One of the old men had brought along a boy of about thirteen who was there not as a guest but as a helper. When the old man flagged on the second course, the boy took over. Then porcupine and raccoon were served. Then stewed squash. This was followed by a whole deer. What misery in that longhouse, what feelings of nausea can only be imagined! Finally the meal was over and all the scraps eaten. Some of the older guests had to be helped out of the longhouse, but after vomiting they returned.

Then the speeches began, which seemed to be an opportunity for the medicine man to rest from his labors. He was wet with perspiration and reeling with exhaustion and collapsed before he got to the door. Someone moved him over a bit so he wouldn't get stepped on. One of the guests gave a long harangue about the life of the invalid. The speaker at long last sat down to approval of the others in the form of "Ho, HHo, HHo."

Another friend of the dying man gave his reminiscences, which were again met with hearty agreement. Then all were able to leave, having done what they could to help the sick man regain his health.

Champlain's Request – July 1615

From a distance Étienne could see the huge canots de maître coming into the little harbor. As they neared the shore, the men on the beach waded out to help unload them. Champlain and his men jumped out and stretched their cramped muscles as they greeted everyone they knew. Since many of them had grown up in the same longhouse in the village, it was like a family reunion as well as a visit by the well-known and respected Champlain. He represented the fur trade and they were all profiting from it in one way or another. He'd gone to war with them against the Iroquois, and it was French help that secured their victory.

Étienne hurried to embrace his employer and said rather formally, "Ah, mon cher Sieur, I am delighted to see you again! We have all been watching along the shore for your canoes. We thought you would be going to Trois Rivières for the annual fur trade, so when some of the men who were fishing told me they saw your canoes about a week ago, we were sure you would be arriving soon. I even have a feast almost ready to be served."

"After nothing but boiled sagamite and dried fish for days, I think I would find even moccasin-flavored soup quite exquisite. Mon Dieu, but I do have a good appetite! Of what does this meal consist, if I am not too bold?" Champlain asked, following Étienne up the path to the longhouses.

Champlain's Request – July 1615

"First we will have soup made with moose fat, boiled pumpkin and wild onions. Then we shall feast on roast porcupine. I asked that the quills be taken off first, and that the animals be gutted. Quite elegant tonight, you see. I told a man that I would give him a shovel if he helped me prepare a pit to roast a deer. I had the good fortune to shoot a young, tender doe."

"It has been a long time since I've had venison, I will enjoy it no matter who cooked it, or how." Champlain sighed in anticipation of a rare good meal.

Étienne said, "I don't like eating raw meat and fish, so if I'm alone I boil most things, it is easier and faster than finding ways to roast food. But here in the village, I can get someone else to do the cooking for me. The women will prepare my food if I add meat or fish for them. They are all happy to help me in exchange for a kettle, or a French shirt, and since I always have both on hand, I eat well enough, but my cooking skills don't improve much."

Champlain said, "I can eat almost anything... and have. But I certainly do enjoy food when I go back to France. After a few days, I hardly notice again. But I always think it will be nice when we have enough grapevines to make wine here in New France."

"The wine this evening, unfortunately, will be cold water, but we will have mint tea afterward, served with maple sugar candy!" Étienne looked pleased with himself. When the meal was served, his employer ate every one of the foods that was set before him and showed great pleasure in being with Étienne.

After dinner, Champlain settled himself as comfortably as he could on a tree stump to tell why he had come.

Champlain's Request – July 1615

"Étienne, the Huron people, and the Algonquins are determined that I should go to war again with them again because the Iroquois are marauding farther and farther afield. They must be stopped or we will have no fur trade, and of course no exploration and no conversion of the Huron or other settled tribes.

"I would like to continue on to the other Huron villages and send you down to the Carantouanais people with twelve warriors as guides. Some of them have been there before, as you probably know. These people have long promised that they would supply five hundred warriors when the decision to go to war against the Iroquois is made. The Huron warriors from here know that you are my agent. Since they are quite familiar down there, you will all get a good reception." Champlain looked searchingly at Étienne when he didn't get the quick and ready answer he expected.

"Mon Sieur, I will certainly go if you think I am needed, but I have been thinking of going back to France for a visit. It has been a long time. I was sixteen when I last saw my sister and I am twenty-four now. I feel guilty when she writes and asks when I will come to see what she has done with the farm and the house, and when she tells me about her beautiful children."

"Next year, certainly, Étienne. But I need you now. Marsolet is good at mapping the country, but he doesn't speak Huron. Grenolle is kept more than busy trying to keep the Recollet Friars alive." Champlain laughed. "Perhaps it is fortunate that you drive Father Le Caron half out of his mind. Otherwise it is you who would be the good father's caretaker."

Champlain's Request – July 1615

"What makes him object to me so strongly" Ma foi! I teach him Huron, I see that he gets a cabin built apart from the longhouses, and other things too numerous to mention. And he thought my cooking, such as it is, was better than he could do by himself. He is right! Is he still upset about the fact that I forget what day of the week it is and end up eating meat on Friday or Ember Days? Or that I don't always say the Angelus? Ah, mon Sieur, that is hard of him." Champlain was amused to see Étienne so indignant and he added a bit more fuel to the fire.

"Of course, I am sure you know that he says you are addicted to women and therefore are a poor example to the savages."

"Addicted, mon Sieur? Addicted? Does he think I want to get myself killed? Either he is mad or thinks I am!"

"So then, Translator for the Huron Nation and member of the Bear Clan, what do you say to my request to go to the Carantouannais to get their five hundred warriors? I will command the Huron in the battle against the Iroquois, well, as much as anyone commands the Huron, you understand. If you go down to Carantouan to collect their warriors, it would also be an excellent opportunity to map the area of the Andaste country, and it would give us an idea of the upper waters of the Susquehanna – and of the Onondaga country as well. You will be uncomfortably close to the Iroquois for only a short while before the actual battle and then the whole Huron and Algonquin army will be with us. I'll let you know exactly where to bring the warriors, and the date, so this time you will have to know what day it is at all times, and not just Fridays and Sundays." Champlain looked sympathetically at him and added, "I can understand well your desire to go to France for a visit, but no one can do the task as well as you. I hope you will go."

Étienne thought hard for a few moments and then said, "Next year – France. I think it is my duty to go to Carantouan. We will need their warriors in a battle with the Iroquois." Étienne paused and then said with resignation, "I don't think I can ever forget the last time we went to war with the Huron against the Iroquois. Each and every Huron was his own captain, attacking and retreating whenever it pleased him. I suppose they are brave enough, you just never know what anyone is going to do. Do you suppose the Carantouannais are any better?" Étienne looked quizzically at Champlain, who merely smiled.

"Yes, I guess I should have known the answer. I suppose I did know it. After all these years I am still looking for signs of civilization among savages. But, mon Sieur, some of the ways of the Huron and Algonquin seem so remarkably civilized to me. I will never be able to see a Frenchman whip his child and feel comfortable with it again. The savages have trained me by their example. Certainly there is the occasional brute of a husband who strikes his wife. But she doesn't have to put up with such treatment. Not unless she is civilized and a Christian."

"Christian women shouldn't have to put up with that either, Étienne."

"Perhaps not, but here the men live in the longhouse of the wife's family. Usually the wife's

Champlain's Request – July 1615

parents, her sisters and their husbands, her younger brothers and sisters and her nieces and nephews. The husband will have to find somewhere else to live, not the wife. She won't be without shelter and food as long as her clan has anything at all. In France the woman often has no escape."

"Certainement," Champlain agreed, "they have many reasonable customs. I start to admire them and then they capture some poor devils and torture them to death. I have saved more than one, but many more have been killed under my very nose and I could not do a thing about it. I'll wager you never got used to that!"

"No. I have seen some of the women here become very testy if they are not given any of the prisoners to torture. They seem to pout about it, like children refused an expected toy. The same women will perform great acts of kindness at other times that would do credit to the finest French lady."

"Speaking of fine French ladies, Étienne, I suppose you have heard that Madame Champlain has returned to France?" Champlain seemed a bit embarrassed.

"Ah oui, mon Sieur. The Hurons and Algonquins who knew her have the highest praise for her and hope that she will return soon. But I can understand that it is a very hard life for a lady like Madame de Champlain. It isn't reasonable to expect her not to return to France for prolonged visits."

"D'accord," Champlain said.

Étienne hoped he had been diplomatic in his remarks and was glad Champlain seemed to like his analysis of the situation. It would hardly have done for

Champlain's Request – July 1615

him to ask, "Why in heaven's name would a man of forty-eight marry a girl of twelve from a noble French family and then bring her out to New France two years later?"

Champlain finished the last of his now cold mint tea and the last crumbs of the maple sugar candy and getting up from his tree stump bench said contentedly, "Mon cher jeune homme, thank you for the fine dinner and now we must rest."

Huronia to Carantouan

Though Étienne hadn't wanted to go to the Andaste country to get the warriors for the battle against the Huron, he had agreed to go. Now in the early morning, he felt a sense of excitement and enthusiasm. This was going to be a grand voyage. Not only was it an area he had never seen, it was an important mission for him. The war against the Iroquois could easily depend on those five hundred much-needed warriors, and he was the translator best suited to bring them, mapping the country as he went.

He didn't want to wait for the women to begin preparing the morning meal. Champlain was still sleeping soundly on the only other sleeping bench in Étienne's tiny dwelling. Étienne started a fire in front of the cabin and had the kettle on.

He rarely kept a fire going because he could start one quickly with a piece of charcotton that he kept in a small tin box and carried with him in his deerskin bag. A tiny piece of the charcloth would catch fire immediately with only a spark from two pieces of flint, then some dried leaves or grass, et voilà! A nice little fire. Above the fire he had a tripod with a kettle full of water, he would have hot sagamite, mint tea, and perhaps some of the venison left over from the feast of the night before and Champlain would see that there was plenty and eat well too.

"Ho, Étienne!"

"Bonjour, Ahouyoche! Are you one of the warriors chosen to go to Carantouan with me?" Étienne asked hopefully.

"I am now! There were already twelve men, but I saw Champlain in your cabin and he asked me if I wanted to go, too. He knows we are friends. I suppose he knows I have the fastest canoe anyone has ever seen, too."

"And you are the most modest about it! So then, the others will go in the two canots de maître, and you and I in your new canot du nord?"

"Yes. We could be there and have corn planted before they arrive. But Champlain wants us to keep together, so we will. He is a war captain, after all."

"Not to mention that this is not the season for planting corn, mon ami."

"I have a wife to plant corn, Étienne," his friend said haughtily.

"Yes, you do. By the way, is everyone up and stirring in your longhouse? I have serious amounts of food left over from last night's feast for Champlain and I would like to take it over to Goes Softly and her little family. Not that her husband is not a good provider, you understand."

"I know. But it is always good to have fresh meat. They will be glad of it. When I go back for the baskets of sagamite and beans my wife is packing for us, I will tell Goes Softly and she will come and get anything you want to give her."

"Good. When will we get started?"

"Very soon. I saw the other canoes being loaded. It

might be that we have to wait for you instead of the other way around."

"That would make a welcome change. I will have my bundle of things ready. Get your baskets and tell Goes Softly to come to my cabin and take anything she finds there, I gave some of the remains of the feast to Champlain last night to take on his voyage back to Québec. I will meet you down by the water after I have said farewell to le Sieur de Champlain. He is always up and saying his morning prayers by now."

The cool, almost windless weather was perfect for canoeing and they skimmed over the water chatting pleasantly about their route. Le Grand Détour that traders usually had to take to avoid the Iroquois country was going to be altered in order to save time, but it would be more dangerous. Penetanguishene to Lake Simcoe, a portage to the Humber, and another to the Grand River, if it didn't seem safe to use any of Lake Ontario, called the Lake of the Iroquois. Then to Cattaraugus Creek, and by crossing the Genesee River they would enter the Canisteo River, and the Cheming would bring them to Carantouan, the main village of the Andastes who were also Huron and enemies of the Iroquois. It was the Andaste Hurons' misfortune to live so near the Iroquois. The people at Carantouan often promised their readiness to send warriors against the Iroquois anytime the Hurons of the Mer Douce (sweetwater sea – Lake Huron) or the Algonquins were ready to take to the warpath.

"Ahouyoche, how does it happen that so many people know how to get to the Andastes at Carantouan? Where did Champlain get the map? I didn't make it."

Huronia to Carantouan

"I suppose, my beloved civilized friend, who can read and write, that anyone he asked could have told him! He probably asked Ochateguin or perhaps Iroquets of the Algonquins. Champlain usually deals with chiefs. You know that, you do the translating! Marsolet is sometimes with Champlain if you aren't, and he speaks Algonquin well, as you know. So, one way or another, Champlain knows how to get to the Andastes. Haven't you ever been in our village when they came on trading trips? They are great travelers, and they do a good bit of trading, too."

"Do they speak Huron just like we do?"

"They speak Huron, but it is kind of strange. They live apart from the main Huron villages and have some funny ways of saying things. And a peculiar accent, if I may say so."

"You may say anything you wish, Ahouyoche. As you keep pointing out, the Huron are always free. What do they have to trade?"

"They go down the Susquehanna toward the land called Florida by the Spaniards. Spaniards are rather like Frenchmen. I met a few of them at Newfoundland. Quite a bit bigger than Frenchmen, aren't they?"

"You saw Basques, Ahouyoche. They are a variety of Spaniard. Yes, they are bigger than Frenchmen, but then, so are most of the Huron. The Basques do not think that they are Spaniards. Still, it is good that they often speak both French and Spanish. It is very fortunate for them, too, since they have a language of their own that no one else can seem to understand. What do the Andastes get in trade down on the Susquehanna River?"

"I have seen pretty round metal pieces called *reales* that make nice necklaces. They brought along big onions. I planted a basket of them in our garden; but some animal got most of them. They were good. I'm going to try planting some again. I also traded them a fine French knife for spicy little red things that you can put in the kettle to flavor food. We planted some of the seeds from that, too. I don't know, maybe they will produce more spicy little red things."

"What did they come up here to get, do you suppose?"

"Probably tobacco from the Petuns. The Andastes have their own corn. They usually have some furs, not great quantities nor very good quality. Not like the furs the people have up along the Ottawa, of course. Ah, but the poor Andastes, stuck there so close to the Iroquois. Every day is filled with fear. They have a very well-fortified village with many longhouses. If they didn't, the Iroquois would have killed them all long ago."

"How many dwellings?"

"Oh, twice as many as there are fires in a big longhouse."

"Well, about forty longhouses. Each will have twenty fires, six people to one fire. Ma foi, that is a very large village of about four thousand eight hundred people!"

"I don't know. You are the one who can tell great numbers. Some day you must show me how to determine how many of anything there are. It would be interesting. Perhaps tonight before we go to sleep you can tell me how to do that."

Huronia to Carantouan

"With anyone else, I would laugh at the idea, but you learn so fast. I never taught anyone else French, just you, and even Champlain understands you when you speak."

"This is good, Étienne. But is it not strange about people? Champlain still speaks no Huron and no Algonquin. Years before I met you, I found ways to learn Algonquin or at least enough to do some trading with them. And here is Champlain always with a translator. Was it hard for you to learn Algonquin, Étienne?"

"Yes. The first language other than your own is the hardest. After that, other languages seem easier. I had trouble with just about everything when I lived a short while with Iroquets. I tried hard not to show it, and little by little, I could do well enough to help in the fur trade. But I think the worst difficulty of all was my very first attempt at Algonquin. The variant the Montagnais use."

"Why do the Montagnais starve every winter, why not just plan ahead?"

"You are asking me! How should I know? You are the savage. I am French, remember?"

"Étienne, I don't think I could live with the Montagnais. Why don't they raise the three sisters of corn, squash and beans? Why suffer so much?"

"I used to wonder about that when they smoked eels for the winter. But never enough eels were prepared. I could see there weren't enough to last the winter, so I am sure they could, too. The Iroquois, I am told, have great fields of corn just like the Huron. Oh well, they are basically the same tribe."

Huronia to Carantouan

"Étienne!" Ahouyoche exclaimed in horror.

"Well, you know what I mean. We both speak the same language, build palisades around villages, live in longhouses…"

"But we are not the same! If we were really brothers, we would not go to war with each other!"

"I agree that Hurons and Iroquois aren't the same in all things."

Suddenly the peaceful sound of the lapping water and dipping of paddles was brokers by a loud cry, shouting, splashing – one of the canoes had turned over dumping its six occupants and their supplies into the water. The other two canoes pulled closer to grab the supplies from the waves. The men of the overturned canoe righted it, and one by one, carefully got back in. Ahouyoche chuckled. "That must have been Small Deer. I like to go fishing with him, but he is always standing up in the canoe. It is better when he paddles alone. I suppose he saw a school of fish and stood up to get a better view."

Without discussion, all of them paddled toward a nearby beach so that their wet companions could take off their clothes and lay them flat in the canoe to dry. Since it was September, it was uncomfortably cool to be naked, so other men lent them dry shirts from their own tiny store of extra clothing. Being half-naked didn't seem to bother them, but the men who had been dumped into the water were annoyed with Small Deer who was apologetic and promised never to stand up in a canoe again.

"Did you ever go up on the Ottawa with the Cheveux Rélévés, Étienne?"

"Not yet, but I am sure I know what you are going to say. You are reminded of them by these six men without pants."

"Oui. It is a strange sight. The women dress like women of any other nation. The men simply do not wear pants. I was there in the summer and the mosquitoes were like thick clouds. The babies were all sick and crying from the poison of those insects, and there the men were "sans culottes" as you say in French."

"Yes, Ahouyoche, that is certainly what we say. I wonder what they do in winter?"

"I don't know, but surely they must cover up then."

"I'll have to ask. Now that you mention it, I cannot believe they could live through a winter up in that cold place without leggings. I traded for some very good thick furs up there. So even the animals dress warmly for winter in the far north."

"Aside from not wearing pants, I have always heard that they are very fussy about their hair, are they?"

"Oh, yes. They spend hours at it. That is why they are called High Hairs. I think they use bear grease, or maybe beaver fat to get the hair to stand straight up. We do. Then they file stone knives as best they can and shave one part of the head for contrast. As you can imagine, they are great customers for good sharp knives. That is how I got the fine furs they traded for French knives."

Each of the three canoes had lines in the water, and they checked to see if they had caught anything. They found several fish, and then settled down to smoke tobacco and rest. Ahouyoche passed around small pieces of the dried meat rolls his wife had packed. They smacked their lips politely to show their pleasure with the treat. Every day that followed was the same: leave early in the morning, and when the light began to fade they stopped when they saw a good place to spend the night. A fire was made, food cooked and eaten. Remains of the food were hoisted into trees by means of cords. If it looked like rain it was the habit of a couple of the men to sleep under the beached canoes. No one mentioned it, but constantly on their minds was the fact that they were getting closer to Iroquois territory. Soon it would be necessary to choose either to do a long portage, or use the far western corner of Lake Ontario. But there had been no sign of Iroquois.

The night before the decision had to be made, they discussed it and everyone thought it would be best to use the water route. They would just stay out of arrow range from the shore, if possible, and not make noise, and have no more fires at night.

Étienne slept uneasily, feeling that there was an Iroquois behind every tree. He couldn't help but think, *Why didn't I go home to Champigny this year. No one would blame me. It's been eight years. Champlain goes home every year. Well, true, I am not Champlain and I don't expect to have an audience with Louis XIII or his mother, Maria de Medici. Champlain always comes back. I would come back. What's that noise?* He sat up, pushed his beaver blanket aside, then quietly got to his feet, found his knife and went toward the sound of the noise. No point in arousing everyone in case it was nothing, but if there were enemies around, he didn't want to be caught unarmed and lying down.

Huronia to Carantouan

The sound was more like a groan than anything else. He followed it quietly down to the water. There was Tall Trees, sitting on a boulder, rocking back and forth and moaning. Étienne said quietly, "Ho, Tall Trees, I am Étienne."

"Can you help me? I have the tooth worm. There was pain all day long. I could hardly paddle. Now I cannot sleep. It is getting worse. Do the French know anything to do?"

Étienne went up to Tall Trees and felt his head. Just as he had feared, a fever. Even his cheeks were hot, his chest was bare on this cool night and it was hot too.

"Is it just one tooth?"

"Who knows about that!" Tall Trees asked crankily.

"I can try to put a cord around the tooth and then maybe Ahouyoche and I can pull it out."

Ahouyoche was asleep but woke up easily, probably worried about Iroquois.

"We have to help Tall Trees. He has terrible toothache. I am going to try to put a cord around the tooth and you and I will pull it out. All right?"

"I hope it is a tooth in front, because if it isn't, a cord won't work. Using a knife or bone to get it out, well, that is bad. I hate toothworm. People die with it and you and I are not medicine men."

"Perhaps that is lucky for Tall Trees. Blowing smoke in his face and making ugly faces never helped anyone. You and I are what is here, so let us see what we can do."

Everyone had cord in his supply bag because each evening the canoes had to be repaired. There was always a stitch that had given way, a piece of bark that

Huronia to Carantouan

needed replacing, or spruce gum that had worn off. Étienne searched their canoe and found a piece of strong cord that was not very thick. He took it and some spruce gum with him and then washed his knife in Lake Ontario, and with those three tools and Ahouyoche, he returned to the suffering Tall Trees.

"Ho, Ahouyoche. Do you think you can help Étienne get the tooth out?"

"I hope so."

They sat their patient with his back to a tree and with the light of the moon reflecting off the water, they managed to get the cord around the aching tooth. Étienne could see the agony on Tall Trees face and doubted that the cord method would work. He said, "Tall Trees, I am going to say a prayer to our dear Lord, and I am going to ask his friend Saint Apollonia to give us strength, too."

"Who is this Saint Apollonia, Étienne?" asked Ahouyoche.

"She is the patron saint of those with toothache. Like Saint Anne with sailors, Saint Odilia with eye problems. You know, a friend to people on earth."

"No, I don't know anything about the woman, but if she will help, she is welcome."

"She will be glad to hear that."

First Étienne held the patient still and Ahouyoche pulled. Then they changed places. It didn't seem to want to move and Tall Trees was getting faint. Finally, either the tooth was more rotten than they had thought or Saint Apollonia lent a much needed hand, the tooth came out with a gush of bad smelling blood. Then Tall Trees fainted. His helpers went to the Lake

Huronia to Carantouan

and got a bowl of water to clean him up and a piece of moss soaked in water to put on his head to cool it.

"I know I have willow bark which I could boil up to make a tea to calm pain, but I am afraid to start a fire. Do you think it would help if we just put some willow bark in cold water?" Ahouyoche asked.

"Well, it can't hurt. And it will make Tall Trees feel as though things are being done for him and that always helps. Let me see that tooth you have at the end of the cord." Étienne walked down to the water and examined it, root and all, and said he could see the tooth worm. Ahouyoche said he could see it, too.

Tall Trees was still spitting out blood. They gave him a bowl of water to rinse his mouth and another with the willow bark floating in it. He dutifully drank it too, and said to Étienne, "Please tell Our Lord and his friend, Saint Apollonia that I will help them if I can some time."

"I will, and I think they will be glad to know that." They walked Tall Trees back to where his companions slept peacefully. Étienne covered him with a bearskin, put the wet moss back on his forehead and then they retired for the rest of the night.

In the morning, Étienne went over to see how Tall Trees was. He was still asleep. The other men heard the story of the bad tooth and let their companion sleep while they ate a simple breakfast of leftover food. They put some in a bowl for Tall Trees who could mix it with water and drink it for a bit of strength. They had to wake him finally, but he didn't have fever and felt better.

They paddled steadily on a blessedly quiet Lake

Huronia to Carantouan

Ontario, no sound other than the dip of the paddles and the occasional jumping fish. Étienne looked around at Tall Trees who was doing well. They saw no other human beings and continued canoeing until they reached the end of the Lake and then made camp for the night.

They were all suffering from too long a time in the cramped canoes. Their muscles ached, it was hard to sleep. But the next day would be a long portage to the Grand River. If that didn't give cramped muscles a chance, nothing would.

★

Portage and river, river and portage, and finally the Cheming River led them to the village of Carantouan. Many people were already awaiting them, so they must have been seen and expected. Étienne marveled again at how fast news could travel in a land with so few people. The number of kettles and fires outside the longhouses said quite clearly that they were going to feast on this day. Étienne and Ahouyoche spoke longingly to each other of deer or bear, but even a well-prepared fish would be nice.

They needn't have worried. The Andastes were delighted to see their Huron relatives who had been expected for two days. They had gathered together the best food the village had to offer. Since it was the end of summer, there was a good store of edibles. Deer roasted in a pit, large fish cooked over the coals, tender ears of fresh corn, squash and stewed pumpkin, and nice little corn cakes made of pounded dried corn,

Huronia to Carantouan

mixed with fat and blueberries and baked over a low fire in a heavy French iron kettle.

The Andastes traded far and wide and they knew that if their women had iron kettles and tools, they would have more time to raise the foods that kept everyone supplied during the winter, and provided a good source of trade goods. The three sisters, corn, squash and beans, were always good to trade with people who had furs to barter, but were usually hungry. With those furs, the more settled tribes could trade the French for the axes, hatchets, knives and other things that made life easier.

The feasting went on for hours that first day, and none of the men from Huronia complained. It was wonderful to have so much good hot food. They were used to long speeches and that was fine, too. The second day it became a bit harder to take. On the third day Étienne found himself begging the chiefs to hurry or they would not get to Onondaga Lake in time for the battle. But still the speeches went on and on. Each orator vied with the last in telling of Iroquois atrocities and of how they would soon be avenged. Yet no one prepared to leave. There were war dances, then just plain dances to welcome the warriors from Huronia, and dances that Étienne always described as basic orgies. More food. Eat-all feasts. Ah, the eat-all feasts, just the thing for men who were supposed to be in good fighting trim. Many of them were half-sick by now.

A week went by; Étienne was frantic and trying not to show it. He remembered the battle with the Iroquois in 1609 and he knew, as did all of the Huron,

Huronia to Carantouan

that this was a battle that must be won. If the Iroquois were victorious, no one but Iroquois would be safe anywhere. There would be no fur trade because no one would dare take the thousand mile, fifty portage trip from Huronia to the main trade centers of Trois Rivières, Québec and Tadoussac. Without the fur trade, there could be no further civilization of the natives. No priests would be able to get to Huronia to convert anyone. Useful skills, learning, Christianity and what little civilization now existed, were all at stake.

Even the least intelligent among the men from Huronia knew that no Huron nor Huron ally would feel safe in his own cornfield and more and more women and children would be kidnapped, more tortures. Finally, after Étienne nearly despaired of their doing anything, the promised warriors and his own Hurons left the village amid a great war-like clamor from the people and the most enthusiastic of leave-takings.

*

Even with constant movement during the day, either by land or by water, they arrived late.

Étienne felt sick at heart. It was obvious that the Iroquois had won. There remained still smoldering Huron fires, moccasins, broken arrows and the devices called cavaliers that Champlain had them build to fire upon the Iroquois village from above its palisaded gates. Those tall towers on rollers remained. No wounded, no dead, no living. Where were they? Scouts went into the woods and came back with the information that the Hurons had fled. The deep tracks showed that some were being carried out on other men's backs. No one was stopping to eat, there were no dead fires on their escape route. They were on their way back to Huronia after a terrible defeat – racing away from the Iroquois and trying to beat the winter storms.

The warriors from Carantouan weren't as disappointed as the men from Huronia, which made the latter irritated. What a long and difficult trip they had made to get those five hundred warriors. How hard they had tried to get them to leave Carantouan in time. Not to mention the hurried and unpleasant march to the battle they had missed. It was likely that the lack of the five hundred promised warriors caused the Huron–Algonquin defeat.

Étienne and his companions thought about what they should do. It seemed clear that Champlain and Ochateguin were not going to welcome them with open arms after they had so clearly failed. It was getting very cold. The people from Carantouan wanted to go home right away, not embarrassed in the least, or so Étienne always said. The Hurons went with them. If winter were to overtake them now, it would not be possible to get back to Huronia anyway.

They began a slower trip back to Carantouan. One day was spent hunting and they had plenty of meat. But nature had not forgotten them either, and it rained a cold and steady drizzle, that changed to hail and then back to rain. It seemed impossible to keep a good fire going and everyone was cold and weary. There was

Huronia to Carantouan

plenty of meat, but since Étienne had never gotten used to eating it raw, it was back to sagamite again.

"Ahouyoche, this country is built on corn. Sagamite is not my favorite food, but at least there is no blood running down my chin while I eat it."

"You are becoming too fussy, Étienne. Perhaps it is your age."

"Twenty-four isn't that old! I am glad we are going back to Carantouan in your canoe. Lucky all our canoes were where we hid them on the way to the battle we missed. I wish I knew how Champlain is... and the rest of that two and a half thousand-man army. If any are wounded or sick they will die if winter overtakes them. September is just too late a date to start for battle with the Iroquois. It is usually cold and rainy anyway, and often gets muddy and then icy." He sighed deeply. "Ochateguin and Iroquets are going to be very difficult to deal with, you know."

"Étienne, the Huron are free. They can go to war or not go to war. During a battle they can leave if they wish. Our villages know the Andaste Hurons are free just like all Hurons."

"But what nonsense it is for everyone to fight on his own account, without regard for time or place or needs of the army!"

"The Huron are free," Ahouyoche said firmly.

"Very expensive kind of freedom. By the way, do you have any idea of who might have gone with Champlain as translator? I know it was not Marsolet."

"Well, two of Iroquet's Algonquins went to France three years ago. They must be back if they are still alive, and they would be with Iroquets, and be able to

Huronia to Carantouan

help Champlain. Ochateguin has Savignon – do you know him?"

"Saw him a couple of times. He is the Huron who was sent to France when I went west with Ochateguin. We were a trade, Savignon went to France, and I went to Huronia. Marsolet told me that Savignon was almost in tears when he had to go back to Huronia after a year in France. But they say he learned considerable French and has been a help in translating for Ochateguin. He is probably with that defeated army of Hurons and Algonquins. I suppose most of them do not realize how much they have lost. I hope none of them were taken prisoner. Better to die in battle."

"Maybe the French will send many ships and an army to defeat the Iroquois," Ahouyoche said hopefully.

"No. The French like beaver hats, and some of them like to hear tales of New France – this country. They aren't interested in coming here to fight. Those who are so inclined have plenty of fighting just with one another, Huguenots and Catholics."

Ahouyoche exclaimed, "So the French call this country New France!"

"Well, yes. It is in the same latitude. Oh, never mind. It just means that France and New France are easy to sail to and from. Perhaps not always so easy, but the trip can be as short as twenty days and the trip from Huronia to Tadoussac is longer than that in days of travel. And often far harder."

"I myself have talked often to Savignon because I like to practice my French when you are not in

Huronia to Carantouan

Toanché, Étienne. His tales of the great French village, Paris, are very entertaining. He has been considering getting a French wife. How many beaver pelts do you think that will cost?"

"Men don't buy French wives."

"How do they get them?" Ahouyoche was obviously prepared to be shocked.

"The woman's father, and the man's father talk about their children marrying each other and then the woman's father says he will help them by giving them land, or something of value."

"Ah, so the women buy the men! That is strange, but not as bad as just getting your friends to help you steal a husband or wife. I suppose in France the girls steal husbands now and then? Especially if they don't have a father to buy a man for them?"

"I have never heard of that." Étienne was thinking seriously about dowry. Did he actually buy a husband for his sister by providing her with a good dowry? The strange ideas he got from his friend were often hard to shake. He paddled harder, and struck up a tune that Ahouyoche knew and they sang and paddled on through the cold drizzle.

Captured

Ahouyoche and Étienne, along with the other Huronia warriors, were anxious to go home, and leave Carantouan and their failed expedition behind them. The warm days had melted the ice on the rivers and lakes. The ground was finally dry enough so that they could make the portages.

Champlain had asked Étienne to try to learn something about the Susquehanna, and he and Ahouyoche took the first opportunity to go farther south. They were now back in Carantouan for a week and rested from their trip down the Susquehanna River as far as the great bay on the Atlantic Ocean. It was a useful trip, and Étienne mapped the area as well as he could. Certainly it was more than Champlain would expect. They considered going farther into the lands held by Spain, but Ahouyoche believed he ought to be getting back to his family in Toanché who probably thought he was dead.

Nothing was likely to soften the awful blow of the loss of the war with the Iroquois, caused in part by the failure of Étienne to get the Andastes to the battle on time, but perhaps the new discoveries would help put him back in his employer's good graces.

The people at Carantouan gave them several baskets of sagamite and some dried pumpkin and onion to give it flavor because the constant diet of cornmeal, usually without salt, tastes much better with vegetables. One of the young women ran up to Étienne and smiling shyly handed him a delicate basket filled with tiny wild strawberries. He wished she had shown a bit of interest earlier, because he liked the company of young women. He never quite knew what they might do next. It was easier to figure out men and children. She watched and waved as he and Ahouyoche set off in their canoe. One other canoe left at the same time.

At the first portage, Étienne, Ahouyoche and the men who were in the first big canoe waited a bit for the latecomers. They smoked their pipes and stretched their muscles, but finally decided that the others must have stayed one more day.

Three men easily bore the large canoe aloft, and the three others carried the provisions. Étienne was carrying the goods from Ahouyoche's canoe. As he trudged behind his friend, he had the small basket of perfect strawberries hanging by a cord looped over his wrist. Ahouyoche looked big and sturdy carrying his beautiful canoe with the colorful designs of trout so carefully worked into intricate patterns on the sides.

"Ahouyoche," Étienne said in a low voice, "I am not anxious to see Ochateguin and Iroquets, I do not allow myself even to think of Champlain. He will be very angry. Aenons will not be easy to be with either. And what can we tell the families of the warriors who didn't make it home?" He sighed wearily.

"You are very strange, Étienne. But then, you are French. Why should anyone blame you because we couldn't hurry the Andaste warriors at Carantouan? And I would like to know how we could have started for home earlier. I suppose you do remember that we left Huronia very late; was that our fault too?" His friend sounded disgusted with him.

They plodded along in silence. This was a part of the trip where there might be Seneca Iroquois. Portages here were dangerous. The Huron felt safe on the water where they could easily out-run the cumbersome war canoes of the Iroquois. There was no noise now other than that of moccasins on damp ground. They portaged on for another mile.

Suddenly, a horrifying, awful war whoop! Iroquois! The Hurons dropped the canoes and supplies and everyone ran into the woods hoping to be able to escape death, probably by torture. Out of the corner of his eye, Étienne saw an Iroquois swing his stone hatchet and strike Tall Trees such a blow that he fell lifeless to the ground. Étienne could hear his friend being hacked to pieces with that hatchet, but knew it made no difference to Tall Trees now.

Running, tripping, steadying himself, he reached a thicket of trees. The ground was wet and thickly covered with the leaves from the previous fall. He slipped on a soft, damp area near a half-rotted log, and with his hands he made a slight shelter by burrowing into the leaves as fast as he could. Then he covered himself as well as possible with leaves and dried branches. He knew it was a poor shelter against determined Iroquois. Fortunately for him, they had taken prisoners and were anxious to get them back to their village.

★

Captured

When there were no sounds of people, he left his hiding place but did not dare go back the way he had come. He thought it likely that there would be Seneca waiting for stragglers to return to their supplies and the canoes. When darkness came as a welcome protection, he could continue his journey without being seen.

But which way should he go? Easy enough to tell north, south, east or west because of the light of the moon and stars and the relative scarcity of heavy woods. The problem was to tell which direction would be safest now that he had to go on without a canoe. He finally decided to head as straight north as he could. There was no path, so keeping on a northerly direction was difficult. By morning, he was tired, but didn't think he had covered much territory. He was also sick-hungry and so thirsty he couldn't think of much else.

Keeping as close to tree cover as he could, he continued north all the next day. There were some edible roots here and there, and in one place he found some half-ripe strawberries, which he ate, thinking he might as well have eaten the luscious, ripe berries the girl gave him as soon as he had them. He spoke sternly to himself, "No wonder the savages do not plan ahead. How can they? Next time you have strawberries, eat them."

Another night in the open. He made a rude shelter under a tree. Slight, constant drizzle with periods of hard rain, his clothes soaked, his muscles ached, and the chill entered every pore of his body. But he was able to squeeze water from his wet shirt into his mouth to slake his thirst somewhat. A flash of lightning showed him a path not far from his resting

Captured

place. It might lead straight to an Iroquois village, but blundering around in the woods was going to kill him, too. He needed food and more water than he could collect in his hands and on his clothes during a rain. No path would go very far without leading to a river or lake.

Inside his shirt, he had the packet of maps he made on the way to the Andaste village at Carantouan, and the maps he made on his journey down the Susquehanna to the great bay that flows into the Atlantic. Perhaps, somehow or other, just seeing and following a river would help him get his bearings. He had to find water and food soon. This was his third day in the open, and he was weak. He was no longer following the path warily and from a distance. Now he was simply on the path. Morning faded into afternoon, the sun was high overhead and still no water in sight.

He staggered along. *Where were the others?* Étienne shuddered. He had heard so many stories of Iroquois torture, and he had seen both the Hurons in his Bear Clan and the men in Iroquet's band of Ottawa Algonquins torture men and women without a shred of pity. It always made him sick, and there was nothing he could do about it. That was probably the fate of his six companions, death by torture. Tall Trees he knew was dead. He could only hope the others escaped or at least died fast. *Oh Lord, protect them, protect me, too.*

He had scarcely uttered this prayer when he saw two men on the path in front of him. They were carrying a pole strung with fish. Impossible to tell what tribe they belonged to, because they were almost naked in the cold of the damp spring weather. They could possibly be something other than Iroquois, but he doubted it. He knew he didn't have much choice, so Iroquois or Algonquin, he had to call out. *Perhaps this is the answer to my prayer, I can go with them and eat fish and drink water, or stay here and starve.*

"Ho, hho, Ho," he called.

The men acted afraid, but looking at him carefully, and realizing he was alone and weak, they stopped and waited for him to join them.

He addressed them in Algonquin, hoping that they would belong to any one of the many Algonquin groups. They looked at each other, shrugged and told him in Iroquois that they couldn't understand him. Étienne's heart sank, Iroquois!

"Chatoronchesta," he said in Huron–Iroquois, meaning he was hungry and thirsty. He hoped the accent had a strong Iroquois flavor, knowing that when living only a few miles apart, each group of Huron or Iroquois sounded slightly different from every other one.

"Come with us to our village and we will give you food and water, and you can tell us who you are," one of them said kindly. A mile or so farther, and they were at an Iroquois palisaded village walled in by three rows of posts about thirty feet high, with a space between each row, and on top, a ledge from which to drop rocks on attackers. True to their word, they provided him with food and water, which tasted so good that he temporarily forgot that he was not safe. After he ate and drank a little, his hosts said he should come with them to their chief.

Étienne tried to seem flattered, but what he felt was

alarm. Naturally, the chief who had been down a few trails himself, merely glanced at him and then asked, "Aderestouy?" (You are French?) He had already determined to say he was Dutch, hoping the chief did not have any contact with the Dutch at Albany and wouldn't know that he didn't resemble the Hollanders.

"Oh no, I am from a better race... Dutch. We are friends of the Iroquois."

The chief looked skeptical, but was willing to let it go at that. By this time a crowd had gathered. They watched him eat and drink again, and then began to question him. He tried to make people think he was Dutch, but no one wanted to believe that story. Absolutely no one. He didn't look Huron because he had let his beard grow while with the Andaste Hurons at Carantouan. None of the tribes liked beards and pulled out any facial hair they might have themselves, usually scant. But since he went to Carantouan as a representative of Champlain, he wasn't expected to look or act anything other than French, so he didn't bother to shave; now he wished he had.

The natives certainly never had the chest hair that he did either, and by now, several people, men and women, had pulled up his shirt to examine him. They made several comments about his having too much hair. He wondered if he should have said he was Basque. The Huron knew the Basques, at least by hearsay, since there were Basques and men from Normandy already fishing the Newfoundland Banks when Jacques Cartier arrived almost one hundred years before. If the Huron and the eastern Algonquins knew the Basques, then the Iroquois certainly did.

Captured

He thanked them for the food and water and asked them where he was in relation to the Lake of the Iroquois. No one paid any attention. They were all convinced now that he was French and they intended to torture him to death. It seemed so perfectly natural. In their place, the Huron would have done the same.

Étienne's mind worked faster than it ever had, but there was no means of escape.

I must be far more stupid than I thought. Why didn't I just follow those two fishermen along the trail? One glance at this palisaded village and I would have known it was Iroquois. Well, yes. But I was dying of thirst. I didn't have much choice. At least I will die with a full stomach. I hope they kill me quickly.

Three large men pulled him outside to a pole firmly staked in the ground. There were rows of longhouses on two sides, the gate on the third, and he guessed there would be a lake or a river on the fourth side, all sides enclosed by the palisades. He was tied to the stake and they made jokes and laughed and eagerly awaited private turns at making him suffer. He knew he should be singing. It was expected. All the Huron sang as long as humanly possible when they were tortured, and so did their Iroquois cousins.

There was a large crowd, young and old, both sexes, waiting and eager for their turn. All except the chief, who wanted them to stop. The people paid no attention to what the chief did or didn't want them to do. The chief's compassion was surprising to Étienne because he had never before known a savage to object to torture. When the chief realized he would not be heeded, he simply walked away. The Iroquois seemed to be like their cousins in Huronia, completely free to do anything they wished. If they wanted to follow their chosen leaders – fine, if not, then they didn't.

A woman ran up with a burning brand to have her part in the torture right away. However, she was pushed back by the crowd and that honor fell to a burly warrior who began to pull Étienne's fingernails out with his teeth. Étienne groaned and writhed but did not scream. How could such a small part of the body hurt so very much? He knew he was expected to sing, any Huron, or Iroquois would.

He took a deep breath and sang as loudly as he could. The song that came to mind was one he and Ahouyoche had sung so often on the rivers. His voice reverberated through the longhouses and anyone who had not already come out to see the torture came out at the sound of his singing. "En revenant de la jolie Rochelle, j'ai rencontré trois jolies demoiselles, c'est l'aviron qui nous mène, qui nous mène, c'est l'aviron que nous mène en haut." *Whoever wrote that song was right, it certainly was the oar that brought me here. The oar, the canoes and the water. And, of course, going down to Carantouan in the first place to bring warriors to help Champlain and the Huron. This trip had nothing at all to do with pretty girls, so the words are wrong about les jolies demoiselles.* He paused in his singing and prayed aloud. The words that came out were those of the grace before meals. He heard himself and wondered if it was an evil omen. Several men now came forward, all trying to pull his fingernails out with their teeth. He fainted.

A woman threw a bowl of water at his face and

laughed delightedly to see him revive. She took her fiery brand and burned little patches of skin from different parts of his body. She was careful not to kill him, she only wanted him to suffer intense, excruciating pain. And she succeeded. The smell of his own burning flesh was sickening. Some of the women were now pulling his beard and chest hair out and sometimes getting pieces of skin with it. *Why don't they just take a hatchet and kill me. Please Lord.*

He started singing again, this time an old hymn he knew from childhood. "Agnus Dei, Agnus Dei, qui tollis, qui tollis, pecata mundi." Then, almost in response to the Latin hymn about the Lamb of God, one of the young men came up to grab the Agnus Dei medal Étienne always wore. It was the one that his mother always wore on a silk ribbon and that Catherine gave him when he left home. Automatically, his bloodied hands went up to the medal and the leather cord from which it was suspended. The Seneca laughed, and Étienne decided not to let him have it without giving him as much struggle as he could. He knew that he would lose and that his death couldn't be more than a day or two away no matter how careful they were not to kill him outright. Disgusted and angry, he looked the man in the eye and said, "You and all your people will surely die immediately if you take this medal. It represents the great God of the French."

Suddenly, and seemingly from nowhere, the cloudless blue sky was filled with black clouds. Lightning flashed, thunder rolled ominously, rain fell in angry wind-whipped sheets. The savages looked up at the sky and at one another in amazement and in utter fear. These people of nature knew very little about nature. But they did know that it wasn't usual to have thunder and lightning and heavy rain from a clear sky. They ran in fear back to their longhouses, leaving Étienne tied to the stake with throbbing and bleeding hands, painful burns and a face and chest that hurt beyond telling, especially from where the hair had been pulled out in handfuls. He was still wearing his Agnus Dei. He fainted again but could not fall down because he was tied upright to the stake.

The chief came out of his nearby cabin and untied him. He half carried, half dragged him back inside. He dressed his wounds with bear grease and gave him a place to lie down on one of the wide, long benches on the side of his cabin. Fever soon raged through Étienne's body, and the memories of his time of torture were so over-whelming that waking from the fitful sleep his wounds allowed him, he was always surprised to be alive. *Why am I alive? What am I supposed to do yet that I have been chosen to do?*

The fever broke at the end of the fourth day of his stay with the chief, and the pain was subsiding bit by bit. He could now lie on his side as well as on his back and move without the agony of the first days, but he was still far from able to care for himself. He wanted to thank the chief who had taken care of him. The chief had helped him to get outside the cabin to relieve himself, and often held his head gently so he could drink water. His host usually gave him a bitter brew also, which seemed to be slightly calming. When the chief came to feed him a bowl of sagamite with a bit of fish in it, Étienne said gratefully, "You came and saved

Captured

me. I would have died out in that cold rain with my wounds still open. I will be your friend always."

He said nothing but sat down next to him and handed him the bowl to see if he could hold it alone. He could. They smiled at each other. Étienne would be able to use his hands, but his fingers would never be the same. The chief grunted his pleasure at his guest's improvement, and then handed him a shell to use as a spoon. Étienne was feeding himself. He sighed with relief and gratitude.

When he had eaten the food and drunk a bowl of water, he asked, "Will the people let me leave the village?"

"Yes. In a few weeks, when you are well enough to travel, they will let you go. Later today, you should join me and some of the others in a sweat lodge they are preparing. It will make you feel better, too. You can only stay in it a short while, but it will help you to rest easier."

Étienne smiled and said, "It is fortunate that you live in this cabin alone. I don't think there are many others who would willingly stand the smell of the bear grease on my wounds, nor even the smell of me after so long without a bath."

The chief avoided the topic of smells, but said, "No, I do not live here alone. My son lives with me. He is away on a hunting trip. I always worry about him when he is gone because all the neighboring tribes are at war with us. And we are at war with them, and with the Huron. We are at war with almost everyone, except the Neutral Nation and they don't like us much either." The chief waited for him to speak.

Captured

"When I first came across the great water from France, I was told of the enmity of the Iroquois toward everyone else. I wished I could bring peace to this land. Le Grand Détour alone is a terrible hardship and makes trading difficult, but who would willingly enter Iroquois lands?"

"No one, but an enemy, and all people are our enemies. It makes our lives hard, too." The chief sighed.

"I have lived among the Huron for years, and with the Ottawa of Chief Iroquets also. I know their fear of the Iroquois. I felt it myself long before I arrived in your village. We must make a lasting peace so that we can all grow our corn, cultivate our vegetables, go hunting and fishing and use all the rivers in peace and without fear. Isn't the winter cold enough? Are the mosquitoes not thick enough? Do we need to torture each other, too? I know that there are people here who will not want to let me go back to Huronia because they fear that some day I will lie in wait for them with a battle axe in my hand, so they will want me to die here. But I swear to you, if I ever get back to my cabin in Toanché, I will always work for peace between our people. It is right that I do that. I have said what is in my heart." Étienne stopped talking and watched the chief who was moving restlessly about the small cabin.

"You have said what is in my heart, too. I am tired of living in fear. I do not want to be at war and there are others here like me. We are not heeded and some are called traitors and are tortured at that stake out in front that you know so well."

Étienne felt comforted by the thought that there were others in this Seneca village who wanted peace.

Seneca Village

Soon Étienne was up and moving freely, first about the cabin, then around the area between the rows of longhouses. He didn't tend to tarry long there because the torture post made him feel uneasy. He didn't want to be too near it for fear of giving the people ideas.

He knew the ways of native children, and expected them to throw things at him, and laugh and jeer because it was not the custom in any of the tribes to correct behavior of little ones and they were never disciplined in any way. Children seemed to learn by example that certain things were frowned upon or made them unpopular, so they stopped doing those things, eventually.

Oddly enough, the children didn't seem to want to do anything he had expected them to do. People, both young and old were glad to see him. After all, it isn't everyone who can call down thunder, lightning and rain, and they were intrigued by a Frenchman that could speak their language and knew Algonquin as well. There were always a few Algonquin slaves and Algonquin-speaking Iroquois living in any village as large as this.

But he was most interesting to them as a person who had such a close relationship with a great oki that a sudden storm was sent to save him. The Iroquois, like their Huron cousins, seemed ready for a more

Seneca Village

developed religion. They were curious both about him and about the god who changed the weather for him.

Without giving it much thought, Étienne soon had the children who were following behind him organized into two teams, and with a bit of ingenuity in constructing a ball, he had them playing the French bowling game, boules. This brought out the young men and soon they were playing, too.

He taught them the game of "dish" or "platters" as the Huron played it. He found six white and six black stones and taught them the gambling game that consists of putting the stones on a dish or board platter, giving the board a blow hard enough to knock the stones off, and according to the bets on white or black stones and their position when they fell, some would win and some would lose. The Seneca Iroquois were great gamblers too, and they liked this variant of their usual gambling games.

It was easy to organize relay races, and running and leaping contests although it was impossible for him to join in any of them because he tired too easily. There were no feasts, and no dances to which he was not invited. Like the Huron, they had dances for every occasion. These often turned into orgies, but this was expected and encouraged in order to increase the size of the tribe.

Étienne was able to plead his wounds to avoid the dances. There was no way to avoid the feasts. Since he didn't like feasts, even among friends, it wasn't a treat to eat with people who had recently tried to kill him. But he went when summoned, and ate what he was expected to eat and listened to the interminable

Seneca Village

speeches. He believed the Hurons were better orators, but was careful not to comment. After a month of recovery, he felt well enough to talk about going home to Huronia.

The chief gave him the food he would need on the trail and a bow and arrows, some stout leggings and a fringed shirt. He looked searchingly at Étienne and said, "Now, Frenchman, you remember our pact?"

"Yes, it is written on my heart. We will work for peace between Huron and Iroquois. It will not be easy, and it would be foolish for either of us to tell our tribes that we want peace. Perhaps later we can speak freely to our own people. Not now. Do any of your men ever trade with the Neutral Nation?"

"Yes, and with the Petuns, the tobacco growers."

"I will leave five French knives wrapped in buckskin with a chief of the Neutral Nation. When I tell him that the package is for you, a gift for saving my life, he will ask the next Neutrals going into Iroquoia to take it to you. It is not the gift that is important, Uncle, it is the pledge that goes with it. Remember that when you see the five knives. They will represent the five tribes of the Iroquois confederacy, Onondaga, Oneida, Mohawk Seneca and Cayuga. I am a member of the Bear Clan of the Huron, The chief is Ochateguin. My employer is the great le Sieur de Champlain. As you probably guessed, I am a fur trader and an explorer."

"I am not young. I may not see you again, Frenchman. But you give me great hope. I know there is a better way to live and my son has that belief, too. If you come back some day, you can ask for my son. He will keep the pact. As for you, I do not believe others in this village will harm you again either."

Seneca Village

Étienne slung the bow over his shoulder and tied the bag of provisions to his waist to leave his arms free. He put one hand on the chief's shoulder, inclined his head slightly, and left the cabin.

At the gates of the palisade, there were four Iroquois warriors, all provisioned and waiting for him. He already knew their names, but was very surprised to learn that they intended to accompany him out of Iroquois territory. That would prevent other Iroquois raiders from capturing him, and by leading him out of Iroquoia they could keep him from becoming lost. He was profoundly grateful.

For four days they guided him along the shortest paths out of their territory. They were near water, and someone always shot some game for food so he didn't have to touch the provisions he started out with. It was a good time for him and for his guides. Every night they made a simple shelter just big enough for the five of them. Étienne could never forget the cruelty he had endured in that village, but the four days of good company helped to restore his faith in the goodness that lies in the hearts of all.

On the fifth day, when they were out of Iroquois territory and he was sure that he knew the way back to Huronia, they sat down to smoke their pipes and ask him again if he had any questions about the correct path. He repeated their directions carefully, because he didn't want to be caught again.

"What will you do when you return to your village?" asked the oldest of the Seneca warriors.

"I would ordinarily go to Trois Rivières for the fur trade, but I am not going to go this year. It is a long,

Seneca Village

hard trip." Étienne paused and thought out his next words carefully. "We have to go north to Nipissing, and then down the River of the Ottawas and thence to the Great River. How easy it would be if we could use the Lake of the Iroquois."

The warrior, who had asked him the question, pretended to be casual as he said in a low calm voice, "Perhaps we will not always be at war with each other."

There had been so many peace efforts, all had failed. But this man seemed so sincere, and the other three warriors were trying to read Étienne's face.

Étienne answered, "I long for peace. You do too. If there are enough of us, we will have it."

They finished their pipes, each put a hand on his arm, and they went south as he continued his journey back to Huronia.

Alone to Huronia

Étienne felt more at ease now that he was out of Iroquoia. Certainly, an Iroquois could be lying in wait at any turn, but it was far less likely this far west of Lake Ontario. The way seemed clear to him, too. It would be easier if he had a canoe, the water way was always his choice, preferably a good, swift canoe moving in the same direction as the stream.

He strode along thinking of Ahouyoche and saying to him, wherever he was, "I hope you were able to escape, my friend. I miss you. It is easier to sing when you are along. Can't say I really like some of your songs because they sound like dirges. But you learn so fast, you sing French songs in beautiful ways and it makes the time pass agreeably. Ah, mon ami."

Étienne reminded himself to rest more often than he had before the torture and to use the grease the chief gave him to keep his wounded skin from being so sore. He had willow bark and made tea with it at night so that he could sleep through the remaining pain more easily. He still had some dried fish and since he was never far from a river or lake he had water. Being lost in the woods when he fled the Iroquois made him doubly careful to be sure not to lose track of where the nearest water was. A shelter at night was easy to make, even with the primitive stone hatchet one of his four companions gave him as they set him on the right direction to Toanché.

Alone to Huronia

Soon he would be back in his Bear Clan village and find out if any of the others escaped. And, as he knew too well, he would also have to learn the unpleasant details of the failed war at Onondaga Lake, the fate of Champlain and of that large army that returned beaten and cold at the beginning of winter.

Even so, thinking of being among friends made him feel more cheerful, and he finally broke into a slow trot. He didn't see the gopher hole. He stepped into it, heard something snap and knew in a sickening instant that it was his left ankle. There was a shooting pain and a sense of shock, dismay and then nausea. He struggled to stand up without putting any weight on his left foot. "No, I can't walk. I don't think I can even hop on my right foot using a strong stick to support myself. Perhaps I can make a crutch. There are women at Toanché who can set bones, but I never bothered to learn how. I am going to have to do something now."

For the first time since he lay burned, and bleeding at the torture post, Étienne felt completely helpless. "I can't have come this far to die because I stepped into a gopher hole!" He took a piece of dried fish out of his pack and made himself try to eat it to keep from adding hunger to his other woes; but his stomach was churning and refusing food. The pain seemed to have filled his body. He looked around hoping to see anything like a trail. Nothing. But he was not in heavy woods and he could hear the water lapping at the riverbank. "Well, I can crawl to the river, perhaps someone will come down it in a few days." Talking aloud seemed to reassure him a bit and he struggled to get up again. Spying a branch near him on the ground,

Alone to Huronia

he used that to help himself stand up again. The branch broke. Here he was in Huronia and helpless.

While sitting there feeling depressed about coming to such an ignominious end after all he'd been through, he heard a woman's voice singing. He thought, I hope I am not delirious, but why should I be, I don't even have a fever. Then he heard the dip, dip, dip of a paddle in the water. Without hesitation he called, "Ho, hho, I am Étienne, I need help. I broke a bone."

His call was returned by a soft, feminine voice. She called, "I am Sarainta." Then the sound of the canoe being beached and hurrying footsteps. "Did you break your leg?" she asked, skipping any further introductions.

"No, my ankle, I fear. I stepped into a gopher hole. I can't walk. I am French, but I am a member of the Bear Clan. Do you know who I am?"

"Yes. I will go now and bring my brother back with me to help you into my canoe. We will take you to his hunting cabin after I see what I can do about your ankle."

"You will be back?" Étienne tried not to sound anxious, but failed.

"I said I would. I have nothing with me to help you and I can't get you into the canoe alone. I won't leave you here," she said reassuringly.

"I've come so far and now I am almost home, but I can't move."

"Don't go away," she said jokingly, and walked hurriedly toward the water talking as she went. "I paddled over to bring my brother sagamite and to help

Alone to Huronia

him with the beaver pelts. Don't worry. We should be here long before dark. I will bring you a bowl of water before I go." She brought him the water and Étienne watched her graceful movements. She was beautiful, tall and perfectly formed. He hated to see her leave. If she did not come back... but somehow he felt sure that she would.

★

"Hho, Étienne!" came a familiar voice from the direction of the stream.

"Is that really you, Ahouyoche?" Étienne sat up and watched as the bushes were parted and there stood his friend. "I hope I am not having a fever dream. How did you get here?"

"My sister Sarainta told me you needed help. She is bringing the canoe up to a better place for you to get in. I did not think I would ever see you again!" Without asking for permission, Ahouyoche examined Étienne's hands, his chest and back and sighed deeply.

"And you, how did you fare?" Étienne asked his friend.

"I kept running until no one was chasing me anymore. I thank the Lord and Saint Apollonia. I believe I shall let Father Le Caron make a Christian out of me. I never had any luck with the gods of the Hurons or the Algonquins. Most of them are devils. What do they care? Ah, here is Sarainta. She was so happy to find you, no one thought you would ever come back."

Étienne looked at the beautiful woman and asked,

Alone to Huronia

"Why didn't you tell me that your brother was my friend Ahouyoche!"

"But I told you my name was Sarainta! Didn't Ahouyoche ever mention me?"

"Certainly. He always called you "my sister". Do you have another sister called Spring Flower?"

"I was called Spring Flower, but then my husband was killed by Iroquois. Now I am called Sarainta." She lowered her head apologetically.

"Are You Crying" is not a good name for you. Should I call you "Sara"?" Sarainta felt Étienne's ankle but ignored his question and just smiled at him. "The break is not bad. It is broken but the bones are not pushed apart. Good that you just stayed where you broke it. I am going to put splints on it now. I brought along two kinds of skins to bind it tight. It won't be comfortable. In a few days I will take the sticks away and just leave the tightly bound skins. She worked skillfully at getting the ankle stabilized and then Ahouyoche supported his friend as he hopped on his good foot. Sarainta went ahead and parted branches and helped get him seated in the middle of the canoe. Then with Sarainta paddling and steering in the back, and Ahouyoche moving the water back strongly in front, they glided swiftly down the river.

A few turns of the stream and there stood a round, bark cabin not far from the water. Outside the hut there was a place for a cooking fire and between several saplings there were beaver skins stretched out by means of leather thongs to ovals or sometimes circles of bent branches. The thongs that were attached to the branches and to the pelts drew the skins taut. The

Alone to Huronia

ovals or circles of bent branches were in turn bound by thongs to the saplings.

"I see you have been busy!" Étienne said through clenched teeth as he gestured toward the skins. His ankle throbbed and he was anxious to get inside and lie down on one of the wide benches he knew would be built into the walls on three sides of the cabin.

The only light in the dwelling came in through the open door. The floor was the ground itself, without the tightly woven mats of the longhouse. But no featherbed in France ever seemed as beckoning as the wide sleeping benches of Ahouyoche's hut.

"This will be your place," Sarainta said. "Ahouyoche can help you get in and out of the cabin and I will be here much of the time, too. When the moon is full again, you will be able to walk using a stick for support. We will have all the beaver for miles around, and a winter's supply of dried fish and berries. Then we can return to Toanché together."

Every time Sarainta spoke, Étienne wondered, Is it just because I haven't heard a woman's voice in a long time? Her voice is sweet and gentle. Huron is not as pleasant to the ear as Algonquin, but with her it is like music.

Ahouyoche cut him a stout stick to help him get around without stepping on his left foot. They spent their days cleaning and stretching furs, smoking fish, and picking over the berries that Sarainta found. Those they didn't eat were spread out on a table to dry. They would be welcome in winter. Ahouyoche told him that he was the only one of the thirteen Huron warriors from Toanché who made it back. He said it was hard

Alone to Huronia

to be around so many grieving families in the village and Étienne understood why his friend wanted to leave it for the peace of the woods, if only for a little while.

"Where did you get the tools to make this flat table top and the benches?" Étienne asked, rather surprised to see a French-style kitchen table outside the cabin.

"You forget, I'm a fur trader. I take tools in exchange. I like this adze – far easier than always trying to do everything with a hatchet. A flat table is good. Very good. There are many in Trois Rivières like this." Ahouyoche looked pleased with himself.

"Next thing I know you will be building yourself a cabin like some of the traders have in Québec!"

"Even in Trois Rivières there is a cabin I like. Have you ever built a French cabin, Étienne?"

"Well, no. I do not like living in the longhouses, so that is why I usually live with Aenons in his cabin. I have built little bark dwellings like this one from time to time, but they don't last long, especially if I'm gone a lot and don't keep them in repair, and I am always gone more than I am in Toanché."

Ahouyoche said, "Marsolet and Grenolle showed me how to build a good cabin when I was with them. They have one at Trois Rivières that they use, not far from where the river pours into the River of Canada. It was Marsolet whom I sold my furs to and he showed me how to use this adze, one of the tools he gave me in exchange. I would build a French cabin, but my wife thinks it would look as though we didn't like her relatives if we moved out of the longhouse." Ahouyoche shrugged and gestured with his arms

123

Alone to Huronia

raised and palms outstretched.

"I would risk their displeasure if I were you, if only to get out of the smoke, away from the dogs and the constant noise of children."

"Well yes, but my two sons say they will be lonely if they are not with their cousins in the longhouse."

"So be it then, Ahouyoche. I myself will build a French cabin and you can use it when you want to breathe during the winter. The smoke makes my eyes hurt. Did you know that Father Le Caron was almost blinded by the smoke? His eyes became infected and if spring had not been early, he would have lost his sight. I was glad to hear that some of you bring him food and help him with repairs to his cabin." Ahouyoche brushed it off as if to say it was nothing, but Étienne could imagine what a relief it was to Le Caron to have some human contact. He simply could not live in the longhouses, few Frenchmen ever could.

"Étienne, you know how to build a fireplace?" Ahouyoche sounded eager.

"I think so. You have made me want to try. I am anxious to be able to walk. Now I want to build a good solid cabin, and have a fireplace, and perhaps a wife?"

"Is that a question? Don't you know if you want a wife or not?"

"No. I'm not sure. I think that Goes Softly's child is mine, but she isn't certain. I will probably know when I see how the little girl looks when she is older. I like her and play with her. I often bring meat and fish to Goes Softly. I don't want to live with her." Étienne chuckled and continued, "She doesn't want to live with me either. I think she will stay with the man she

Alone to Huronia

is with now, they understand each other well and are happy together."

"Don't you want a French wife, Étienne."

"Ma foi! What would I do with a French wife out here? Even if I already had the cabin with fireplace, she would probably die the first summer of mosquito bites, and if that didn't kill her, loneliness would. The woods, and especially the rivers always have beckoned to me and I do not get lonely. Or, I thought I didn't. Now I don't know. When I came here years ago, I was sick until the mosquitoes finally had me thoroughly filled with their poison. Now, I don't suffer any more than the Huron. What fevers I had that first summer! It is hard to say whether I suffered more in my first years because of the winter hunger, or the summer insects. I would not like to see a wife suffer like that. And she would be so lonely."

"Don't you have mosquitoes in France?"

"No. But then, you didn't used to have measles or mumps or poxes, or the coughing and spitting blood disease or colds. And we always have those diseases and others."

"You are the first Frenchman who has admitted to me that those awful plagues came from across the sea. The Frenchmen don't die of them so easily, I notice. Here, the closer we are to the French, the sicker we are and the earlier we die. But you don't seem to bring sickness, Étienne," Ahouyoche added hurriedly.

"I don't think I do either. But I don't spend much time in Québec with people newly arrived from France. I had many of those diseases and won't get them again. It is also true that the closer the relationship with the French, the less hunger in the winter, the less silly worshipping of rocks and other nonsense and all the crazy stuff about having to do something because it was in a dream."

"True enough. Father Le Caron has helped me to see that it is foolish to fear the spirits of the woods and water. I was never very sure of them anyway. Do you know the things Father Le Caron knows, Étienne?" Ahouyoche asked eagerly.

"Some of them I know. Le Caron is usually disgusted with me. He thinks I am too much interested in women and that I will be severely punished when I die if I do not change."

"But you haven't even had a woman companion other than Goes Softly, and that was for such a short time. Nice, of course, if that child is yours."

"Well, I think so, and the Huron think so, but Father Le Caron is always shocked. Fortunately, he doesn't know about a couple of pretty girls up along the Ottawa. You see, Ahouyoche, in France it is not permitted to have more than one woman. Well, unless you are very rich, then there are exceptions made. Like with the King."

"Oh certainly. That is reasonable. But the Huron and Algonquin and even the miserable Iroquois love children and are glad to have them born into their people."

"The French love children, too."

Ahouyoche looked very skeptical at that remark, but said merely, "Then why aren't they glad when women have children by different men, if that happens, especially before the woman has settled on any one man?"

Alone to Huronia

"Because of inheritance. How could a man know for sure whether a child was his or not? Like, how can I know about Goes Softly's little girl?"

"Why don't you tell them to do like we do? We know that our sisters' children are related to us. So we leave our belongings to our nieces and nephews. Of course, we can leave things to our children too; the Huron is always free. But inheritance is through the mother. Couldn't the French do that?"

"You and Father Le Caron should have a great time with that problem." Étienne laughed thinking of these two men, each moral in his own way, trying to see the other's point of view. "I can hardly get Le Caron to forgive me for eating meat on Friday, mon ami, I don't even try serious questions."

"Since you know some of the things Father Le Caron knows, you can have me ready to be baptized when we get back to Toanché. I believe I would like to be civilized."

Étienne said playfully, "Then you should learn to read, too."

"Well, I am not busy now. You can teach me to read while we wait for Sarainta to come home to make our supper. Is that all I will have to do?"

"One thing at a time, mon ami!"

Étienne had planned to ask Ahouyoche for Sarainta's hand, but considering the conversation they just had, he decided to postpone it. If he were going to ask anyone for that hand, it would have to be Sarainta herself. It was obvious to him that no one would marry Sarainta unless she wanted him.

Huron Romance

Sarainta arrived in Toanché before the other two and beached her little canoe carefully, because she knew her brother would be right behind her and it annoyed him when she didn't take good care of it. She made several trips to the longhouse carrying the berries, fish and meat they had gathered and dried at Ahouyoche's hunting cabin. Her mother, who was pounding corn in a hollowed out tree trunk near the shore, came down to the water to help her.

"Where is your brother?"

"He is very close behind me. I was showing off and managed to beat him back."

"Why would you bother to do that?" her mother laughed. "Aren't you old enough to stop trying to keep up with men?"

"Well, Mother, you remember Étienne? You know that Ahouyoche thought he was dead. I thought so, too. He was captured, tortured and then released by the Iroquois! He was already back in Huronia when he stepped into a gopher hole and broke his ankle. He wasn't far from the water and called out to me for help as I paddled along on my way to Ahouyoche's camp. He's with my brother now... I find I like to show off a bit when he is around. I think he will be a good husband."

Her mother chuckled, but then said warily, her eyes

Huron Romance

narrowing, "Why did the Iroquois let him go? Because he is French, perhaps? But they are at war with the French, too! And why would you like to be a wife to a Frenchman? If your father were alive…"

"I suppose he wouldn't like the idea?"

"Probably not. You know how your father was. He always did the traditional thing. But since you are a widow, you can do whatever you like. Basically, you could do whatever you liked even if he were alive. But think the matter through carefully. Frenchmen seem to have a lot of hair. Except the priest, Le Caron. He has a bare space on top of his head. They even have hair on their chests and faces. Étienne is always off on a trading or exploring trip. Will the two of you live in our family longhouse?"

"No, I think we will live in a cabin alone. I once saw a French cabin when I went to Trois Rivières with my husband. I liked it. I think I will have one of them. They are bigger and more solid than Étienne's little hut. He knows how to build a French cabin. He knows how to do all kinds of things, he can read and write, draw maps to show where he was and direct others to the same place. I don't really know why I would like to live with Étienne. But I know I want to. I like his curly black hair."

"That's a great start, curly black hair." Her mother shook her head.

The sound of laughter and the hoots of surprise made it obvious that Ahouyoche's canoe was back. People were crowding around him and Étienne.

"How did you escape from those devils, Étienne? Is there anyone else still alive from that trip to

Carantouan? What happened to Tall Trees?" Several people were calling out questions at once. The tension and hope were all too real.

Étienne drew a long breath and began his account of that awful time. "Tall Trees is the only one I know about. I saw him killed by an Iroquois stone hatchet on the day that they ambushed us in the woods – our first portage in Iroquoia. It was very quick, and he did not suffer. I don't know what happened to the others. They were probably taken to the nearest Iroquois village. I hid and was not found that day. I was captured three days later, but I was all alone and I know I was not brought to the same village where the others were taken. I am sorry not to have any good news. I hoped that some of them might have returned, but Ahouyoche told me no one else escaped with him that day."

The father of Tall Trees, and parents and wives of other men who did not return, went to tell their families the bad news. No one was really expected back. It was probably a consolation to the family of Tall Trees to know that he hadn't been tortured, but his father walked slowly and his head was bowed. Tall Trees was really gone.

Chief Aenons had been told of Étienne's return and he hurried down to the shore to greet him. "Ho, Étienne, I rejoice to see you! I was sure you were dead! Come to my cabin and tell me everything. Your cabin is empty, dirty, and raccoons probably play in there."

"Thank you, Aenons, I will go with you gladly." Étienne helped beach the canoe, and seeing that there were many hands to help Ahouyoche with his baskets

Huron Romance

of provisions, he took the stick he used as a cane and walked with Aenons toward the cabin they had so often shared. Aenons seemed older and was limping noticeably.

"Were you wounded at Onondaga Lake, Uncle?"

"Yes, nephew, in my heel. The trip back from there was very hard. Champlain was in great pain, too. One of our warriors carried him for three days in a basket on his back." Aenons sighed. "Good that Champlain is small and there are some big Huron warriors." He tried to smile, but the memory was too bitter.

Like the considerate host he had always been, Aenons found a place on a wide bench for Étienne to rest. This cabin was certainly more comfortable than the longhouses. The tightly woven mats that covered the floor were always clean, there were no dogs, all the cooking was done outside the cabin, and he lived there alone most of the time since his wife died. On occasion, there was a grandchild or a visiting son or daughter, but it was far more peaceful than the longhouses with people constantly entering and leaving and moving about inside. Even a very small longhouse with only five fires meant ten families, about sixty people, and perhaps five dogs. Some baby was always teething. Sickness or injury always had its grip on others, and that required the services of a shrieking sorcerer. Yes, Aenons's cabin was much more to Étienne's taste. He told his story of being captured, tortured, the sudden storm and that he was later even helped on his way back to Huronia.

"I have trouble believing the Iroquois would let you go. I know, I know. There was the business of the storm that made them think you had a link to the Great Oki, but after they had started the torture? It is just so hard to believe. Did they ask you for anything?" Aenons eyed him suspiciously.

"If they had, I would politely have promised them the moon. But what could they ask?"

"That you help them get the Huron trade for the Iroquois." "No. No one asked that."

"It might be hard for others here to believe that."

"I suppose. I never thought of people not believing me! I am a member of the Bear Clan, but I am a Frenchman, too. Doesn't everyone realize that the French are also on the warpath with the Iroquois? The Iroquois are friends of the English, could one Englishman captured by us make any difference if we let him go?"

"I don't know, Étienne. I believe you, and I think your story is true. There was no need to return here if it wasn't. But you had better be watchful of some of the others. It is always hard for the families of those who did not come back, they might resent the fact that you were released."

"Yes, I knew some would resent my good fortune when their own men were tortured to death. I just did not think anyone would blame me for living!"

"The Huron have long memories. So you must be on guard. When least you expect it, someone might accuse you of treason, even years from now. But perhaps no one blames you for being able to come back. I wish you had waited and told me your story first. I could have told you what to leave out."

Étienne was glad he had not confided to Aenons the

pact he made with the Iroquois chief to try to work for peace between the two tribes. That would be too much for his host to accept.

Étienne and Aenons were invited to have dinner at the fire of Ahouyoche's family. The invitation came, as invitations always did, at the time the meal was ready. No one ever refused an invitation because that would be insulting. It was easy enough to go to the fire of a friend for an evening meal, but sometimes it took heroic endurance to get up from a sickbed and go to an eat-all feast. Ahouyoche's wife and sons were glad to have him back and pleased that his good friend was still alive. Étienne looked around the little gathering hoping to see Sarainta. He thought he was not observed.

"Your friend is looking for your sister!" Speaks Loudly yelled. She laughed delightedly to see Étienne's embarrassment. Speaks Loudly was feeling playful, apparently. Ahouyoche shook his head and shrugged his shoulders. He had little influence on his wife.

Aenons said pleasantly, "Everyone is always pleased to see your sister-in-law, Speaks Loudly. She is a fine young widow, a great help to her mother and brother."

"Of course, Uncle. I like her too. I invited her to help me serve the meal. She is in my mother's longhouse bringing down some of the things that I need. Does everyone have his bowl and spoon? I thought Étienne might not have one, so Sarainta is bringing an extra one."

Étienne settled himself on a stump near the cooking fire. It was not as easy to get up and down as it used to be before the Iroquois burned parts of his body. His skin was healed but the muscles felt strained. His beard had grown back in and it hid most of the scars on his cheeks. His back and chest would always be deeply scarred. His ankle was stronger every day, but he tried not to sit on the ground if he could avoid it. It felt good to be among friends.

He watched Ahouyoche's two sons, so rowdy that any French father would have told them to behave and if not, they would have felt the back of the parental hand. But this was not France. Ahouyoche was delighted with his wild young sons, and merely smiled as they ran around knocking things over.

Sarainta finally appeared, carrying a basket of provisions and walking with more of a swishing movement than he remembered. Perhaps she just did that to make the fringe on her dress move more? She was wearing a buckskin dress that was so pale in color that it looked white by the light of the fire. The dress was heavily beaded with purple wampum shells, and had beaded fringe all across the bottom. Her moccasins matched her dress, and had higher sides than her usual footwear. They came up above her ankle, the sides fringed and heavily decorated with purple and white shells. Étienne looked at her and grinned. He knew that she was pretending to be just as usual, but he had lived in the cabin with Ahouyoche and Sarainta for a month, ever since she found him with the broken ankle, so he realized that this elegant outfit was far from being her normal wear.

It made him happy to be able to admit to himself that Sarainta was dressed like this for him. He wished he had something more attractive than the clothes given him by the Iroquois chief that were still sturdy,

Huron Romance

but dirty and a bit greasy. For the first time in his life in the wilderness, he felt underdressed. He looked to see what Ahouyoche thought of all this. His friend was watching Sarainta pridefully and gave Étienne a meaningful glance. Unfortunately, Étienne had no idea what he was supposed to do, so he carried on as though this were simply another evening meal with friends in the Bear Clan.

When the women had served the men all the food they wanted, they took their own bowls, served their own meals and sat apart to talk among themselves. Speaks Loudly, as luck would have it, was talking quietly, so Étienne couldn't catch even a word although he certainly tried. Now and then he would look at Sarainta and sometimes she would smile back. How beautiful she was, how sweet, how graceful. And then too, she was intelligent and his best friend's sister. He knew he would have to arrange this marriage quickly. Suppose some other man also had his eye on her? There must be many who did. That made him feel angry, but why? He certainly always admired Goes Softly, and he felt glad that she had a good husband. He liked her husband. But Sarainta was not Goes Softly.

When Aenons and Ahouyoche were smoking pipes after the meal, Étienne rose as inconspicuously as possible and took the bowl Sarainta had brought him for his food, and under the guise of returning it, went up to hand it to her. She shook her head and said she wanted him to have it. Without waiting for another more romantic occasion, Étienne whispered, "Will you be my wife?"

Huron Romance

She looked into his eyes as though she was savoring the moment, and then said very quietly and firmly, "Certainly."

"What do I do now? Do I speak to Ahouyoche again or do I arrange a feast?"

"You will have to arrange a feast, and since you do not have anything, we will use what we gathered near the hunting cabin. I have corn set aside for winter. We will have to replenish the stocks after the feast. Or, we could wait until you have something available to serve at the feast." She looked at him questioningly.

"It doesn't sound good to have the feast before I can really give it, but I am afraid someone else will get you if I don't speak now." He had never been more sincere.

Sarainta laughed delightedly. "Goes Softly told me she will help me get your cabin ready to live in. First, we have to get rid of the little animals. She has many skins you have given her. I have many things. You must remember," she said proudly, "I am a widow and have my own household wherever I am."

"I am glad you have household goods and food. As soon as the feast is over, I want to go up to the Nipissings and maybe even on toward the Grand Lac."

"Are you just going to take me into your cabin and then leave?" Sarainta was shocked and surprised.

"Oh no, I thought we could go together! On the way back, I will leave you here, and then go on with the other canoes to Trois Rivières. That would not be a pleasant trip for you with only men. But it will be beautiful going up to Lake Nipissing together. I have some trade goods. Goes Softly still has them. She could

Huron Romance

have used all of it by now, but Aenons said she still has everything. We will use that to buy furs from the Nipissings. I want to get some information from them about the Great Lake. I think I will need several men to go with me on that voyage, but you and I can go together to the Nipissings if you'd like." He looked at her hopefully.

"Oh yes, I think that sounds wonderful. I will talk to Ahouyoche and Mother after you and Aenons go back to your cabin, and we will have the feast in just a few days."

"Thank you. Sarainta, I feel so happy, I have never felt like this before."

"I know. I feel very strange, too." Then she laughed and said jokingly, "Well, perhaps it is just your curly hair."

It was dark on the side of the fire where they stood, so he felt free to run his hand over the curve of her cheek.

"And perhaps I feel this way just because of your fringed and beaded dress." He laughed, and went to suggest to Aenons that they go back to his cabin.

Huron Wedding

Étienne still used his walking stick, and Aenons hobbled along beside him. They were about the same size, a generation apart, and centuries distant in outlook, but friends nevertheless.

"So, translator for the Huron, you will soon have a wife!"

"How did you know? Did you hear me ask her?"

"Oh, I knew before we arrived at Ahouyoche's fire. A beautiful woman is with her brother and you for a month. She is lively and intelligent. You are injured and have no wife. It is time you have one. Then you and I are invited to a meal. You bathe and comb your hair and beard carefully. All this for Ahouyoche? No. Then, of course, when I saw Sarainta in that beaded dress and watched you nervously spilling your stew and trying to make conversation, it wasn't hard to guess what you had in mind."

"There are no secrets in a Huron village, are there?"

"Not for long. When will the feast take place?"

"Very soon. Everything will be done by Ahouyoche, Sarainta, and her mother. I know that it is my duty to give the feast, but at the moment I have no means of doing so. Also, Sarainta, her mother and brother know who must be invited."

"I am sure everyone will approve the marriage."

"So am I. It seems foolish to have a feast to settle what we all know will be agreed upon."

Huron Wedding

"Don't you have a feast to celebrate a wedding in France?"

"Yes. But we have the wedding first, then the feast."

Aenons laughed delightedly. "How strange the French are. First the wedding and then the feast! What if the guests don't think the marriage should take place?"

"If they don't think it should take place, they must tell the priest beforehand. And, if there is good reason for the couple not to marry, there would be no wedding and no feast."

"Do you miss your far-off land and peculiar customs?"

"Sometimes I miss them very much. I would like to be married in a special ceremony with a priest to give the speech. Like we do in France."

"Well, we have Father Le Caron here now. You could ask him! He would probably like to give a speech. No one understands anything he says, except you and Ahouyoche."

"I will think about that tomorrow." By now they were back in the cabin and settling themselves in for the night.

★

After a hurried breakfast of cold sagamite and water, Étienne walked over to the cabin that he had paid some of the men to build for Father Le Caron. While still several feet from the door, he called out to Le Caron in Huron fashion. The brown-robed Recollect friar was quick to appear and very glad to see Étienne, whom he invited to sit and visit with him on a bench outside his bark cabin.

He told Étienne of his hardships during the winter. His food was stolen, no one cared to try to teach him the language. He was sometimes fed by charitable savages, but knew daily hunger and cold. It was difficult even to keep a fire going with the wind whistling through the cabin during stormy weather. Then, as might be expected, he fell ill and had a hard time recovering...

He asked all about Étienne's escape from the Iroquois. The news of his survival had reached him, but he couldn't understand much of it, and he was hungry for news, and to hear French spoken again.

Finally Étienne got to the point of his visit. "Father, I am going to marry the widow Sarainta, sister of Ahouyoche. They are arranging the feast. It will be soon, I am sure. Just when, no one knows. It will depend on when the food is prepared and ready to serve. I would like you to have a wedding mass for us. Could that be done?"

"I couldn't do that without permission from Champlain, and besides that, Sarainta is not a Christian."

"Believe me, Champlain does not object to marriage, mine or anyone else's. And Sarainta would be happy to be baptized, if that is the problem."

"I think that I would baptize her if we had not had the bad example of the first priests in New France baptizing so freely that it gave religion a bad name. When we saw the lists of the Christians and contacted the so-called converts, they did not know anything at

Huron Wedding

all about Christianity. Could you postpone the wedding until she has been accepted into the Church?"

"Father, have you seen Sarainta? She is beautiful, and now that she thinks she wants to have a husband again, I am afraid I will lose her if I do not marry her very soon."

"Marriage is not to be entered into lightly, my son," the priest said reprovingly.

"Oh, of course not! Then, you cannot marry us?"

"Not now."

The priest hesitated a moment and then asked, "Will you have the savage ceremony?"

"It isn't a ceremony. Just a big meal. First we eat, and then various men stand up and give speeches. It is boring, but the effect of it all is to say that we have the approval of the Bear Clan. Then Sarainta is officially my wife."

"For as long as she feels contented with you and you with her, is that not right?"

"Yes. I plan to see to it that she is contented. I know I will be." Étienne sighed.

"Instruct your wife well. I would like Champlain to give permission since you are his servant here."

"Thank you, Father. I will instruct her, and her brother, too. Soon after the feast, Sarainta and I are going up to the Nipissings to encourage them to go to the fur trade at Trois Rivières, or to entrust furs to Huron traders to take there. I would like to learn something from them about the way to the Grand Lac. I keep hoping someone will have heard about a passage to the Far East. I am sure that the Grand Lac is sweet

141

water, so that is not the way, but someone might know."

The priest was so glad of his company and the chance to speak and be understood that he pressed Étienne to stay and talk for a while.

"How is the Huron language coming along, Father?"

"Very poorly. I get someone to help me – even in just naming things – and that person eats the food I have for payment, or smokes the tobacco, and then I am left without help in learning." The priest shrugged his shoulders helplessly, and added, "Perhaps if I could live in the longhouses. But I cannot. It almost destroyed my eyesight when I tried. The smoke injured my eyes so much that I was unable to see for a few days. I thought I would never see again."

"I know. I will find someone to help you, and I will pay for it. You won't learn Huron in two months, but it is the beginning that is so difficult. After that, you will see a pattern in the language. You need this cabin apart from the others. It is harder to learn the language this way, but easier for you to keep your health and sanity. Where do you say mass?"

"Come in, my son, and I will show you."

Half of the tiny cabin was set apart as a chapel, with colored holy pictures adorning the bark walls. A crude altar was set up and on top of it was a gold monstrance and a set of candlesticks with uneven wax candles in them. Father Le Caron knew how rude it all was, but the Hurons who saw it were always so impressed that he had begun to feel quite proud of his little chapel in the wilderness.

Étienne thought of his parish church in

Huron Wedding

Champigny, and of the comfortable rectory and saw what terrible sacrifices this man was making to bring Christianity to the Huron. First he would have to learn the language, and somehow he had to stay alive during the winters, not an easy task for anyone.

"When I come back from Trois Rivières, I will do as much as I can to teach you Huron, or hire someone else to do it, mon père. You have a difficult task, and deserve some assistance out here."

"Thank you, my son," the priest said with feeling, "come back to see me soon!"

Étienne was on his way back to Aenons's cabin when he saw several people around his own rough bark dwelling built in a semi-circular shape. Curious to see what was going on, he walked over and saw Goes Softly and her husband, Standing Bear, carrying in the bundles he had left with them for safe-keeping.

Étienne greeted them with, "I could not know how long I would be gone, but I never expected it to be for so many moons. People thought I was dead, but you did not sell any of the goods I had! I need them now, and I cannot tell you how grateful I am to you both. Why did you not use them in the fur trade? A dead man does not need trade goods."

Goes Softly said, "I thought you might be alive. Especially after Ahouyoche came home. Water Song refused to think you were dead. She believes you are her father. She has curly hair! Her eyes are light brown, and her skin is whiter than mine. She is inside your cabin trying to chase out little animals with the help of the dog you gave her. It isn't a puppy anymore."

143

Huron Wedding

Étienne had always loved Water Song and played with her often. She liked the stories he made up for her. She learned French nursery tunes to please him, singing along after him until she could remember all the words. He didn't know if he was her father, but he had always provided meat and fish for her and gave Goes Softly and her husband things they might need, too. He was their good family friend. Now his heart was beating faster, was it true? Was Water Song his daughter? He stood by the door of the cabin and looked inside.

The cabin was small, so the light from the doorway was enough to show a little girl of six with a sheaf of cedar bows in her hand trying to sweep the cabin floor clear of dried leaves and rabbit droppings. She looked up at him and yelped with joy as she raced into his arms. "Oh, my Uncle, I knew you would come home. Did you miss me?" With a pang of conscience, he realized he had not really missed this bundle of unadulterated love. He held her close and said, "Only an idiot would not miss you, Water Song."

He carried her outside to where Goes Softly and her husband were trying to decide where they should set up a new fire pit for him outside the cabin. "Yes, Goes Softly, I know she is my daughter. She resembles my sister Catherine too much to be anything but mine."

He looked intently at Goes Softly's husband and said, "I am your brother in the Bear Clan, but I am more than that to you. I have never had a brother. You are now my brother because you care for my daughter." The Huron punched him playfully in the

Huron Wedding

shoulder and said, "If you are my brother, then you had better let me give you something to wear to the wedding feast. Greasy Iroquois clothing would shame the family! Come up to our longhouse, and I will dress you well. Getting the feast ready is keeping all the women busy, so you will have to fit into my clothes without any changes. Fortunately, you are tall for a Frenchman."

There were others bustling about his cabin now, and a constant stream of young women with firewood on their backs were dumping their loads behind the dwelling. Ahouyoche and Sarainta were there, too. Ahouyoche knew a place where deer bedded down at night, and wanted Étienne to go with him to that general area to see if they could get a tender young doe for the meal. Sarainta smiled lovingly at Étienne and said she thought the feast would be very soon. A boy had been sent off to Cahiague, the biggest of the Huron villages, to invite the most prominent men. They would be told that the time of the feast was two days hence. Of course, who could say with certainty? If the meal wasn't ready, the dignitaries from Cahiague would just have to wait when they arrived in Toanché. But they would be entertained well.

Sarainta went behind the cabin and exclaimed over the quality of the firewood the young women had brought her. It had taken serious time and effort to gather the bundles of wood and carry them to her, but every young woman felt it her duty to provide a load of firewood to any bride. Sarainta chatted with the young women, and there was the usual teasing banter as they sat on a grassy spot behind the cabin and talked and

145

rested after their labor. Étienne glanced at the women and could see that Sarainta was happy, and not nervous at all.

Goes Softly and her husband had gone back home, but Water Song was sitting with the young women. Her dog was at her feet, and she had taken up a position next to the bride-to-be. Étienne smiled to himself. His daughter certainly knew her place in this celebration! Sarainta was braiding some daisies into the little girl's hair. Now that Water Song was no longer a baby, how obvious it was that she was not completely Huron!

Two days later the feast was about to begin. Sarainta's nephews were happily going from longhouse to longhouse inviting those who should attend – all the men over fifteen in Sarainta's mother's longhouse, and all those over fifteen in the longhouse of the mother of Speaks Loudly, Ahouyoche's wife. There were also the friends of Étienne and of Ahouyoche. Aenons had provided the names of the men who should be invited from Cahiague.

The night before, Étienne had been in a long sweat bath with his best friends. His Huron "brother", Standing Bear, had insisted on giving him the new clothing he was wearing, they were not merely a loan. It felt good to be wearing clean and attractive clothing. Ahouyoche wanted to attach various colored feathers to his friend's hair with porcupine quills, but Étienne told him he really did not want to do that. He had already shaved off every vestige of beard and his hair was cut to just above his collar. He wished he had something from his home in Champigny. Then he remembered the medal which still hung around his neck. Goes Softly came into the cabin to collect Water Song who refused to leave earlier and now was asleep on one of the benches by the wall.

"Do you happen to have a ribbon or a beaded cord that I can put my religious medal on? This old cord looks very dirty with the new clothing your husband gave me." Goes softly laughed, "I think I probably do. If not, I can always take a slice off the wampum belt you gave me before you moved in with me!"

"Please do not tell me that you still have the wampum belt I gave you when you were single! Shouldn't you trade that, or give it away, or something?"

"Why should I give away my wealth? You gave it to me. My parents would not have let you stay with me without something! What strange ideas you always have!"

"Doesn't your husband object?"

"Why should he object that I was a popular young maiden? You were not the first to give me a wampum belt, and you were not the last."

"I do not want to think about that now. I do want the cord, though."

"I'll be right back with it, and I'll collect Water Song then."

Finally, dressed to his own satisfaction, and wearing his medal on a red silk ribbon that he or someone else had given Goes Softly, he took his bowl and spoon, stopped for Aenons who was awaiting his arrival, and they went to the clearing.

The great clearing near the water was where

important meetings took place as well as large feasts. It was surrounded by the immense cornfields that provided the mainstay of Huron diet. He was glad the affair would be outdoors, the smoke would not be so gagging, nor the dogs so bothersome. But there was something about this lovely field facing the sparkling blue water that gave him chills up and down his spine. He said so to Aenons.

"Men are almost as worried about taking a wife as women are about accepting a husband. It is just your way of thought that is bad. What did you do when you had Goes Softly? There was no feast? I have forgotten."

"I gave her a wampum belt. I stayed with her in her parents' longhouse for three days. According to strictest custom, we did not exchange one single word in all that time. I didn't mind that. I have never had much to say to Goes Softly anyway. And I don't think she finds me entertaining either. After the silent days, I think we both felt we would probably have a feast, be really married. But the more we knew each other, the less pleasant that prospect seemed. Then I kept going off on trading trips and she found someone else. Or, more likely, he found her. When I came back and she had a different man, I was relieved. When her baby was born, no one knew who the father was. By then, she was living with Standing Bear. They love each other, and he cares for Water Song. But it is clear now that she is my daughter. See her over there with Ahouyoche's sons? She looks just like my sister did at that age."

Aenons glanced at Water Song and said approvingly,

"It is good to have sons and daughters. Come, we must greet the visitors from Cahiague first, then your companions of canoe trips. Do just what I do. Oh yes, don't talk about your captivity, even if someone asks. Just shake your head sadly. Do you think you can smoke a few pipes?"

"Perhaps I won't have to."

Aenons looked skeptical.

There were many cooking fires. The women were laughing and talking and seemed to be enjoying themselves in spite of doing most of the work. The deer that Étienne shot while hunting with Aenons was well cooked and smelled delicious. The blueberry cakes had already been passed around ceremoniously in a basket someone had decorated with leaves and flowers. Sarainta's mother was ladling stewed squash into bowls, other women had set long rough-hewn boards in front of every few men and placed roast beaver and squirrel on them. An old woman went around with a large basket filled with baked fish. A young woman poured hot sagamite into the bowl that each guest brought with him. The boiled beans had been seasoned with hot peppers someone had got in trade with the Tobacco Nation. They sold tobacco as far south as the Spanish people. There was great merriment over the poor diners who got too big a piece of the red things in amongst the beans, and then had to call for bowls of water.

Étienne made a mental note to find out who it was that journeyed that far south, he always wanted to know who was traveling to places he was not familiar with, so that he could increase the fur trade and his

Huron Wedding

own knowledge of the country. Hours passed, people got up from their meals and visited with friends they hadn't seen in some time. Usually, it was the custom to wipe the grease from their hands onto their hair or perhaps onto the family dog. Today, pieces of moss were distributed for that purpose. Great effort had gone into this meal. The visitors from Cahiague were treated like royalty. But it was clear that this was a wedding feast, and that he was the reason for it.

Sarainta was helping out, but would probably go back into the longhouse before the speeches began. She was wearing the heavily beaded dress she wore the night he asked her to be his wife. Her hair was elaborately braided with blue and white ribbons interlaced with her midnight black hair. Étienne wished he could disappear before the speeches, preferably with Sarainta, but he knew that would never do. The Huron, as famous orators, needed the occasional audience to give their talents full play.

Finally the meal was over. The women gathered up the remains and went off to enjoy their own part of the celebration. Sarainta told him it was not uncommon for the women to have a few things set aside for themselves as special treats. One of those treats was ears of corn that had been buried in a swamp until they were truly "prime," the corn worked in such a way that it was a sweet treat and much enjoyed by women and children. It smelled so bad that no one could hope to eat it without others knowing. Sarainta would not indulge. After all, this was her wedding night. He smiled in happy anticipation.

The speeches were every bit as long as he had

feared. They covered everything from the long enmity with the Iroquois, to the alliance with the Great Champlain. And then kind words had to be said for Champlain's translator, who was a member of their very own Bear Clan, and marrying a widow of that clan. In an effort to be fair and just, it was mentioned that no one knew a thing about Étienne's family in France, but his daughter, Water Song, was bright and healthy. It was mentioned, as it always was, that the French were a bit puny and small. But, the speaker said reasonably, their small size was an advantage when their strength wore out as it so often did, and they had to be carried on the backs of Huron warriors.

Wedding Feast

One of the orators remarked charitably that although it was well known that Étienne was inclined to be more hairy than the Huron, he was clean-shaven on this day. His great abilities with canoes, especially his endurance and skill with the grand canot de maître was detailed by men who had been on long voyages with him. His facility with Huron and Algonquin was praised. The fact that he could read symbols and write them so that others knew his thoughts was admired by several speakers and always drew a long drawn out "Ho hho" from the audience. Sarainta was mentioned in flattering terms, and the marriage was approved without anyone even bothering to ask for contrary opinions.

Étienne went back to his own cabin, far more tired, he thought, than he had any reason to be. After about an hour, Sarainta appeared. She was not smiling and it looked as though she may have been crying.

"Oh, little darling, why are you sad?" Étienne felt alarmed.

"Because, my husband, I cannot stay with you for the next four days! It has turned out to be my time of the month and I must go and stay in the small longhouse with the other women who are likewise afflicted. My mother will bring me food and water." Sarainta was sobbing.

Wedding Feast

Étienne felt disappointed, but more for her than for himself. He had never been called, "my husband" before, and he knew the separation would only be for a short while. The ridiculousness of the situation made him chuckle slightly. This infuriated his new wife, who was almost too angry to speak. Almost.

"It may be amusing to you, but it isn't for me! I have been dreaming of living here in this little cabin with you. Now, when I am so tired and upset, I am going to have to be with lots of foolish women!"

"Surely, they can't all be foolish," Étienne suggested, to pacify her.

"Well then, you live with them the next four days and find out for yourself!" Sarainta was certainly telling the truth when she admitted she was tired and cross. She seemed like a petulant little girl, not the reasonable young woman he knew. He took her by the hand and said as kindly as possible, "I am going to walk over there with you. Do not sit and talk to the other women. Tell them that your husband has ordered you to lie down and sleep and that you are not feeling well. I will bring you food and water. I'll ask your mother to bring you something to sew or maybe I can find something myself. How do you feel about making a leather pillow filled with pine needles? I could get the materials for that."

"Oh, what does it matter! Let's just go to the women's lodge and I'll start my married life over there with them."

Étienne held her close to him and kissed her beautiful smooth face and tear-filled eyes, and said, "Ma petite, do not think about anything serious

Wedding Feast

tonight. I have learned to postpone some worries. I dwell on other things and often the matter resolves itself. Your problem is limited to four days! Do not torture yourself. Make a pillow for our cabin, talk with the women when you are rested. I will come over and call for you to come to the entrance every morning where I'll bring you food and things to pass the time. Now let's go and you can start getting the four days out of the way."

Nipissings

Étienne was drawing a small map of Penetanguishene Bay that he knew well, when he heard Sara call his name outside the cabin. She was out of breath from running. Only four days had passed, and every day he saw her for a few minutes when he delivered food and water, but it felt wonderful to have her back in his cabin. He put down his pen, pulled her close to him and groaned. "We aren't ever going to go through this silly nonsense again, Sara."

"We will have to. Everyone does."

"*Everyone* lives in the longhouses except the occasional chief, Father Le Caron, and you and me. *Everyone* goes to *tabagies* where all the guests eat until they are sick and every so often someone dies because their poor bodies can't take crazy superstitions as well as their minds can. Everyone is not you and me. I have been able to do things differently because I am French. You might as well join me in being French, it is far easier."

"I will think about that, Étienne. See how I am doing what you tell me to do? You always say I should think about everything and sleep at least one night before deciding. I will do that. Perhaps I will be French, perhaps not."

Finally alone in their cabin for the first time, Étienne felt vaguely embarrassed. What did she expect

Nipissings

him to do now? That was not a worry for Sara who asked, "What do we need to do so that we can leave early tomorrow morning?"

"Nothing. Your mother gave me a bag of pounded corn, Goes Softly gave me some dried fish, your brother and his wife sent the boys over with corn cakes. I was never so well cared for as a single man. Do you suppose they think I might fail to feed you?"

"No. They are just happy for us. You have everything packed, I see. I will spread the mats on the sleeping bench and put the pillow I made of pine needles there. The French like pillows, so you can use it. It made my neck hurt. Considering being a French woman is not going to be easy."

"Don't let the pillow change your mind. French women sleep without them too, if they want to. We have no rules concerning pillows." He laughed, thinking again how happy he was to have this lovely woman for his own.

The visit to relatives and friends to say goodbye before leaving for Lake Nipissing was mercifully short. Étienne doubted he could take much more distance from Sara without getting angry at someone. He gave Water Song some little wooden animal figures he had for her, and she let him go without fuss when he told her he would bring her back something pretty from the Nipissings. Not that he could think of what that might possibly be.

When they came home from visiting relatives, Étienne asked his wife as they entered the dark cabin, "Shall I light a candle from the embers of the cooking fire?"

The Indians knew where the beavers lived, and the European fur traders relied heavily on Indian guides.
Harper's New Monthly Magazine, LXXXIV (Feb., 1892)
Permission of State of Mich. Dept of History Arts and Literature.

MAP SECTION 01

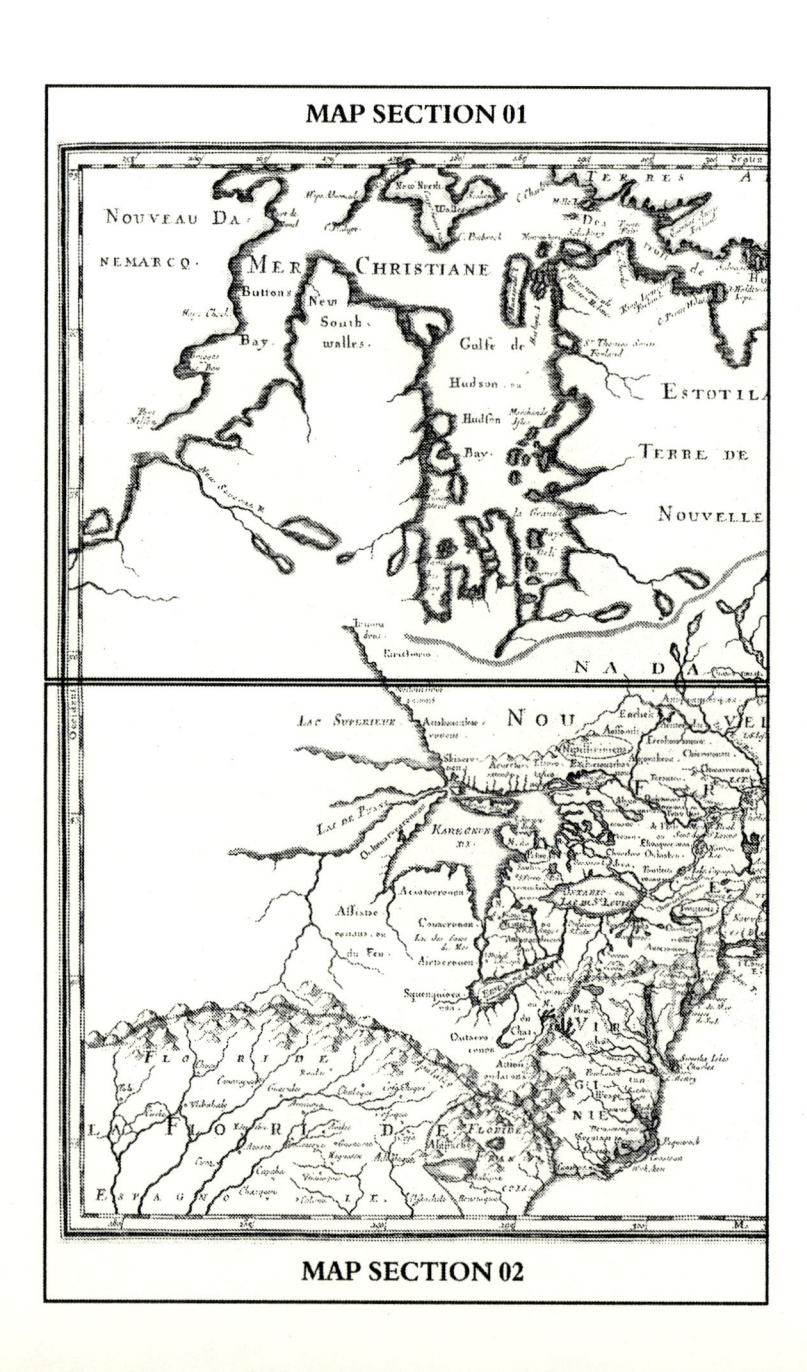

MAP SECTION 02

MAP SECTION 03

MAP SECTION 04

NOUVEAU DA=
NEMARCQ.
MER CHRISTIANE
TERRES ARCTIC
Buttons
Bay.
New
South-
walles.
New North
Walles
Golfe de
Hudson, ou
Hudson
Bay.
troit de Hudson
ESTOTILANDE, ou
TERRE DE LABORADOR, ou
NOUVELLE BRETAGNE.
LE CA=
LE SAGUE
NAY.
NA DA
OU
NOU
VEL
CANADA.
LAC SUPERIEUR

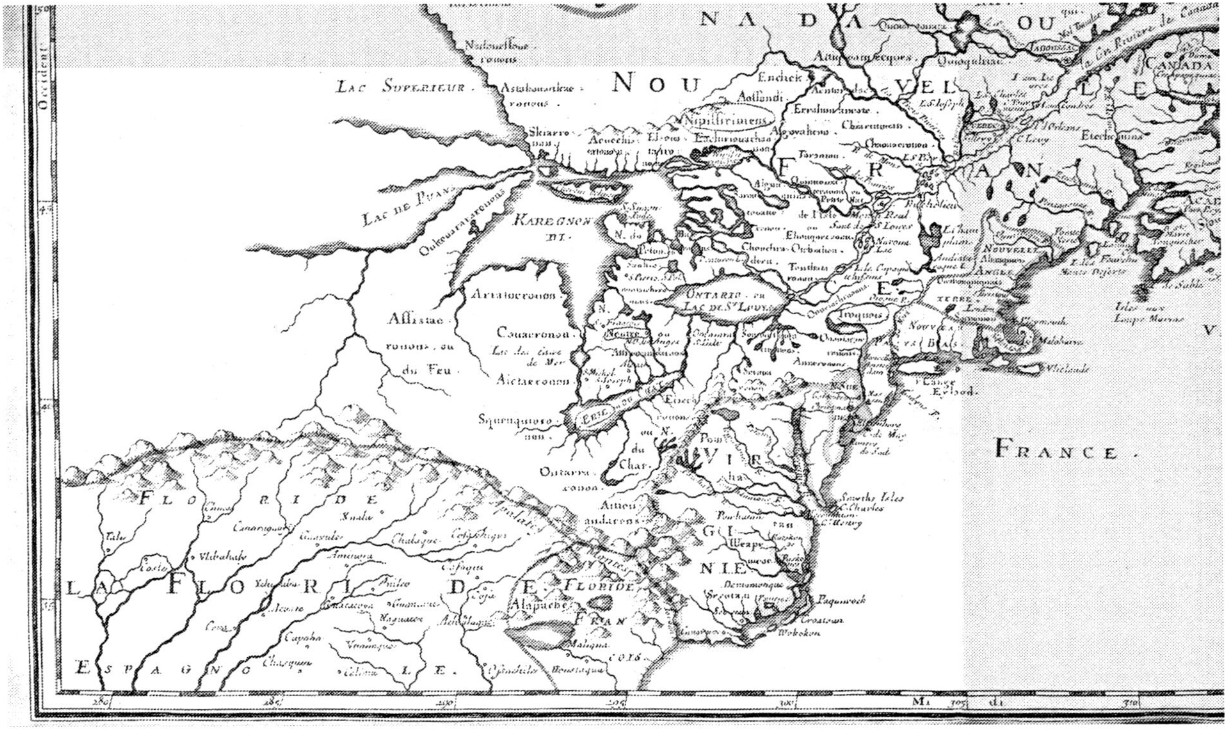

Occident
LAC SUPERIEUR
LAC DE PUANS
NOUVELLE FRANCE
CANADA
KAREGNONDI
ONTARIO ou LAC DE St LOUYS
ERIE
Nipissiriniens
Iroquois
NOUVELLE ANGLETERRE
NOUVEAU PAYS BAS
VIRGINIE
FLORIDE
LA FLORIDE FRANCOISE
ESPAGNOLE
FRANCE
Assistaeronons, ou du Feu
Attiouandarons
Ouitarraronon
Alapache
Paquiwock
Croatoan
Wokokon
Mi

Terres Arctic
Groenlande
Destroit de Davis
Destroit de Forbisher
Hudson
Estotilande, ou
Terre de Laborador, ou
Nouvelle Bretagne.
Mer
Mer de Canada
Le Canada
Le Saguenay.
Golfe de Canada
Isle de Terre Neuve
Belle Isle
C. Farwel
C. Christian
Elsabetes Forland
Lage Hoeck
Hollandsche Bay
Port de Quartier
Schild padde.
Buttons I.
Isle de Resolution
Oupapinachouek.
Bersiamites.

LE CANADA, ou NOUVELLE FRANCE, &c.

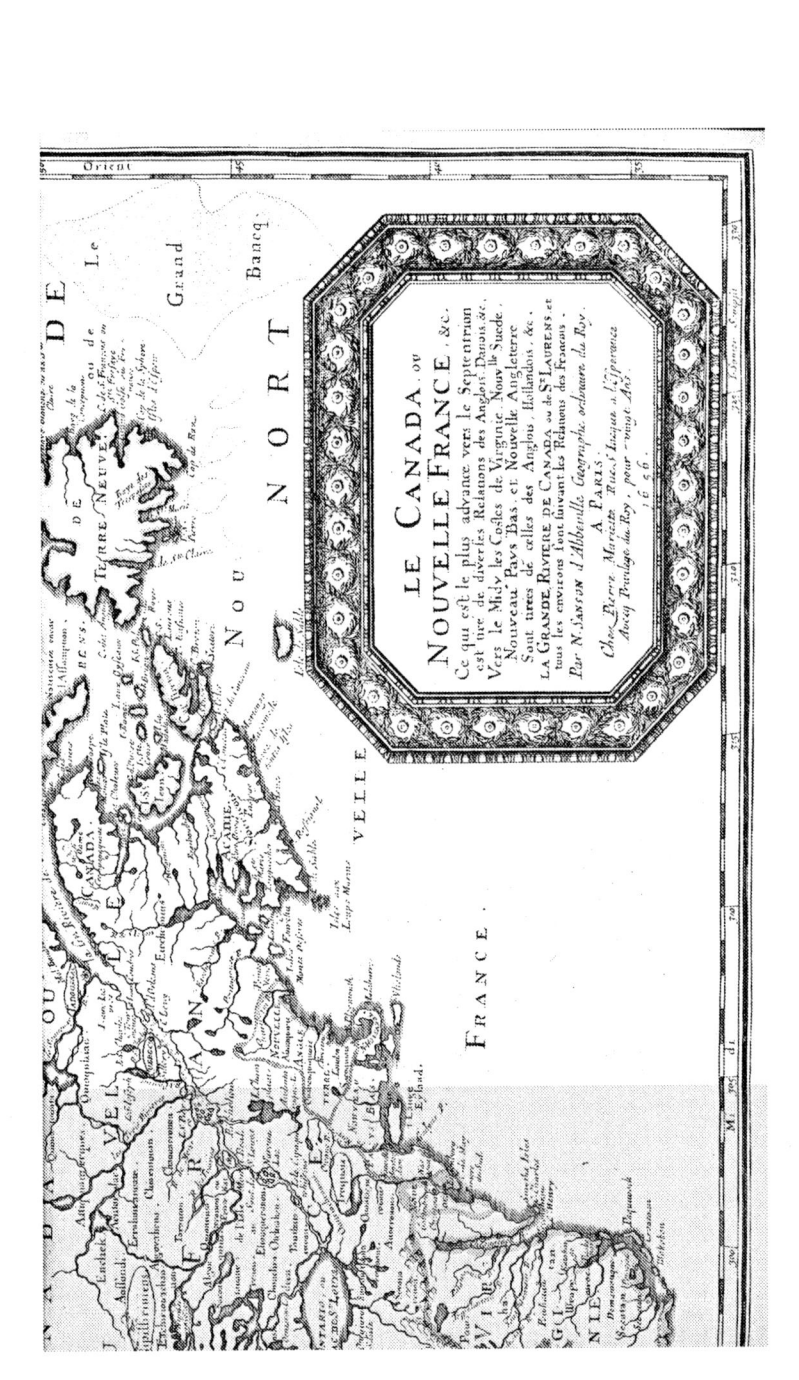

Ce qui est le plus advancé vers le Septentrion est tiré de diverses Relations des Anglois, Danois, &c. Vers le Midy les Costes de Virginie, Nouv. Suede, Nouveau Pays Bas, et Nouvelle Angleterre Sont tirées de celles des Anglois, Hollandois, &c. LA GRANDE RIVIERE DE CANADA ou de St LAURENS et tous les environs sont suivant les Relations des François.

Par N. Sanson d'Abbeuille, Geographe ordinaire du Roy.

A PARIS.

Chez Pierre Mariette, Rue S.t Iacque a l'esperance. Avec Privilege du Roy, pour vingt Ans. 1656.

Algonquin village scene at the time of the arrival of the Europeans in the 1600's.
Michigan Historical Commission
Permission of State of Mich. Dept of History Arts and Literature.

Catholic priest with Chippewas at Sault Ste. Marie.
Castelnau, Vues et souvenirs de l'Amerique du Nord
Permission of State of Mich. Dept of History Arts and Literature.

Ancient copper mine, Lake Superior area.
Michigan Historical Commission
Permission of State of Mich. Dept of History Arts and Literature.

"Oh no, don't waste the candle. We are tired anyway, aren't we?" She laughed.

"Tired of waiting for you, my love," he said tenderly as he took her hand and led her to the sleeping bench.

★

The morning dawned cool and quiet, even the children weren't crying. Although the kind of dogs the Hurons had did not bark, there were sometimes dogs at Toanché that did, but not this morning. There were bears kept in a pit where they were fattened up to use for feasts, and they made strange guttural noises when awakened, but they were quiet, too. Étienne turned to his sleeping wife and marveled at the perfection of her features and body. She half opened her eyes and asked sweetly, "Shall I move closer?"

"Well, yes, if you don't mind."

"I don't." She pulled him close to her.

Finally they noticed that the village was all awake, children crying, mothers clanging pots and kettles, and men calling to one another.

"Sara, let's take our supplies, load them into the canoe and then paddle out of Matchedash Bay into the Great Bay of the Sweetwater Sea and then find a pretty place to stop and eat."

She slid over him onto the edge of the sleeping bench, felt around on the floor for her dress, slid it over her head and tied the cord around it. All dressed, she slipped her feet into her moccasins. Then she took the braids out of her hair, reparted it with a wooden

Nipissings

comb, and quickly re-braided her shiny black tresses. Étienne watched her and enjoyed the show. She left the cabin to take care of other needs and to bathe, using some of the big pot of water he stored near the cooking fire.

The problems of sanitation and smells made it essential that villages move a bit at least every ten years. Water for cooking and washing was usually kept near the fire pit in large clay jars, if water was at any distance from the cabin or longhouse. But garbage and human and dog wastes became a problem. Leaving palisaded villages to relieve oneself or to get water was not easy. Étienne often wanted water to drink so he had it at hand. The Hurons rarely drank water with meals, but needed a great deal of it for the usual sagamite and for the fish and meat stews. That was another reason for wanting French cooking utensils – they didn't leak.

"You take the small packs, Sara. Leave the big ones for me." He shouldered a pack of trade goods and started off. Then he turned and saw Sara with a tumpline across her forehead attached to a heavy pack of supplies. He felt horrified.

"Put that down! Take off that tumpline! Do not ever use it unless your life depends on it. I don't want you looking like a beast of burden."

"Work goes faster this way, Étienne. I'll have to make more trips to the Bay without it."

"No, you will not! Just take small packs and then wait for me to finish. I did this alone before. Remember, you are considering being a French woman."

"Well, perhaps that is not practical here?"

Nipissings

"We will make it practical, Sara. Why should you be worn out and tired? I love you!"

The use of the words seemed strange to her. Clear, but strained and as though they had been translated from a different way of thinking, and, of course, they were. The Huron did not speak like that to their wives. She smiled and took off the tumpline. When they were settled in the canoe, there was plenty of room to stretch their legs, even with trade goods and extra baggage. Sara took the usual woman's seat as steersman and Étienne took the paddle in front. Easily and quietly they skimmed through the still waters of Matchedash Bay.

"You must have canoed this with your husband?"

"Oh yes. With both husbands."

His hands froze on the paddle and Sara laughed and called to him to paddle hard left or they would be pushed onto the rocks.

"I didn't know about any other husband. Who was he?"

"I was married to a fishing net when I was ten. It was a very nice ceremony. They gave me a pretty dress too, it had porcupine quills dyed bright red in a band along the top and bottom. Everyone said I looked lovely. My cousin was married to another fishing net the same day. Then we had a small *tabagie*, not a horrid eat-all feast, you understand, just a nice meal even though it was what you would call a religious feast. I had a pleasant time. So did my cousin. She was twelve. We had a fine fishing season. The best in years. Your daughter Water Song is pretty, perhaps she will be chosen to marry a fishing net when she is older."

Nipissings

"We will think about that," he said, knowing he would never agree to it. "But I suppose I should not be jealous of a fishing net. While we are talking about such things, I would like to know if you ever went to the side of a sick friend and spent the night there with a young brave?"

"No, but it was not easy to escape that duty. My friend was sick and the old women thought she would live if all her friends went to her cabin and each brought a young man along. There were many deaths among the people here that year and my mother was sick, too. She would have nothing to do with medicine men so I was needed to care for her. She had one of those sicknesses the French brought with them. I felt quite fortunate that I didn't have to go to the longhouse of my friend. Have you ever heard the din of those ceremonies? Bad enough with all those young men and women in the dark without also having a medicine man on each side of the cabin banging on a drum and having visions all night long. You would think that with what was going on in the longhouse, there wouldn't be time for visions."

"I am glad you never had to go to one. What happened to your friend?"

"She died. Two moons earlier her father went to Québec to trade, came home with little red splotches all over his body. He lives on, but she took care of him and then she was too sick to live. The French certainly have a lot of illnesses. I hope you won't start to be like that." She sounded reproachful.

"I will try to stay away from people newly arrived from France. Sara, I have already had the diseases that are killing people here. Some of those diseases people only have once, usually when they are children."

"The coughing sickness?"

"No. People can have that several times a year. I don't often have it."

"I hope you will continue that way. I will try to be a little bit French, and you must try to be Huron and not bring sickness."

Her request seemed reasonable because the more the tribes traded with the French, the more sickness they had. The French could plead innocent as much as they wished, but the facts were that the Huron and Montagnais were losing many people to diseases they had never seen before. The tribes that didn't see Europeans didn't have colds, whooping cough, mumps, measles, smallpox, chicken pox, or tuberculosis. Of course people often died of starvation or of wounds.

Étienne usually plied these waters alone, and when he had companions he always let them decide when they were going to stop to eat. The weather was fine, only the most gentle of breezes disturbed the calm blue-green water of Matchedash Bay. In less time than it usually took him paddling alone, they were on the shores of the great Bay of the Lake of the Hurons, the Mer Douce or Sweetwater Sea.

"Ho, Étienne, are you still there paddling, or is it an evil oki who has taken over your body? You are not singing, you are not talking, and I am getting very hungry. Is this going to be another one of those strange things French women do – go without food on canoe trips?"

Nipissings

Étienne enjoyed knowing Sara was behind him in the canoe, he liked the way she steered and the smooth dip, dip, dip of her paddle in the water. His mind was full of pleasant thoughts and dreams, and somehow he had forgotten that he had said they would eat breakfast in the first pretty place they saw. "Oh, Sara, I am sorry. I was so happy I forgot we also have to eat. We can land here at a place I call Moose Point because I once saw a moose there. They immediately beached the canoe and he said in what he thought was a calming tone, "You can rest all afternoon now, as soon as you have had your very late breakfast. There was no need to encourage her to eat, she pushed some corn cakes toward him, but was already muching on one. She was still feeling annoyed about the long time between meals.

Because it was already August, Étienne had decided before leaving Toanché that they would go up the French River to the Nipissings, and if the weather held and the Algonquin war was over, they could learn about the best route to the Grand Lac, but important business first. The Huron wanted the people at Lake Nipissing to bring their furs to Toanché to let Huron traders sell for them at Tadoussac or Trois Rivières because they were the more experienced traders and particular friends of the French. They also expected the lion's share of the profits. Still, Étienne understood quite well that Champlain wanted all the tribes to think of themselves as friends of the French. No hope with the Iroquois, but all the Algonquins, especially those who had gone to war with the Huron against the Iroquois, seemed likely trading partners.

Later, when they came to the only serious portage on the river, Sara acted surprised when Étienne began hiding some of the supplies and trade goods. "Will they try to steal our things? Will you remember where you put them?"

"No, they won't steal from us. They know I am allied with the great Champlain and that he is their friend and protector. We will be returning this way. I don't want to be tempted to sell everything I have at Lake Nipissing. Perhaps we can visit the Cheveux Rélévés, they live between the Great Bay of the Huron and the Sweetwater Sea.

Their country isn't far from Manitoulin Island. The more I think about it, Sara, the more I know it is too late in the year to go any farther than that. Winter would stop us, and we would have to spend it right where we found ourselves. I have lived with Algonquins, and it is hard to do, especially in winter. You think the Huron have many superstitions? The Algonquin people have them too, but theirs change from day to day. Now that is hard!"

"Étienne, everything that isn't French isn't necessarily foolish!" Sara said teasingly.

"Oh, I know that, and some groups of Algonquins do provide enough food and wood for winter. Not all of them. They seem to be surprised when it gets cold. They are always hospitable, but often have no food. No, you and I will go back to Huronia. But I do want to encourage large groups to go to Tadoussac and Trois Rivières with their furs. I think it always helps to have some French merchandise to show them. Watch where I am putting goods and then if I forget, you can

163

Nipissings

remind me." Étienne laughed happily. It was fine to have a partner.

They rested and spent the day fishing. After a good meal of fish, sagamite and berries, they made a shelter for the night. Étienne found a place near the water where there were low-growing saplings. He bent some of them over a small space, covered them with woven mats in case it rained, and placed spruce bows on top. Mats and furs covered the small space they needed for sleeping.

It was the duty of the Huron man to build the shelters and the canoes, to go to war and to hunt. They were also expected to get the soil ready for planting by clearing out old vegetation. Huron women did everything else. So Sara took care of the food, hanging it by cords out of the way of most animals. Bears might be anywhere and probably were.

Étienne had made this trip several times with Ahouyoche or with Grenolle, usually alone. It never before seemed so easy nor so pleasant. Still, he reminded himself, he needed to be very careful mapping every cove, and every change in the river that people were starting to call the French River because by taking it to the Ottawa, it was possible to arrive finally at the French settlement at Québec without going through Iroquois territory. Meantime, Sara liked his attention, and he enjoyed providing it.

The next morning Sara said determinedly, "We are going to eat before we leave. I am not ready to give up food until you find the ideal place to beach the canoe. Yesterday morning my head ached until we finally ate." She sounded like every wife he had ever known

Nipissings

in France. She was going to bring up that morning's "starvation" all her married life. Étienne smiled. He would find some little peculiarity of hers and never let it drop. Marriage was a good idea.

The day they arrived at Lake Nipissing there was no one fishing and no one on the shore, but not long after they brought the canoe up onto the beach, there were swarms of people around them, all asking questions.

Sara knew very little Algonquin and it was obvious to Étienne that she was frightened by the foreign sounds. The Nipissings were all asking him, "Where were you?"

They drew in their breath, shouted oaths, or just gasped in horror when Étienne answered by saying "Iroquois", holding up his mangled fingers. He had to tell again the story of how the Iroquois warrior reached for his religious medal and how he believed he had been saved by the intervention of the great God he believed in. Since the Iroquois didn't let captives go, his escape caused great wonder. He followed his story with the spoken hope that soon there would be a servant of that God living among them and teaching them Christianity. Naturally, he mentioned how much Champlain would appreciate that.

Suddenly, a pretty girl whom Étienne had noticed on previous trips, asked boldly, "Who is the Huron woman?"

"My wife," he said simply. Sara had put on her dress with the dyed porcupine quill and beadwork embroidery and looked both well-dressed and very Huron. Her dress and moccasins were much finer than any the women in the crowd had seen. The pretty

Nipissings

Nipissing girl looked Sara over from head to foot, shrugged, and decided to help her unload the supplies. Then she took her by the hand and led her away from the noise on the beach. Étienne was glad that the girl was being friendly. He knew it was upsetting to Sara to see so many people gathered around, speaking a language she couldn't understand.

This group came to camp by the shores of Lake Nipissing every summer, then went farther north for the winter. They were known to other tribes as the Sorcerers because there were so many medicine men and so much superstition among them. Because they didn't have palisaded villages and lived in small cabins, their settlement seemed much larger than a Huron town with the same number of inhabitants. He could understand how threatened Sara would feel.

All the men who were gathered around him looked toward Sara who came racing back down to the beach a few minutes later. She said quietly but angrily to him, "You should have told me you have a child up here."

"I certainly do not! Who says I do? I usually was here on the beach with Ahouyoche, and once with Grenolle. I do remember the pretty girl. But I would remember more about her if, well, you know."

But Sara was angry and trying not to show it in front of the Nipissings although they all seemed to know exactly what the problem was, and they grinned and talked among themselves enjoying the discomfort of the newly-married Étienne.

"I am going to do some trading here right now, and you certainly have drawn their attention! Now sit down and listen. It is time you learned Algonquin.

Nipissings

Don't even think about anything else, and don't quarrel with me in front of them. One or two of them are sure to understand some Huron, you know."

Sara smiled sweetly and said through clenched teeth, "Oh yes, great Sagamore, I will do your bidding, but you must explain to me later." She spread a large bearskin on the shore, and put trade goods on it – not helter-skelter as he had always done, but in neat rows, and just one example of each piece.

Étienne spent the rest of the afternoon trading for furs which he would sell on his own at the trade fair next spring. He always sold some pelts on his own account and now he had greater use for wealth because he was beginning to think seriously of bringing Sara back to France with him for a visit. But his main purpose on this trip was to make the Nipissings want to bring furs to the Huron at the end of winter. It was important to Champlain that they accept a missionary into their settlement, and if the people here went to Trois Rivières themselves, they could take a priest back with them. While he talked to the men, his mind kept reverting to the problem of the child who Sara told him was half-Nipissing, half French. The pretty Nipissing girl was able to say that much easily with sign language. Why had the girl decided to call him the father? She must know he was not. Nipissing braves would not be deterred from courting that girl just because she had a healthy child! For some reason, she wanted a Frenchman. Why? He could easily insult the whole tribe if he did the wrong thing. After all the trade goods he had with him were sold, and he extracted promises from one band to bring furs to

Nipissings

Toanché, and from another group to go to Trois Rivières to trade, and even a half-hearted promise from a chief to bring back a missionary, he told Sara to show him where the girl and her child lived.

She hurried along at his side, muttering and complaining as they went. He ignored her. These people rarely called out in front of the cabin, but simply entered. He stood politely in front and Huron-like, he asked to be admitted. The girl came out immediately. She was carrying a boy of about four months who wasn't all Nipissing because his black hair was curly. Étienne grinned when he saw the child, and said aloud, "I am sorry this beautiful baby cannot be mine. I never slept with you. It is part French, I can see that. Any man would be proud of this baby. I do not blame you for picking out the first Frenchman you see after the child's birth. But unless Grenolle was here alone after he was here with me two years ago, it is not his either."

The girl looked taken aback, as if it surprised her that a Frenchman could do a little female arithmetic. She paused a moment, and then said flatly, "It is a French baby, and I am its mother. I want to live in a French cabin and I want French shirts and many kettles."

"That is reasonable. I will see Grenolle and probably Marsolet when the ice melts in the spring. I will tell them about this handsome child. If neither of them is the father, perhaps they can help you find the fur trader who is. Do you know?"

"No, I am not sure. The man was here alone; he bought many furs. He laughed a lot and said he would

Nipissings

come back soon. He gave me a French shirt."

"Show it to me." She soon came back with a French peasant's blouse which had been carefully worn and wasn't yet greasy. "I will tell Marsolet and Grenolle that whoever it was, he gave you a French shirt. Do not worry, we will find the baby's father because they know the other men who trade up here. They all go to Trois Rivières or Québec every year and there are very few of us. No more than the fingers on both your hands. The child's father certainly will give you trade goods, and if he wants to, he might take you with him and build you a French cabin. I will find the father for you, but you must tell the people here the truth. Champlain would be angry with me if he heard that I had a baby up here because he insists on marriage first. Do you have food to last until spring?"

"I think I do. My mother's brother still lives near. He will help me through the winter. I will tell everyone that you are searching for the baby's father. She accompanied Étienne and his wife back to the beach. Sara was fascinated by the half-French baby, and it was easy to see that she planned to have one of her own. She understood the girl's reasons for choosing Étienne. After all, she had chosen him herself.

Sara was going to prepare food for their meal at night, but he told her it would be best if they just visited several cooking fires.

The weather was still not cold, the people would be moving farther north for the winter soon, and all had plenty of food to share. They would consider it a courtesy if Étienne and Sara ate a bit with several

169

Nipissings

families. It would be considered rude to eat alone. Also, at one of the fires someone might give him more of an idea who the child's father could be. Some of the no more than a dozen traders had wives with them.

Others, like Grenolle and Marsolet were better known and easy to find because they worked at least part of the time for Champlain. Étienne was the first white man to learn Algonquin and served as the first translator of it, but now he was the translator of Huron, so he was not as familiar as Marsolet and Grenolle were with the Frenchmen at Tadoussac and Québec that were Algonquin areas.

Étienne asked one of the Nipissings about the danger of encountering war parties if he went to Manitoulin or down to the Cheveux Rélévés at the top of the Sweetwater Sea.

His host, who was an old warrior with the scars to prove it said, "Who can tell what the Winnebagoes might do? They are the farthest outpost of a great warlike nation that lives far away toward the setting sun. I cannot understand a word they say, I have traveled much. I have been to the Great Green Bay. It was many years ago, perhaps they have learned to speak a reasonable language by now. Do you understand them?"

Étienne had been asked this question or variants of it for many years. If he could speak Algonquin, Huron–Iroquois, and French, then people thought perhaps he could speak other languages as well. "No, I don't think I have ever heard a word of Dacotah. I have been told of it. Do you think they are warring on the Cheveux Rélévés?"

"The people at Manitoulin will know. If the Puants, (Stinkers) who are also called the Winnebagoes, are warring on the Cheveux Rélévés, go back to Toanché. Oh, and I am sorry to hear you aren't the baby's father." He laughed gently and shook his head. How quickly news spread!

He and Sara had planned to sleep on the beach, but his dinner host insisted they share his cabin. Étienne brought their furs and spread them out on pine boughs. His host and wife were talkative and when sleeping, they snored. "Don't worry, Sara, tomorrow night we will be in Manitoulin and you can rest well. I told you this fur trading wasn't all as pleasant as you thought."

"I will be able to understand the language at Manitoulin?" she asked hopefully.

"Oh yes! I am glad we came here because I think we will see Nipissing canoes at Trois Rivières in spring and they will take back a priest who knows at least some Algonquin. Marsolet will have taught one of the priests by now. Champlain wants to have a mission here. Maybe Grenolle will accompany the priest, they often get him to look after clergy. I hope he comes this way because I want to take him with me to the Grand Lac, probably right after the fur trade next year at Trois Rivières." Étienne laughed and added, "Grenolle will solve the mystery of the baby's father."

Manitoulin

Étienne was encouraged by their successful visit to the Nipissings. None of the sorcerers there had accused him of witchcraft – no one had even mentioned evil manitous. He knew there would be more Nipissing canoes coming down the Ottawa in spring because he had convinced them to make the voyage. Champlain would be pleased.

Now he could devote his time to exploration. He could travel as he pleased. It was impossible to journey safely into Iroquois territory, and always foolhardy to go anywhere when winter might set in. No matter how much he wanted to explore the land to the west, first he had to get the natives enthusiastic about going to the fur trade in the spring, because it was always the fur trade that paid for exploration. But he had done all he could for the fur trade this year.

Distances were so great. He sighed as he looked at his map. Rivers and streams are never straight. It would be wonderful if de Monts or any group of rich men would hire him just to explore. But first the fur trade. If the natives received him kindly, it was because everyone wanted French kettles, tools and even shirts and blankets. He had visited Manitoulin before, but knew his maps were not accurate enough. Now he would correct them, renew acquaintances with the Huron on Manitoulin Island and find out about any

Manitoulin

Algonquin wars that would hinder trade.

The scent of the forest, different in every season of the year, now was full of the smell of recently fallen leaves. The foliage decaying in the fall rains, the increasingly cold water of the great bay of the Mer Douce, and the indefinable feeling that he and Sara were all alone in the world made him quiet and pensive. It seemed to energize Sara who was paddling too fast. He finally asked, "Do you want to work this paddle and I will do the steering?"

"No."

"Then relax. You must never get worn out over nothing, especially when we are on the water. We might need your strength later, and where will it be?"

"All right. You teach me religion so Père Le Caron will baptize me when we get back to Toanché. I cannot be part French and not be baptized."

"D'accord. You, your mother, Ahouyoche and many others have noticed that the medicine men are silly, running around with flaming torches in crowded longhouses to frighten devils. Then they try to make friends with devils to drive out sickness! I am going to start your instruction by showing you how right you are already, and how much better off you will be if you give up all superstition and believe in one good God instead of so many devils."

"Don't you believe in devils at all?"

"Yes, I believe in a devil and that he has followers, but God is greater than all. There is no devil vomiting and causing thunder, for example."

"What does cause it?"

"I was afraid you were going to ask that. I can't

Manitoulin

explain it, but it isn't a devil. In France sometimes mothers tell little children it is the sound of angels playing boules, but that is not taken seriously by adults. Père Le Caron will know. God can cause thunder and lightning anytime, but the natural thing is that it is due to the weather." By the time they reached Manitoulin, he thought he had removed enough superstition so he could begin teaching religion next time they were alone on calm water.

No surprises awaited them at Manitoulin, and no one seemed to know anything about Algonquin wars except that they certainly were taking place up along the Ottawa in an area about two weeks away. After a day at Manitoulin, repairs to the canoe, and a night's rest, they set off for the land of the Cheveux Réléves.

"Sara, don't get upset with these people, or at least try not to show it. They know I work for Champlain. They can give me information about going to the Grand Lac which I hope to do next summer with Grenolle, and well, you see–"

Sara said with a laugh, "These are the people who don't wear pants, but you don't want me to embarrass them! I already know that. They aren't concerned about embarrassing me!"

"Well, I suppose. But don't look too startled about their skin either. They cut it into intricate designs so that it looks like embroidered deerskin. Most of the men do that. Not the women, fortunately."

"Doesn't it hurt them?"

"Yes. It is terribly painful. Many die. I don't see that it is beautiful, but they think it is. They wear their hair in elaborate styles, usually arranged to stand straight up

Manitoulin

on top, and since they are tall anyway, they seem to loom over me like giant animals."

"What do the women wear?"

"Oh, they dress simply, and much like any Algonquin tribe, like the Nipissings or Ottawa that you already know. I have often wondered if the men wear pants when it gets cold. I suppose they must, or there wouldn't be any Cheveux Relévés to talk about or visit. They are eager for French goods, and we want them involved with us, in the fur trade. Some of them are even farming and raising corn, beans and squash. But not many do that yet. It takes a while."

"Why? It is awful to be without corn!"

"I keep telling you that people are all different, you keep wanting to believe they are all the same. They all get hungry, not all provide for hunger."

"Well I would. Of course I am Huron. I thought it was going to be a long, hard journey and you keep telling me to be sure to keep close to land. How are we going to get anywhere without going across the Bay?"

"I want to ride along Manitoulin's shore until we can see another island where we will spend the night. No one seems to live there. From it we can see the top of the great peninsula where the Cheveux Relévés live, between the Lake of the Huron, our Sweetwater Sea, and the lake with the green bay where I intend to go next spring with Grenolle. Today, I don't want to risk getting lost in a fog. It is much easier when you can paddle straight for land that you can see. I have sat for hours on end waiting to see where I want to go when the fog hangs close to the water."

"My brother said you have a piece of French magic

Manitoulin

that will always tell you the direction of the setting sun. Why didn't you bring it?"

"It isn't magic. It was abandoned with Ahouyoche's beautiful canoe when we were attacked by the Iroquois. I will get a new one next spring. But just in case we have a sudden storm, or thick fog, it is better to paddle farther along the shore than to take a chance in the open water. Did you ever have to swim when the canoe overturned?"

"Only once. Not far. Did you?"

"Too often to remember. Water in the canoe from sudden squalls, leaks in the bottom I couldn't bail fast enough, once some idiot stood up to show me how he caught a moose in a trap, and often in rapids. I've been alone on many shores – wet, cold and hungry. It has made me cautious."

"Can we make the trip across in one day?"

"We must, Sara."

"If we get lost and can't see after dark, what do we do?"

"Nothing. Never wear yourself out foolishly."

"Do you absolutely have to make your maps and go to new places all the time?"

"Yes, I think I do. Does Ahouyoche need fine canoes? Does Le Caron have to convert savages? Do you want to live with me?"

"Oh, all right. Paddle hard right," Sara said resignedly, but she was smiling.

★

After a night spent on the island above Manitoulin,

Manitoulin

they finally started toward the Cheveux Relévés. Étienne, as he had promised, was teaching Sara basic Christian doctrine.

"I know you are wiser than I," Sara said diplomatically, "but are you sure about the virgin birth?"

Étienne laughed, paddled strongly and replied, "Oh yes."

"I ask because we had two young girls in our longhouse last year who insisted they had never been with a man and it turned out to be false."

"I think I am going too fast with my teaching and skipping too much. I shall tell you first about prophets telling about what would happen. Then you will understand."

"Oh good. I like prophecy. I was disappointed that none of the sorcerers at Lake Nipissing did any of that. I always heard they did."

"Yes, sometimes they put on a wonderful show. They build a little cabin and get in there and wrestle with devils and moan and groan a lot and some of the people believe what they have to say. Unfortunately, there are so many sorcerers among them that it is sometimes hard to get a believing audience. Not to mention that they are usually wrong. Too many in any trade make getting work difficult.

"I was there once when a sorcerer told a young hunter about abundant game one day's journey to the east, and no Iroquois to trouble him. He barely escaped with his life when a raiding party saw him. And the only game he saw was a chipmunk."

"Well, chipmunks shouldn't be considered game.

Manitoulin

The Huron are descended from a little chipmunk."

"Do you really believe that nonsense?"

"Not really. Are your prophets different?"

"The ones I will tell you about were. None were chipmunks. Sara, do you see land ahead?"

"Yes. How long will it be? I am hungry."

"Reach across the pack of beaver pelts right in front of you and get out the rolls of pemican and a corn cake or two. We are a long way from land, but the sun will last till we get there, and we don't have to work hungry. I want a bowl of water, too, don't you?"

"No, but I know you want me to drink water. The French have quite strange habits. I think water should be mixed with food, but I have often had a drink of water when I was in a canoe. I hope it doesn't taste too bad today."

Two hours later they pulled the canoe out of the water onto a beach that was quickly filling up with the curious who had seen them while they were still a long way off. The natives helped unload the canoe, marveling at the wonderful things that it held. Champlain always held himself a bit apart, waiting for the chief men of the village to present themselves. That seemed right for Champlain, but Étienne thought he himself should state who he was, what business he had there, and the fact that this was not his first visit so that anyone who had an interest in meeting with him would know about his arrival. He had learned the hard way that people can be very touchy, even in the deepest forest. It didn't matter which set of manners he used, French, or Huron, but everyone expected a certain amount of formality.

Manitoulin

He finished his few remarks, bowed ceremoniously as he had seen Champlain do, and then waited.

Several men said they had met him on his last trip. An old woman who was looking covetously at the French kettles, volunteered the use of a cabin that her son was not using because he was off at the wars.

"How bad are the wars, has this area been attacked, and who are you fighting?"

The woman looked perplexed and said, "For some reason, the people living across the water on the other side of us, not the Hurons, the other side, don't want us to hunt or fish or even travel in their country. I personally think it is hard enough moving camp when we absolutely must, so believe me, I will let them rot in their great green bay. I don't know what else is causing problems. I didn't want my son to go to the war, but you know how young people are today, no one pays attention to old people who know how life is."

"Do you think I will be able to go in that direction next spring? Are they warring with the Huron?"

"Oh, just go and see. You can never say what will happen. By spring everyone should be fed up. I don't think the Ottawa and the Cheveux Réléves, the Chippewa, and the Ojibwa people will let the Winnebagoes drive them out of any land. Besides, the few Stinkers that live there can't do too much harm."

"Why does everyone call them the Stinkers?"

"I usually call them Winnebagoes, but some of them don't smell too good, perhaps that's it. I never met any of them myself, but I know they are a part of the Sioux people. I wish my son would come home

Manitoulin

instead of going off to fight them. Since he has plenty to eat here, why bother?"

The Cheveux Rélévés had a dance that night. Étienne sat with the men, Sara sat with the women and both tried to look entertained. Huron women had such a high position compared to women of the Algonquins that she found it impossible to relate well to their status somewhere between slave and free and she couldn't understand them anyway. She used smiles instead and that helped.

The dance was held after only one speech. What a relief! No Huron dance or feast could avoid the orators. But then, no tribe that knew them considered themselves equal to the Huron in oratory.

Like all native dances, the steps varied little. The tempo changed now and then, but even so, it became hypnotic. The mosquitoes were unmerciful and the dancers were continually scratching themselves. This was all the more obvious since none of the men were clothed, although some were wearing animal headdresses. Most of the women kept their clothes on. Some did not and had been led off to various cabins. That part was like Huron dances, and encouraged by the chiefs who wanted to keep the population growing. The drumming was monotonous and trying to stay awake didn't work. Sara fell asleep on the shoulder of a large matron who was sitting close beside her.

Some of the people were singing along with the drumbeat, there was a good bit of noise caused by the pounding of feet on the packed earth and the rattles that the dancers held. The large fire in the middle of the clearing was the only light and it was kept burning briskly by the addition of dry branches which snapped and popped as they were thrown into the flames.

Suddenly someone screamed. Étienne looked around in time to see painted warriors with hatchets throwing themselves into the center of the dancers. Three of the dancers were hacked to death amid wild war whoops and cries of pain. A handful of arrows hit others. Étienne looked to where Sara had been sitting and thought she was dead or wounded as she sat slumped against a woman who seemed paralyzed by fear. He ran around the edge of the clearing and straight to Sara. She was sitting up now and looking startled. He grabbed her hand and took the arm of the woman she was near and led them into the woods.

"We will stay here in the dark. Be quiet. I think it was probably a raiding party. They will go before the people can arm themselves." The noise from the clearing that had been deafening just a few minutes earlier, was now reduced to the groans and cries of the wounded. Étienne crept quietly through the underbrush and seeing the clearing now filled with Cheveux Rélévés again, he called to the women to come out, too.

The plump matron patted Sara's arm by way of farewell and hurried off to her own family. Étienne and Sara looked to see if there was anything they could do, but the dead and wounded had been taken away. Sounds of grieving were heard and the cries of frightened and confused children were heartbreaking.

"Who were those warriors?" Étienne asked one of the men who just minutes before had been a principal dancer.

Manitoulin

"I thought at first they must be Sioux because I didn't understand their words. Then I heard one of them yelling in Algonquin. Could the tribes along the Ottawa have done this awful thing? Why?"

"I don't know. Do the Stinkers have any Ottawa or Ojibwa allies?"

"I can't see why they would." He looked around him stupefied. "We don't know who attacked us or why!"

Étienne took Sara by the hand and led her off to the cabin. She was sputtering with indignation, her usual reaction to shock or anger.

"What is the matter with those people? There we were, trying to have a nice time, and in they came with hatchets. I must have fallen asleep because I didn't see or hear them till they were in the center of the clearing. What do you suppose they wanted?"

"I don't know, but I am taking you home tomorrow. We will have to know more about the Algonquin wars before we go anywhere."

Trois Rivières – 1618

The River of Canada, now called by some the Saint Lawrence, was crowded with canoes where the Saint Maurice empties into it by three mouths... seemingly, three separate rivers, so the French called the place Trois Rivières. The natives had come from the farthest reaches of Huronia, encouraged by Brulé whose job it always was to get them in the mood to go to the trade fairs. The approximate date was easy to guess because French vessels left Honfleur in April, but if there were icebergs on the Atlantic, or if it had been a very cold winter, it would be June before the ships could even get past Tadoussac to go up the river to Québec. Now on July 7 1618, the trade was in full swing.

Étienne was eager to talk to Champlain whom he hadn't seen since before the battle at Onondaga Lake in 1615. By now, Champlain would expect him to be dead. As Étienne walked up the beach, noting who was there and who was missing, he reasoned that Champlain's surprise at seeing him alive would allow him to explain why he didn't get the Andastes to the battle on time.

There were the usual Huron canoes with their well-known owners, and some brightly painted Algonquin canoes big enough for several men and many pelts. This did not please the Hurons since they wanted to buy and sell directly to the French

Trois Rivières – 1618

themselves, and then buy French goods to sell to the Algonquins in exchange for furs that they then sold along with their own. Hurons also bought furs from the Algonquin tribes in exchange for corn, pumpkins and squash. They always tried to have a good surplus of foodstuffs so there was something for barter with other tribes. They wanted a monopoly on going to the French trade fairs for themselves.

The Algonquins on Allumette Island charged a hefty fee to let Huron traders pass. Naturally, the people on Allumette had some furs to send along with the Hurons who were going to Québec or Tadoussac. They expected French goods in return as the traders returned to Huronia. The lure of going themselves to Trois Rivières was finally strong enough for them to risk Huron displeasure. There were also canoes belonging to the Neutrals and to the Tobacco Nation, the Petuns. The Petuns were accustomed to selling everyone else tobacco, and getting the other things they needed in trade. Perhaps the Huron had underestimated their neighbors. First the Algonquin selling their own furs, and now the Petuns planning to sell tobacco directly to the French. Étienne groaned. *Bad enough we have to live in a swirl of foul-smelling air here all winter long when they smoke. Now I suppose they will get the French to do the same thing. Well, no. The French won't do that.*

Everyone was in a festive mood because it was the end of the long and often painfully cramped voyage. The canoes were not made with seats in them, and paddling on the knees, very close to the man behind and the man in front, quickly became serious

Trois Rivières – 1618

suffering. Now it was time for feasting and dancing and lots of tall tales.

Étienne reflected that the Hurons were already ashore when the Algonquin canoes appeared. *Well, what's to be done? For one thing, none of the Algonquins whom I see here speaks French, and I wager that most of the merchants haven't caught on to the fact that they can sell directly to other nations without going through me, or Marsolet, or Grenolle, or some Huron who speaks Algonquin and French.* He chuckled and continued making his way through crowds of natives and traders as he looked for familiar faces.

He was particularly searching the crowds of men for his sailor friend, Jean. It would be wonderful to talk with him and hear the news from France, and Jean probably had a letter from Catherine for him. Étienne had a pair of snowshoes for Jean, who would enjoy using them whenever there was enough snow on his little farm in France.

Étienne wanted to tell him about Sara, and it would be interesting to hear how Jean was adjusting to his arranged marriage, and to farming.

Along with the bulky snowshoes, Étienne had a box made of birchbark under his arm. It had been carefully and artistically painted and decorated with quills. Inside it, there was a blanket made of beautifully matched beaver skins. No one in France would have anything like it. Catherine would be delighted.

His pay of one hundred pistoles per year was always delivered to her because he didn't need it. The money he made in the fur trade more than compensated for it, and he knew how much the money meant to

Trois Rivières – 1618

Catherine. Étienne wanted her to be a prosperous farmer on a fine family farm. In the last letters he had seen from her she said that her husband was very proud of his voyageur brother-in-law. Étienne planned to retire to that farm and build a house for himself and his family near his sister and her family. *I probably should have gone to France in 1615; I'd have escaped an awful lot of pain.* He shuddered and put that part from his mind.

Still, I would not have met Sara the way I did, so I would not have my beautiful wife, I would not trade anything for her. In the letter he had for Catherine, he related the romantic story of how he had found the woman who was now her sister-in-law. He told her that he was teaching his wife to read, and that she already knew quite a bit of French, although it was certainly funny to hear her mangle it. Someday, he promised, he would bring her back to Champigny with him, if the Lord allowed him to live and prosper.

Suddenly up ahead, but still at a distance, appeared what were obviously Frenchmen. Étienne shielded his eyes against the sun to see if he could distinguish anyone he knew. Yes! There was his sea-going friend Jean Girodet, running down the beach toward him.

"You are not dead! Ah Étienne, we have had you killed by the Iroquois, drowned in the rapids, dead of fevers, eaten by bears."

"What, no one suggested I just said my evening prayers and closed my eyes to die peacefully in my sleep?"

"Ma foi, no! Champlain is going to be here soon. When I spied you at a distance, one of my shipmates

Trois Rivières – 1618

ran off to get him. Ah, mon cher ami, it is wonderful to see you. Where were you? I have not told Catherine anything. I just said I had missed seeing you. I have letters now for you from the last three years! But I know she must have despaired of ever seeing you again on this earth." Jean sighed deeply.

Étienne brushed his hand across his eyes, perhaps it was only a bit of dust in them. But as he did so, his mangled fingers were evident to his friend who sucked in his breath and murmured softly, "Iroquois."

"Regarde, Jean, there comes le Sieur de Champlain. He certainly can move fast for a man of his age. Perhaps because he is so small? It certainly isn't because he has had an easy life." Étienne and Jean then walked down the beach toward him.

Champlain looked at Étienne with his Huron clothing, tanned skin and healthy aspect and said, by way of greeting, "Where were you?"

"Let's go and sit under a tree and I will tell you everything that happened in the past three years." The three men walked toward the nearest comfortable place to sit and then Étienne told them about the trip to the Andastes, the difficulty in getting them to hurry, their late arrival, the sad trip back to Carantouan.

Jean had work on the ship that had to be done; he was now a first mate, and needed to attend to goods brought over for sale. He left carrying Catherine's beaver blanket in its beautiful box and his snowshoes, which he considered a great gift.

Left alone with Champlain, Étienne could hardly find words to apologize for the Andastes failure to comply with their promise to join the others in the war.

Trois Rivières – 1618

"They just could not be hurried. They were good to us and we had a pleasant enough winter with them. I never have found out what happened to the Hurons who went to Carantouan with me. At least half of us were discovered by Iroquois on our way back home. We ran in every direction and I know some were taken that very day. I don't like to think of what happened to them. But we know what their fate probably was."

Champlain bowed his head and said sadly, "How I wish they had been converted before their terrible time of torture. To think of their suffering on this earth and to know that they are damned for all eternity."

Étienne said, "No, mon Sieur, that does not have to be so. We know our God is good. Why would he torture people for all eternity?"

"Without baptism, Étienne, we are all doomed."

"I doubt it will be any consolation to you, mon Sieur, but I think that is sheer nonsense."

"I will pray for you, my boy, so that you accept all the teachings of our holy faith!"

"Please pray for me, but don't ask for that. I could not live with the savages if I thought God would damn them for what they cannot help. It is the Huguenots who are always damning people for every last little thing, aren't you Catholic?" Étienne spoke pleasantly and smiled mischievously at his employer.

"Étienne, you are incorrigible. I hope you have not become as irreligious as the priests say."

"Well, of course I haven't. I have even had a miracle to prove it." Étienne told the story of the Iroquois trying to snatch away the religious medal that Catherine gave him before he sailed from France, of

Trois Rivières – 1618

how the weather changed with remarkable abruptness, shocking everyone, and of the lightning that kept the Iroquois from grabbing the medal. An occurrence, which so frightened everyone that they left him, tied up, but alone. He told how the chief had come out, untied him, treated his terribly wounded hands and his burned flesh as well as he could, and how he lived with him until he was well.

"Didn't they ever try again to torture you?" Champlain's voice was trembling with compassion and with that sense of religious fervor that so marked all his life.

"No. I was invited to every feast and dance until the day I left. Four of their men accompanied me part way so that I would be able to get safely back to Toanché. I did not meet more enemies. I did break an ankle, but I can walk well again." Étienne considered telling him about Sara, it was the ideal time, but somehow he didn't, and since Champlain didn't ask how he had managed to travel on a broken ankle, he lost the proper opportunity to mention his married state.

"Mon Sieur, the chief who took me into his cabin is a man who would like peace with the other tribes and with the French. You must not mention that to anyone, but you and I can remember it and realize that there are Iroquois who agree with him. I have always hoped to be able to bring about peace. I know I can't do it alone, but you and I and the priests and all the men who have to take the Grand Détour, can agree that we must make every effort we possibly can. The Huron would kill us if they thought we wanted peace with the Iroquois. The Iroquois would surely kill that chief."

Trois Rivières – 1618

Champlain looked at Étienne in what seemed to him like a mixture of astonishment mixed with hope. "Ah, Étienne, I hope we can be instruments of peace. I had no real choice but to side with the Algonquin against the Iroquois. If I had not, we would have no allies at all, and no fur trade either, certainly no chance at converting the settled tribes." They sat companionably in silence while both of them reflected on the ways of God and man.

Finally Étienne said, "I have other news that you will like. I have gone down the Susquehanna River as far as the great bay that disgorges into the Atlantic Ocean. I've made maps of the country, too. It is very fair, it rarely snows there and when it does, the snow melts in a day or two. There are many tribes of savages living all the way from there to Spanish Florida. I did not get that far. But I didn't want to waste the whole winter with the Andastes in sleeping, fishing and hunting, so I made that voyage and I have brought you maps." From a new leather pouch that Sara made for him, he drew out the maps he so carefully brought back from his long voyage. Maps he had saved and fortunately had not lost even during his torture although some were blood stained.

Champlain looked at the maps eagerly. He asked Étienne many questions and seemed to be memorizing the answers. He absorbed the information, and was as grateful for knowledge of the land and rivers as other men might be for a large gift of gold. "I know that you are in no way to blame for the failure of the arrival of the Andastes. Did none of the Hurons who went with you survive the Iroquois attack?" Champlain asked.

Trois Rivières – 1618

"Yes, Ahouyoche came back. He found his way back to Huronia alone and without a supply of food or weapons, and without his beloved canoe. He was fortunate to have escaped the Iroquois with his life, it would hardly have been wise to go back to where we had to drop the canoes and run for our lives. He told me himself that he credits his finding his way back home to Our Dear Lord and Saint Apollonia."

Étienne didn't want to laugh so he was careful not to look at Champlain, who digested this bit of information and asked, "Well, Our Lord, yes, but why Saint Apollonia?" Étienne told the story of Tall Trees and his bad tooth and the help received from the patron saint of those with toothache. Champlain chuckled and admitted he was both amused and edified and hoped that Ahouyoche would soon be baptized. He promised to pay Étienne for the years he had not been able to get to Québec or Trois Rivières and said that he hoped he would continue his good work encouraging both Hurons and Algonquins to come to the trade fairs. Étienne didn't bother to remind him that he could hardly do that any more openly than he already did. It helped that he was a member of the Bear Clan, but if they found him unworthy, he wouldn't live long. Naturally, Champlain admonished the younger man to be more pious and to set a better example so that the priests wouldn't complain.

"I shall try, mon Sieur. But I think they enjoy telling wild tales about me. Père Le Caron is very easily scandalized, if I may say so. All of the Recollect Fathers seem to be greatly surprised at human nature, and far

191

Trois Rivières – 1618

more easily upset than our good old parish priest in Champigny! Too much time spent away from women and children, and too much time swinging their beads, do you think?"

Champlain, who was not easily shocked, just laughed and said again how glad he was to see him alive and well and still doing great work among the savages.

When Étienne left Champlain, he walked down to Jean's ship and finding his friend free to visit with him, listened to his stories of life on the farm. Later, Étienne told Sara how glad he was that Jean spoke truthfully. In New France it was easy to remember the milk, cheese and meat of France, the cream tarts, the wine. But as Jean talked, Étienne remembered the drudgery of life on the farm, the sameness, the bouts with colds and far worse diseases. Jean told him how his yearly trips to New France made possible the purchase of more livestock and poultry. Étienne congratulated his friend, but was glad not to be at the beck and call of cattle and chickens himself.

"Jean, I can't tell you how much I look forward to talking to you every year. Sometimes I wonder if I will forget French. No, that's an exaggeration, but I know I must be missing the new jokes and certainly all the news. It's been so long since I've seen Champigny, my sister and friends there." Étienne sighed.

"Then come home on the ship when we return in two weeks! You've been here now for – must be eight years since we left France together at Honfleur."

"I would, Jean, but I have a wife here." Étienne waited while Jean pretended to faint and recover.

Trois Rivières – 1618

"Where did you find a wife out in the wilderness?"

"She found me. I broke my ankle on my way home from the Iroquois country, and I was very lucky that she did find me. Her brother is my friend Ahouyoche, the only other man to come home from the Iroquois capture. We are very happy, but I don't think she should go to France until she is able to speak French, and she should be baptized and our marriage blessed. I want her to be treated with respect."

"Does Champlain know you have a native wife?"

"No. He wouldn't mind that she is Huron, but he wouldn't consider her my wife because we weren't married in a Christian ceremony. She is beautiful; tall and graceful, quick-witted and able to steer the canoe for hours. It is wonderful not to be alone."

Jean stood up and embraced his friend and slapped him on the back congratulating him and said, "Good for you, Étienne. When you go back to France with her, perhaps you will have a little Étienne to take along with you. That would certainly please Catherine and her family."

"Thank you, Jean. I knew you would be happy for me. Now I must go off and see if I can find Grenolle or Marsolet or both. I told a pretty girl up among the Nipissings that I would find the father of her baby for her, and one of them will surely know the fur traders who have been up in that area."

"When you find them, bring them back here with you. I have to remain aboard ship so no one gets any ideas about stealing things. Bring cooked fish or venison back with you. They are roasting both meat and fish on shore and I have plenty of wine. That will

Trois Rivières – 1618

be a change for the three of you, good French wine!"

Grenolle was easy to spot. His short, stocky figure and the red cap with tassel that he always wore over his black curls made him stand out from the taller, and generally more slender natives. When he saw Étienne he stretched his arms out wide and ran along the beach bellowing, "Finalement, mon ami! Where have you been for so long? Everyone said you were dead. Everyone but me."

Étienne recounted the story of his adventures and of his marriage. Grenolle was delighted.

"Now tell me, Grenolle, why have you not gone back to France?"

"To France?" Grenolle looked as surprised as if Étienne had asked why he had not gone to Brazil. "I live here, Étienne. I have no family left in France. No work there that I want to do, no wife, no children. Here I am free, and I suppose I am rich. I give my money to the Recollects to take care of, and they do. Some of it has been invested in that very ship you just climbed down from. The fur trade has been good to me, at least when I am not shepherding visiting priests from place to place. Ah Étienne, that can be very hard. Very hard." He sighed and looked resentful.

"Stop feeling sorry for yourself, and reflect that if it were not you, it would have to be me or Marsolet. By the way, where is he?"

"Down on the beach here with about a thousand others. Let's go find him."

Marsolet was happy to see his old friends and glad of the invitation to dine on Jean's ship where wine would be served. He had a store of trade goods in the

Trois Rivières – 1618

small ship he'd come up the river in. They went with him while he rummaged around and found a colorful French shirt, which he folded neatly and the three of them went off to buy hot fish and venison, knowing that the shirt would get them plenty of anything they wanted. A deal was soon struck with a woman who had both meat and fish to sell. Jean heard the boisterous laughter of his friends and set a table with the French wine he had promised. Étienne enjoyed the evening, it had been so long since he had seen his friends or spoken French. He told the story of the half French baby, and with little reflection, Grenolle and Marsolet said together, "Pierre!"

"Who is Pierre?" Étienne asked his laughing friends.

Grenolle answered, "They call him Pierre Le Noir. He is very dark, very quiet. He travels alone, but doesn't always spend his nights alone. He isn't supposed to be trading in this country, but who can stop the traders who come in without permission from Champlain or the French Government?"

"Do you think he will go and get the girl and baby up at Lake Nipissing?"

"I'll ask him," Marsolet said. "But why shouldn't he? I imagine he will… It is one thing to have a French wife. Very proper. But when you live like Pierre, it is better to have a native wife. Good, of course, to have a son too."

Le Grand Lac – 1623

All the maps Étienne could find, no matter how worn, no matter who made them, were spread out in front of him on a long wooden table. He was walking around it trying to envision the area from the point of view of the different Huron, Algonquin, and French traders who had ventured anywhere near the lake they called Lac Supérieur. So named because it was higher than the others, or sometimes Le Grand Lac because some of them believed it was larger than the lake of the Huron people.

After the miserably hard and pointless trip with an inveterate liar up to find the Northwest passage, Étienne was determined to have this journey as well planned as possible. Canoes can always leak, enemies of any kind can be anywhere at any time. The provisions can be soaked or stolen. He wanted to ensure that he and Grenolle wouldn't get lost, no matter what else happened.

"Sara, go ask Ahouyoche, or anyone who might know, if Grenolle has been seen in this area." The weather would hold only so long, and it would be colder up on the peninsula above the bay of the Winnebagoes. He wanted to go with Grenolle who was not only cheerful and strong but knew two Algonquin dialects well and could make himself understood in Huron. Best of all, he spoke French and

Le Grand Lac – 1623

liked to sing the old songs. Ahouyoche would be fine, but Speaks Loudly didn't want him to be away from home long. Besides, Étienne was glad to have him and Speaks Loudly in Toanché when he was away so there would always be someone to look after Sara and Petit Étienne.

Sara sighed dramatically, and slowly left the new cabin he had built especially for her. She wasn't gone long. "My brother says several of his friends saw Grenolle near the French River a few days ago. He said he'd be here soon. He's been trading up at the Lake of the Nipissings. Do you think he found the father of the half-French baby we saw up there?"

Étienne laughed and said, "We will know soon. I'm glad he's on his way. The weather, the weather, always the weather. You can only travel easily for six months, and it is more like five months when you get farther north in the Grand Lac area."

"Étienne, we have this large cabin now with room for that huge table you have maps on. We have our little son. I have provided enough corn, beans, squash and dried fish for a very long winter. I'll ask again, why do you insist on going to faraway places and risking our happiness here?"

"That's my work, Sara. Some men are warriors. I am an explorer. That's why Champlain paid me, that and the translating."

"Champlain doesn't pay you anything now, and we both know it. You are paid by Guillaume de Caen these past three years. Even when Champlain wanted to pay you, often he couldn't. We don't need the money, we need you!"

Le Grand Lac – 1623

Étienne looked at her and began to add up a few things. *"Sanderiq?"* (Are you pregnant?) he asked.

"I don't know. I feel awful." Sara started to breathe rapidly and he could see she wanted to cry. "I asked Water Song to take care of Petit Étienne today so he wouldn't bother you, and so I could rest."

"Shouldn't he be able to take care of himself? Ma foi, the boy is four years old!"

"Listen to yourself. You sound more savage than the savages. A boy of four is dangerous to himself and others. Especially this boy."

"Petit Étienne is with Water Song, and Grenolle won't be here for a while, so let's rest and talk and you can tell me what is bothering you."

More sighs, and grumbling, but Sara went into the large bedroom off the main room of the cabin and lay down on her side of the bed he himself built. Étienne had intended to build the cabin alone, but that seemed foolish when the big Algonquin who often helped Ahouyoche was available, so together they built the cabin in the pièce sur pièce style. The tree trunks were cut in small enough sections so that one man could handle each piece alone. Everything was held together with dirt and clay mortar, and if one part rotted, it could easily be replaced. The bark was left on. Étienne intended this house to last. It even had a smooth, flat, wooden floor. Sara wove mats to cover it and to make it a bit warmer. There was a large main room with a fireplace for heat and for cooking. There was even an outhouse. It all seemed quite elegant.

Their Huron friends enjoyed bringing visiting relatives over to view it. Knowing glances were

Le Grand Lac – 1623

exchanged when they saw the matrimonial bed in the main bedroom. The unspoken question seemed to be, "What do Frenchmen do that requires so much room for sleeping?" The quizzical looks always offended Sara and that made Étienne laugh uproariously. He built the bed with headboard and footboard, and lashed thick sinews horizontally and vertically to support the furs they put on top of the ropes. Over it all were sturdy French sheets and blankets.

He lay down next to her and took her into his arms, gently rubbing her back and singing a little lullaby he used to sing to Petit Étienne. Sara dissolved into tears and sobbed her unhappiness. "I feel so sad when you are gone. I liked it when we went on your trading trips together. I love Petit Étienne dearly, but now I am left behind and life seems like it did after my first husband was killed. I loved him, too, you know!" She sounded resentful, as though Étienne had something to do with the death of her first husband.

"Of course you did, my little Sarainta. Everyone knows you did, that is why they called you Are You Crying. But you are Sara now. Everything in your life has changed. You are my wife, you are a Christian, you have a son. You even agreed to be half French, and you speak my language better all the time. You live in the best cabin between here and Québec. You know I love you. I am not going east to the Iroquois country, I am going west. You want me to be the first to make real maps of the area, and to find out if there is the slightest chance we can reach the Pacific through the Grand Lac. You do want that, don't you?"

"I don't care! All I want is for you to get home soon. What if I am pregnant?"

Le Grand Lac – 1623

"If you are, we will both be happy. If you feel tired or sick, get Water Song to come here and help you care for Petit Étienne. She likes it here and loves P'ti Étienne. Do you want to stay in your mother's longhouse while I am gone?"

"Étienne, I think it is impossible to live like that now that I am half French. Don't you remember?"

"Certainly I remember. But I am all French, and I am about to go on a voyage where I will surely have to sleep outside much of the time. Even the Montagnais live better than that! So don't feel ashamed to go back to the longhouse if you get lonely or feel sick. I wouldn't normally ask you this, but do you want a rotted ear of corn right now to cheer you up? If you do, I know where I can get one. But please, use leaves to hold it and do not bring it into the cabin."

She hesitated momentarily and then said haughtily, "No, I don't eat that anymore."

Grenolle arrived only a few hours later, laughing and marveling at Étienne's living quarters. "Par Dieu, mon ami! This is not a cabin, it is a palace! I was directed here by some of the men down on the shore. They are watching me to see if I am impressed. Well, I am!" Grenolle waved at the young men and held his arms wide to show surprise at the size of the house Étienne had built.

"I am very glad to see you, mon vieux! I didn't expect you for a few days yet, but the sooner we leave, the safer." Étienne embraced his friend warmly.

"Don't tell me the Puants (Stinkers, or Winnebagoes) are warring with the Ojibwas!"

"No, no, no. I am just concerned about the weather.

Le Grand Lac – 1623

It is perfect now, and I'd like to get going."

"Tomorrow is soon enough, Étienne. I am very tired. I had company on the French River, someone to help in the canoe. But this last part of the voyage I was alone. I need food. I want to rest. Can just anyone spend the night in this fine cabin or will I need dispensation from the Pope?"

"You can sleep in my son's room. He can have a bed on the floor in our room tonight. What would you like to eat?"

"Anything that generally passes for food will be fine." Grenolle walked behind Étienne into the bedroom and reaching the bed, stretched out full upon it and said simply, "Call me if you find something to eat."

Sara had awakened, and came out of their bedroom much the better for having rested and for having confessed her fears and worries to her husband. "I suppose that is our friend, Grenolle, in P'ti Étienne's room? I am going to see what I can prepare quickly for us all to eat. Grenolle always has a good appetite."

Two hours later, Étienne had the maps put away, except for those he planned to carry with him in an oilskin pouch. Sara had visited the fires of her brother and one of her friends, and with the sagamite that she was boiling over the fire outside, she was able to serve the usual corn soup, but with roasted onions and pumpkin in it. Grenolle would have been content with that, but she wanted him to know how well off his friend was since he had married her. So she had traded a basket of parched corn for a large fish that one of her neighbors had completely encased in clay and then

Le Grand Lac – 1623

cooked in the coals of a cooking fire. A sharp blow with a stick, and the covering shattered, leaving the fish in its steaming perfection.

Grenolle waited for Étienne to lead the grace before meals. It didn't seem to be forthcoming so he launched into the usual prayer with additions of thanksgiving for having the company of Étienne and his family. They were seated on benches around the table. Grenolle, Étienne, Sara, P'ti Étienne and Water Song who had decided to stay for dinner. Water Song said she liked eating with the men, and she didn't mind bouncing up to get more food for them, but thought it was a pity her father and Grenolle weren't speaking in Huron. She was learning French, but not enough to follow the conversation.

Sara asked, "Did you find the father of the half-French baby up with the Nipissings?"

"Certainement, Sara. Pierre Le Noir went right up there and collected his little family. Better him than me! That girl is pretty without a doubt. But she is not going to be easy to live with. She demands that Pierre take her and the little boy along wherever he goes so she can keep her eye on him. She wants a French-style cabin like one she saw at Trois Rivières. She wants French clothes, and insists that Pierre jump to her every wish. Ahhh, quelle femme! Still, poor Pierre seems to think he is the luckiest man in the woods. She will probably make a rich man of him before he dies young of overwork."

Water Song returned to her mother's longhouse quite happily after Étienne promised that he would remember to bring her a present from the area of the

Grand Lac. It was agreed that he would bring P'ti Étienne a toy canoe to sail on puddles. Water Song left the cabin wearing a red cap with tassel, a gift from Grenolle. Her father couldn't resist a proud, "Elle est belle, non, mon ami?"

"Oui, Étienne, no one can deny she is beautiful, and lively!"

"Eh bien, now to business. I have two canoes of men contracted to make the journey with us, and four more to help in our canoe. I've been on rivers and lakes with most of them. All are strong and good voyageurs. We can count on bad weather at least part of the time, no need to have to endure bad companions. I've seen to the loading of supplies and some trade goods. Do you have much to take?"

"I suppose we are going in your canot de maître?" When Étienne nodded, Grenolle continued, "Then let's take lots of food. I seem to have been cursed with bad luck lately when it comes to provisions. I have noticed that going hungry doesn't improve anyone's disposition, Savage or French. Guillaume de Caen pays at the end of the trip, I suppose? Or did he give you enough to pay the men something now?"

"He gave me enough to pay the men half of their wages. It was an afternoon's work trying to figure out how many hatchets, adzes and blankets each man would get instead of French money. When we get back, I will owe them the second half. You and I will be paid when we see Le Sieur de Caen at the end of the voyage, or next spring. Do you want to take some trade goods along?"

"Oui. I brought along a bundle of red caps like my

Le Grand Lac – 1623

own, and a packet of tobacco pipes that have hatchet, hammer, or adze at the other end. They are much valued all the way from the River of Canada to the Lake of the Nipissings. One of the traders told me he has made as much as seven hundred percent profit on the pipe-hatchets. Since this is a voyage of exploration, and not a trading trip, I don't intend to bring much. Are you taking trade goods, Étienne?"

"Some. I have noticed that people are far less wary of me when they see I want to do business with them, because it explains my presence. Everyone profits from trade! I have heard many a Huron laugh at French traders behind their backs because they were given a hatchet in exchange for a few skins. I know the trader thought he had made a good bargain, too. I plan to use any available space for canoe repair supplies and not trade goods this time. If there are as many rapids as I think there are, it is going to be a problem getting canoes ready for the water every day. D'accord?"

"D'accord. I detest leaky canoes. Eh bien, mon ami, it is now time to blow out the candle and get a good night's rest." With a slight bow to his hosts, Grenolle went to P'ti Étienne's room to sleep and Sara made up a bed for their son on the floor next to his parents.

★

The whole village seemed to be down on the shore to see the three great canots de maître start out for le Grand Lac. No one in the village had been that far west, although some said their fathers had been there, and one or two of them had copper ingots to prove it.

Le Grand Lac – 1623

Since the Huron were great traders, and considered themselves a few stages above their neighbors, the people of the Bear Clan were pleased to be involved in this important voyage of exploration and discovery. The fact that Champlain was still in charge in Québec overshadowed the information that it was now Le Sieur de Caen who had a monopoly on the fur trade, and that it was de Caen's money that was paying for the voyage to le Grand Lac. For them, Frenchmen were Frenchmen, and the Huron were allied with the French. That some French were Huguenots and allied with the English didn't matter.

Sara was carrying P'ti Étienne so he wouldn't get hurt in the crowd around the canoes. "Étienne, do not stay up there any longer than you must. I will miss you and your children will miss you." Water Song, who was there with her mother, took this as her cue to start to sob. Étienne looked at her darkly and told her to set a better example for the children of the other men. She immediately changed her attitude and became the picture of long-suffering heroism. Goes Softly and Étienne exchanged glances and shrugged their shoulders.

★

The three canoes pushed off from the shore with the help of wives and children who waded into the water to help. No rocks must damage these fine canoes that would have to transport them for a thousand miles each way. Père Le Caron took off his sandals and went into the water to bless each canoe and all the men. The

Le Grand Lac – 1623

paddlers drew strongly away from shore, and in a few minutes they couldn't see the people they'd left behind.

"Grenolle, it was good of Père Le Caron to come down and bless us. Would you believe he says my wife is ready for baptism but he won't give her the sacrament? He wants Champlain's permission! He and I had words… again."

Grenolle shook his head in disgust. "You would think that Champlain was the bishop. Or that we had a bishop. Or that Québec was only a league or two from Toanché."

"I took care of that, and baptized her myself. I baptized P'ti Étienne at the same time and if Water Song had been in the cabin I would have included her. When Champlain says he approves the baptisms, and he will, of course, then I will mention that I want the marriage blessed and recorded in the church at Québec. I can just see Père Le Caron's face when Sara tells him proudly that she and our son have been baptized. She will want to receive communion. Ah yes, I have created a problem for the good father." Étienne didn't seem particularly repentant.

Grenolle chuckled and then added seriously, "Ah the poor Recollect Fathers. They suffer so much and then we add to their miseries. I was in Québec when the Iroquois attacked their mission in early June. Did you hear about that? Is it all right for me to tell the story in Huron so the other men can understand?"

"Oui, and then I suppose we both ought to go silent. You know how they resent anyone who talks much in a canoe. I don't know why. It passes the time better. That's why you and I are together in one canoe. So tell us your story, Grenolle."

"Ho, hho." The Huron call to attention caused the others to give him a fleeting glance as if to say, "We are listening." Grenolle continued, "I was in Québec to get a priest to start a mission at Lac Nipissing. And one night, out of the darkness, there appeared thirty Iroquois canoes filled with warriors who hoped to destroy Québec. They headed toward the Recollect mission shrieking and howling like wild animals. It would freeze your blood to hear them. Then, as the warriors ran toward the mission carrying burning brands, we were able to see to direct our fire. Every able-bodied man in Québec was there to save the gentle priests and their mission. After many Iroquois were killed, the others retreated, and pulled away as fast as they could in their wretched excuses for canoes. Still, we were all worried. Suppose it had been sixty and not thirty? Suppose there had been only six armed men in Québec and not twelve?"

The men directed the usual curses at the Iroquois. One of them spoke up. "The great chief in France should send the Huron clans muskets so we can kill Iroquois like the French do." Étienne and Grenolle said nothing. The paddles continued in perfect rhythm, but everyone seemed to have something serious to think about.

Grenolle said in French and in a very low voice, "Étienne, the English and the Dutch have already armed some of the Iroquois. Both nations sell them brandy. Did you know?"

"Oui, I knew. That's going to be as much trouble as

Le Grand Lac – 1623

the firearms. When they get a bottle or two of wine there's no restraint, then they blame any action on the wine or on the person who gave it to them. We have to find the way to peace with the Iroquois before it is too late. Guns and brandy aren't the answer."

"If you find a way, don't hesitate to tell me." Grenolle didn't sound expectant.

Three hours later, the wind had whipped the waves to a froth, and the men were all straining to make headway. It was work just keeping the canoes headed in the right direction and they were sweating and finding the paddles difficult to work. Étienne put his back into it, with much effort. He had a reputation to uphold, he had to do more than his share. Not for the first time, he considered that he did not have to live like this. He could go back to France. Or he could live at Québec, someone else could make the rough trips, and certainly someone else could go to unexplored places in his stead. He had money saved and could continue to trade from Québec. Finally in disgust at making no headway, he called, "Pull for the shore here, we are going to stop early today. The wind is taking too much of our strength."

No one argued about making it a short day. Soon a fire was built, the fish that had been caught on lines trailing behind the canoes were cooked under the coals and a kettle slung over the fire had a rich soup flavored with bear fat. Since they had just begun the trip, there were still corn cakes thickly studded with pecans. The Petuns (the Tobacco Nation) didn't only trade in tobacco; they often had pecans from the people farther south. Pecans weren't as common as hazelnuts, but

Le Grand Lac – 1623

both made excellent additions to corn cakes. The men ate all parts of the meal at once, corn cakes, fish and sagamite. Each had only one bowl and it was used for physical needs while on the water, then rinsed out to use for food. The inevitable pipes were taken out and the air around the cooking fire was thick with smoke.

"Grenolle, let's take off our clothes and go for a swim, the water is cold, but then, it never is warm." Grenolle and Étienne and a few men went into the cold waters of the Bay of the Lac des Hurons. The waves made swimming impossible, but it was enjoyable leaping into them and feeling like little boys again.

The next day the waves were even higher. Étienne suggested a day of hunting, and that seemed better than fighting with the water. They had success, and dinner the second night was fresh venison and the rest of the corn cakes. Finally, the third day of the trip dawned clear and warm with no wind. They left their rude lodges of pine boughs, and resumed the voyage, rested, well fed, and with roasted venison wrapped in deerskin.

That night their sleep was broken by shouts from Grey Lynx, who seemed to be having a nightmare. His companions woke him and he insisted on telling his dream. "I dreamed we went to Manitoulin, and there we met a chief who gave a tabagie for us. Not an eat-all feast, just a good meal. He had a daughter who was serving us the food, but she wasn't a woman, she was a small, light-brown fawn. She wanted me to go away with her, and I wanted to go, but I was held fast by thick branches." Grey Lynx was upset and wanted to

Le Grand Lac – 1623

know the meaning of the dream. The Hurons, always prone to rely on dreams, were even more reliant on them if they were on a journey, or going to a war.

Étienne undertook to interpret the dream. "You are called Grey Lynx because of the legend of the original man who went hunting with two lynxes, his brethren. The two lynxes drowned in a flood. Some people say the animals were wolves." Grey Lynx nodded his assent to this, so Étienne continued. "A young woman and a lovely fawn are both objects of beauty, so you wanted to follow the fawn and couldn't because the tiny hut you slept in held you fast unless you went out of the opening. You were asleep and your flailing arms didn't hit the opening. That is what made it seem like a nightmare, like a trap." Grey Lynx was pleased with this interpretation and everyone was able to go back to sleep.

The next day, smooth waters under a placid sky brought them to Manitoulin just before dark. Many people had seen them from far off and were there on the beach to greet them. Fortunately, no one talked of war as they had when he was there with Sara. A good sign. The Ottawa and the Winnebago must have made peace. And the Huron weren't at war with the Winnebago. As usual, the community put together what was left in the firepots, and prepared more food for them also.

The chief invited them to sit down in front of his cabin, which was a bit apart from the longhouses and called on his daughter to help the women serve the guests. Étienne and Grenolle started to laugh when they heard her called Little Fawn. This wasn't funny to

Le Grand Lac – 1623

Grey Lynx who seemed to be so overcome with love and longing for this girl he had just met that he couldn't eat his food. The daughter kept spilling the sagamite she was trying to ladle into bowls, she tripped over a stone and generally acted quite nervously, especially while serving Grey Lynx. The chief told them that was because his daughter recently dreamed she fell in love with a very tall man who arrived in a canot de maître. Grey Lynx was taller than the next tallest man.

Étienne and Grenolle stopped laughing. It all seemed too unreal, too like a tale told in the longhouse on a cold winter night. Their Huron companions were excited by the chief's story and told him about Grey Lynx's dream. The chief then stared quietly into the fire. This seemed to the Huron like a dream that required fulfillment.

The men were invited by their hosts to spend the nights in the longhouses. Some of the travelers were glad to rest indoors, and some decided to stay near the shore and sleep on pine boughs and the furs they brought with them. The rhythmic sound of waves hitting the rocks on the shore, the sight of moonlight on the water, and the smell from the surrounding forest made the beach attractive. No one would admit it, but it was a pleasure to occasionally be away from the longhouse, with its smells, crying babies, dogs, smoke and bugs. Grey Lynx had accepted the invitation to spend the next three nights in the cabin of the chief, his wife, and Little Fawn.

Grenolle asked, "Étienne, did you notice that none of the men made any jokes about Grey Lynx and Little Fawn?"

Le Grand Lac – 1623

"I didn't think they would. This is dream fulfillment. They always hope for it, and now and then it actually takes place! They are happy for Grey Lynx. I wish it had not been this way. They have so many superstitions, and this just makes them all seem like sound reasoning. I think it was simple chance. It is fine that Grey Lynx has found a wife. I believe there will be a marriage feast before we leave, or perhaps when we return from the Grand Lac."

"When do you want to leave here?" Grenolle asked.

"I'd planned to leave tomorrow. But you don't order the Huron to do anything. Grey Lynx is going to live with Little Fawn for three days, totally silent, both of them. We will leave after that. No one can object that I haven't given them time to be sure of their choice. Though as superstitious as they are, I wonder how much freedom of choice is actually involved after two people dream of each other."

Grenolle shook his head bewildered by it all. "I can't see how three days of total silence will help much."

"Ah, mon ami, tu n'est pas romantique!" Étienne said, laughing at his friend.

"Of course I am romantic! I am French. I simply am not superstitious."

Three days passed fast enough because Étienne and Grenolle went from cooking fire to longhouse, to the surrounding cultivated fields, talking to any men they could find. They wanted them to get a flotilla of canoes together to go down to Trois Rivières for the next fur trade in spring.

Conversations about more trade with the

Le Grand Lac – 1623

Algonquins living south of the Ottawa as well as along it, brought the complaint that the people living on Allumette Island on the Ottawa River were charging too much for passage down the river. Was there anything Étienne could do?

"I think I can modify their demands a bit. They are dependent on French and Huron protection from the Iroquois. They don't have muskets, and their village is not palisaded. I will talk to them about maintaining good relations with their friends in order to ward off enemies better."

Grenolle added, "If you would rather meet us where the Ottawa and the Mattawa meet, or at the Lac des Nipissings, that could be arranged. Then your furs could go down to Trois Rivières with ours – for a part of them, of course."

There was a good crowd of men by now, all listening. They wanted to have a full meeting concerning all of this and would let Étienne and Grenolle know their decision in two days.

"What did I tell you, Grenolle, they are going to let us know in two days, just as I thought! That will be the end of the three-day visit of Grey Lynx in their cabin. They will have a feast for the happy couple, and they'll let us know how they plan to do business. I think they will choose to go down the Ottawa if I can get to les Allumettes first and talk the people there into charging a more reasonable toll. It will be a problem to get word back here. I hope they decide just to trust me to do it."

"Since you are playing guessing games, Étienne, please tell me how bad the feast will be, I mean, how many speeches?"

Le Grand Lac – 1623

"There will be so many speeches your life will flash in front of your eyes, you will forget your own name. It will be boring beyond anything you've ever endured." Then seeing the look of dismay on Grenolle's face, he said, "I always talk to myself like that before feasts. Then, expecting the worst, it isn't so bad."

Grenolle suggested they all go hunting or fishing to add to the store of food for the tabagie. Somehow or other they would also have to find a serious gift for the father of the bride. "I told you, Grenolle, that this was going to be difficult for all of us. Those silly superstitions! Now we are going to have to use what few trade goods we have in order to get together a gift for Grey Lynx to give to the father of Little Fawn."

"Oh, all right. I donate ten red caps with tassels, and a smoking pipe with a hatchet at the other end. No one else better dream of anything." Grenolle was feeling ill-used.

Étienne added, "I'll donate a kettle, an adze, an axe, and I think both you and I should give short speeches extolling the virtues of Grey Lynx. I don't see why the parents of the girl should expect anything at all since they get the services of a strong young man."

"C'est vrai, in France the girl's parents have to come up with a dowry and they don't get the services of anyone! Yet we will probably be expected to drop off the bridegroom on our way back like we might drop off a load of venison. His parents are going to be surprised to find he is living on Manitoulin instead of coming back to Toanché."

Grey Lynx himself understood full well that he

214

would have to live with his wife's parents in their cabin and that he would very rarely see his Bear Clan at Toanché, but he seemed happy with his fate. Little Fawn followed him around with the air of one who is delighted with what some great spirit Oki had given her through dreams. Étienne was eager to be on the way, but ordinary courtesy seemed to require that they spend the last of the three days there helping with the feast and then attending it. At the wedding feast the speeches weren't as long as they had feared. The short courtship did not allow for relatives from afar and since no one knew much about any of the visiting Huron or Étienne or Grenolle, that shortened speeches a good bit. It would be hard to speak about the bridegroom's life when all they knew of it was the last three days and all of that with the bridegroom silent. Grenolle gave a short speech, Étienne a slightly longer one since he knew the young man better. The assembled men listened intently as Étienne mentioned his fellow member of the Bear Clan's good qualities, and they answered with encouraging, "Ho HHHo's" when Grey Lynx's amiability was extolled.

Étienne used the occasion to congratulate his hosts on their hospitality, on the beauty and value of Little Fawn, and on the advisability of meeting the French flotilla in spring at Trois Rivières as soon as the ice was well off the water there, or of letting him know before morning if they would meet the French elsewhere. As a final remark, he mentioned that they would be leaving at dawn but that they would return Grey Lynx to them on the way back to Toanché.

Then, taking advantage of the fact that he and

Le Grand Lac – 1623

Grenolle were forever French, and therefore always a bit odd in everyone's estimation, he gestured to his friend and the two of them went down to the beach to get the canoes and equipment set for an early departure.

Grenolle said, "That wasn't a bad feast. Even the food was good. I like pit-roasted venison, and the speeches weren't too long. We used to have some long speeches in France at weddings, if you remember. We should try to get to the great rapids at the joining of the Lac des Huron and Lac Supérieur by the end of the week or sooner."

"Oui, this time we will pray for good weather, but keep going even if the weather isn't good. We are all rested and well. There is a long portage. We will be glad to put the canoes back in the water, and get them off our backs. I think we can stay one or two days after that with the Ottawa people. I would like to head straight across the water from there to the long strip of land an Algonquin map shows extending far out into the water. We should do that to save time and energy, if the weather is good, and we are in no danger of getting lost. If not, we will have to paddle along the shore and that will take much longer. We will decide that together when the time comes."

★

At the rapids between the great bodies of water, they shouldered the canoes or carried supplies and plodded along. Grenolle asked, "Étienne, have I ever told you that I hate portages?"

Le Grand Lac – 1623

"Many times."

"Je les déteste! I am either trying to help carry a huge canoe through the wilderness without damaging it – not easy when you can hardly see where you are going, or it is my turn to carry provisions and a roll of birchbark. In either case the mosquitoes are unmerciful, and I can't even swat at them. I nearly died the first year I was in Tadoussac. My eyelids closed with the mosquito poison. My body was swollen and I had fevers. Mosquitoes don't make me so sick now, thanks be to God."

Étienne tried to get a better grip on his precious oilskin-covered packet of maps, and said, "Thanks not only to God but to the Franciscan Fathers and the Jesuits for telling the truth about this place. They ask for settlers to come out and talk about land for the asking, but they always tell the truth. Mosquitoes, scurvy, hunger, Iroquois. Oui, there is money to be made in the trade. I've made it and so have you. There is land for the clearing, but it takes two years of hard work for one man to clear even two acres of it.

"If all anyone heard about in France was the profit, the woods would be swarming with traders not connected with Champlain or les Sieurs de Caen. Most of those men are money hungry and ignorant of everything including the weather, and the languages. They do nothing to further the colony at Québec or help with native relations."

"And we do, Étienne?" Grenolle asked, sounding surprised.

"Oui. We have made studies of the area, the people and the languages. We are constantly trying to think of

Le Grand Lac – 1623

ways to make peace with the Iroquois. You, especially, are a great help to the priests. And I am a full member of the Bear Clan, the most important of the Huron nation. Without the furs we get to Trois Rivières and Québec, there would be no Québec, no French foothold here."

"For my part, Étienne, I find this better than France. I can understand fighting Iroquois. I have trouble getting angry at the French heretics. Ma foi, I am working for them! Of course, I'd prefer to work for Champlain, but even he accepts the de Caens because they have the fur trade monopoly now. There should be many people willing to come out and start farms near Québec. Here Frenchmen are allowed to buy arms and can hunt and fish anywhere. I'd hate to go back to bowing before the nobility... and not being able to hunt or fish because the land belonged to them."

"Am I supposed to believe that your family didn't do any poaching?" Étienne laughed.

"Certainly we did! It is the idea that we were supposed to beg first for the chance to go hunting or fishing that makes me angry. But to have plenty of land and be able to hunt and fish like we do here is better."

"D'accord. Many Frenchmen would prosper here, if they came with enough resources to last for two years. But what poor man has that? And whoever reads the priest's accounts or Brother Sagard's journals can almost feel the mosquitoes and biting black flies. They must see in their minds the seven or eight months of snow and cold and guess at the suffering from scurvy also."

Le Grand Lac – 1623

"C'est vrai, Étienne, of course. I miss a glass of red wine, a beefsteak, a loaf of good French bread and something sweet that isn't sucre d'érable."

"Good you mentioned that. I'll see if I can get some maple sugar candy for my children up here. You should get married and settle down, too, mon ami."

"Mais oui! If this is called settling down." Grenolle called to his Huron companions to stop because he was too tired to go on. So they stopped and Grenolle continued his conversation about the beauties of France but now in Huron so all could understand. None of the men believed a word he said.

Grey Lynx seemed to be speaking for all of them when he said, "But your poor country is so sad and so ugly that you are happy to live here in our beautiful land in peace and plenty." Grenolle laughed and shrugged his shoulders. Some things are hard to explain.

The Ottawa village they expected to find was completely deserted, but they stayed one night and rested, and wondered what happened to the village they expected to find there. Some of the men found an untended corn patch. This intrigued Étienne because the Ottawa weren't known for raising crops. He had often suggested that they try growing corn, but they never did. "Viens avec moi, mon ami, we are going to see what Ottawa corn looks like."

Grenolle shrugged his heavy shoulders and said, "Bien. I'll go with you, but I can tell you ahead of time that it won't look like much. Did you hear that some of the people farther south now have ears of corn that are as big as my middle finger? They only planted the

Le Grand Lac – 1623

very best kernels from the last crop. Usually there is so much work, so much plant, so little grain."

"C'est vrai. My wife works very hard to raise the corn we need during a long winter and it's no secret that our growing season is really too short. She plants squash around it which she says keeps the corn company and keeps it warmer but the ears are never large."

The Ottawa corn patch looked like someone had taken great trouble to keep it alive, Seeds had been planted in hills and each hill had the skeleton of a dead fish put there to fertilize the plants. The smallest hint of ears could be seen, and perhaps this patch would yield enough to make it worthwhile. "Grenolle, we need a crop up here that will mature in four months or less. The ground is too cold to plant before the middle of May, and even so, some of the grain rots; and it isn't really mature when the freezing weather comes. But why did this village disappear? Do you think the Ottawa were frightened away by their Winnebago enemies?"

"Probably, Étienne. I'll guess that they moved farther north up along the Ottawa River, but someone will come back to bring in the harvest in September. There never is enough food in any of the Algonquin tribes, as you know all too well."

"We won't be here when any harvesters come. I will be glad to leave this ghost village. I think I will ask the men to share guard duties with us tonight and we will all sleep around the fire together."

The Huron did not take kindly to the thought of guard duty and said they were always sleepy at night,

Le Grand Lac – 1623

unlike the French who didn't have trouble remaining on guard. Therefore, they would sleep and Étienne and Grenolle could keep watch.

"I'm not going to insist, Grenolle, they would just fall asleep anyway if they aren't in favor of guard duty, and they certainly aren't. I will stay up as long as I can, so if you will kindly fall asleep almost instantly and remain sleeping and get as much good from it as you can, then you can cheerfully keep watch while I sleep."

"Well, why not. I wouldn't be surprised if there were Winnebagoes skulking about in the bushes looking for someone to scalp. I want to sleep closer to the canoes, too, if you please."

"D'accord!"

They never knew if their guard duty was what kept off marauders, or if they were just being overly careful. Still, they were all alive and ready to leave at sunrise.

"We will keep paddling toward the setting sun. Our first stop will be when we see an Ojibwa village." Neither Étienne nor Grenolle could tell whether that seemed like a good plan because the Huron didn't offer any opinion. The weather was perfect, the lake placid, the canoes in top condition, and all the men were rested, with the exception of Grenolle and Étienne.

A Huron with an attractive singing voice began to sing. Unfortunately, the words didn't make much sense and the tune was monotonous. Étienne suggested a song he and Grenolle knew from childhood and soon all three canoe loads of men were booming out "A la Claire Fontaine". The two Frenchmen looked at each other and smiled. The

Le Grand Lac – 1623

people in his Bear Clan were very patient with him in the years he was learning Huron; he would be the same with them and their French songs, which seemed to the Huron like nonsense syllables set to music. But they liked music.

The towering rocks to the south side of the canoes were a wonder to behold, like huge rock pictures. They all looked and marveled while gently paddling. Then it happened. A terrible sound, more like breaking than like tearing, and one of the canoes was filled with water. The men in it paddled hard toward the shore trying to bail as they went. It was useless. The canoe sank with everything that was in it. The other two canoes came in close to pick up the men. Étienne and Grenolle immediately slipped into the water and kept swimming and searching and one of the Huron who could swim tried also to find the lost men. Where were they? One surfaced, he was grabbed by his long hair, pulled to the nearest canoe, dragged inside it and placed face down with bundles of skins under his stomach so that his head hung down and the water that he had swallowed could be vomited out. The other man seemed to be pushed to the top of a wave, but it was obvious that he was dead.

"Étienne, je crois qu'il est mort de peur!" Grenolle declared with horror.

"Ah, bon Dieu! To die of fear! I always tell them to learn to swim because anyone's canoe might sink." The earlier happy feeling was now a sense of desperation and shock. "Pull for the shore as soon as we pass this rock formation. There must have been a sharp submerged rock there that tore out the bottom

Le Grand Lac – 1623

of the canoe. Good luck that we were all in about the same place. We can manage with two canoes now. Put Chattering Squirrel in our canoe, we will build a scaffold on shore and put him on it. I don't want him left in the water, his relatives would be angry with us."

The men were somber and seemed to be huddling together around a fire that they kindled to dry out wet clothing. After a long period of passing around pipes of tobacco, and talking about how quickly all this happened, one of the men said he thought perhaps the dead man had hit his head on something. They looked at the body, and it showed no injury. If it showed no injury, then he must have drowned. In that case, they would have to remove the flesh from his body and throw it into a fire built for that purpose. Then the bones would be buried near the fire. This made them all sick at heart, but they would do it.

One of the men suggested that Chattering Squirrel's death was due to the Oki of the waters who wanted him left at the bottom of the lake. Étienne said firmly, "No. This was not caused by spirits. And he did not drown. Chattering Squirrel knew he couldn't swim. He was afraid of the water, and when he fell in, the shock and the fear that he felt caused his heart to stop beating. He could withstand an Iroquois attack better because he would know what to do. He was helpless in the water. Today we must place our companion on a scaffold like good members of the Bear Clan. Tomorrow let's try to swim a little before we get into the canoes. Grenolle and I and any of you who can swim will teach the others. I hope all of you will join us."

Le Grand Lac – 1623

The next morning's swimming lesson didn't amount to much, but those who could swim stressed that it was important to try to hold onto any part of the canoe that was still afloat, and not to panic. Each of the two remaining canoes had four more men, but only two extra paddles because the others were lost in the lake.

The men fanned out into the surrounding woods looking for a tree that had recently fallen and could be used to make two paddles. Lightning had toppled a small pine tree that was wide enough. The bark was peeled and the trunk then cut into the right length and width with a hatchet. The handle part was wrapped with cord to protect their hands because these were very rough paddles.

They embarked again. This time they believed they were only two or three days from the peninsula they sought. The Huron were perfectly content to travel far more cramped than they now were, so they didn't complain, but they certainly weren't as comfortable as before the loss of one of the grands canots de maître. The wind was growing colder and everyone wore shirts. The light of the sun was no longer bright on the water but glinted in silver slivers that seemed to hurt the eyes. They plied the paddles, rarely speaking, and lost in thought.

"Doesn't anyone want to sing?" Étienne asked. No one answered. "Then I will sing a song for our lost friend." The only funeral song he knew was a dirge "Dies Irae" which Grenolle joined in singing. The Latin dirge didn't sound too different from some of the Huron songs, which also tended to be minor key

Le Grand Lac – 1623

and mournful. It was received with quiet "Ho's" drawn up from the pit of the stomach. Then another man broke into a song he composed as he paddled. It was the story of the life of Chattering Squirrel. All knew he would not be mentioned again. In the future, other words would be used in place of it. If he had been a great leader, warrior, or medicine man his name might be used by someone else who was also renowned, but he had died too young for that.

Étienne suggested they tell stories. Chattering Squirrel's death had disturbed them all. Oskeendi told a story about a man who died and went to the beyond with his dogs. He told of the man's hunting exploits, the people he met in the spirit world and the food that he ate. This was considered a philosophical tale because only people went to the afterworld along the Milky Way. Dogs journeyed there too, they used The Way of the Dogs. The story passed the time agreeably. Then another man told a story. They paddled and listened to those voices strong enough to be heard in both canoes. When the travelers felt tired and hungry they stopped for the night.

The fish caught on the lines behind the canoes were the great whitefish of the Lac Supérieur. Some of them had heard of this fish, and all enjoyed eating their fill of it. It would be mentioned at many a campfire long into the future. They would tell of their voyage far to the west, of the dangers they had lived through, and the sights they had seen. Some of the cooked fish was tied into skins and looped by cords high over trees to serve for the next day's breakfast. Shelters were quickly made of pine bows. Some of the men brought woven

Le Grand Lac – 1623

mats from the canoes to put on the sandy shore, a fur rug below them, a fur blanket over them and sleep was instantaneous.

When the two canoes of bone-tired men finally reached the great green peninsula called Keewenaw by the Ojibwas, it seemed to loom before them like the end of the earth. Both Hurons and Algonquins living from Georgian Bay to the east, always wanted to see people from a distance before they arrived, and to be seen by them. In the experience of the Huron, only Iroquois arrived by stealth. So they called out their arrival noisily, and then built a bonfire on the beach to let people know they meant no harm.

The man called Oskeendi in Huron or Anguille in French because he was long and slender like an eel, was the first to say in a very soft voice, "There are many people in the woods around us, watching us closely. I suppose they think we may be Winnebago."

When Étienne was told, he was able to say, "I know. They have been there ever since we started building the bonfire. If they truly want to be undetected, they will have to leave the little children at home. Unless warriors have started saying, "Mama, I'm hungry", this is just a group of the curious."

Since they had the fire going well, they boiled their sagamite and put fish on sticks to half-smoke, half-fry in its own fat. Finally, a boy of about fourteen came out of the bushes and strutted about to show that he wasn't afraid. One of the men offered him a fish and moved over a bit so there was clear space for him to sit and eat. The boy ate warily, but when Grenolle, Étienne and some of the others spoke to him in

Le Grand Lac – 1623

Ottawa Algonquin which was easily understood by these people, he seemed to lose all fear and talked and laughed freely.

Grenolle said in Huron, "You had better eat heartily, mes amis, because soon the beach will be swarming with Ojibwas all planning to share our food, and you can imagine the attitude they will take if we aren't willing to give it to them."

The rate at which the jaws and teeth moved was stepped up, but not soon enough because from having one guest, they soon had fifty. None of the Ojibwas suggested their visitors share the sagamite they had in baskets in the canoes, probably because they weren't as familiar with it as the people living farther east were. Difficult to raise corn that far north.

"Where did you come from? Why are you here? Why do some of you look so strange?" Since it was Étienne and Grenolle who looked peculiar to everyone, they undertook to explain that they were from far across a sea, and that it was normal to wear facial hair and have hair on the chest. There were the usual questions, "Do the women also have all that hair?" "How bad was it in your country that you are now here?"

"No. Women don't have any more hair than your women do. We are here to find out how you live, what your country is like, if there is a passage through this Grand Lac to the west that would take us to a western sea. None of us are going to hurt you." As soon as Étienne made that little speech, he had to admit to himself that although they didn't want to hurt them, disease followed the European just as winter follows fall.

Le Grand Lac – 1623

"How do we get from here to the area of the copper?" Étienne asked.

"Just take the path through the woods and when it ends you will be at the other side of the peninsula. Not far from the path and the beach there are people bringing copper up from the ground. What are you going to do with copper?"

"I want a little of it to prove that I have been here. I would like to have ornaments made of it for my wife and daughter."

"Why don't you take Red Lance with you? He is the boy who first came to your fire today. He has been across the peninsula many times and knows some of the people."

"Is it a long walk from here?"

"Two, three days' journey."

Étienne was amused when the Hurons didn't want to leave their canoes unguarded. "Grenolle, they are afraid the people here are as inclined to thievery as they are. Some of them will stay here with the canoes and those who want to can come with us on a long walk."

"I don't mind walking, just so I don't have to carry a canoe." Grenolle answered.

"D'accord. Tomorrow morning we will leave some of the men behind to visit with the Ojibwas, and learn anything they can about the surrounding area and the history of the people.

They saw no one on the path, and yet there were people expecting them when they reached the waters of the Grand Lac again. The people involved in the mining process had to hunt and fish in order to

Le Grand Lac – 1623

survive, so it was not surprising that the travelers had been seen a long way off. For many generations, the Ojibwas of the peninsula had used copper to trade for tobacco or stone axes and arrowheads, but because they were so isolated in their cold and remote peninsula, visitors were a treat, as long as they were not the dreaded Dacotah from the west, or the other part of the Dacotah people, the Winnebagoes, come up from their great green bay. They had heard of the Iroquois, but had enough to worry about with the Dacotah Sioux.

Grenolle brought along some of his red tasseled caps to trade. He, too, wanted to prove he had been to Lac Supérieur by bringing copper back to Québec. Étienne carried small adzes with him, and two French knives.

The men at the mines were delighted to exchange pieces of copper for red caps and one of Étienne's adzes brought him two copper necklaces.

"Grenolle, should I bring a necklace to Goes Softly, too?" Étienne asked.

"Only if you want to be in trouble with Sara. She will be pleased with whatever you bring her, and expects you to remember your daughter. But Goes Softly is not your daughter! Who would think you would need advice from a bachelor?" Grenolle laughed heartily.

They watched the miners take the copper out of the ground in its pure form. Sometimes they heated and pounded the copper into sheets, and sometimes it was pounded cold. The area around the Keewenaw peninsula was very sparsely populated, and at a great

Le Grand Lac – 1623

distance from the settled tribes who might want copper kettles. The people who mined the copper scarcely used it themselves. A few wore copper bracelets, and there were some kettles and pans to be seen. The red caps were an instant delight and looked oddly disconcerting on the tall slim men who were working almost naked in the open mines.

The work was done in trenches that usually were only the height of a man because it was so hard to get dirt to the surface. Étienne made a mental note to suggest in Québec that stout rope would be a good seller at trade fairs. The Ojibwas brought up the dirt in wooden buckets by climbing short ladders. Not too difficult, but very time-consuming and uninteresting, so no one ever worked at it for long. There were a few richer veins where the mining was going on in deeper trenches.

Their guide, the ever-curious Red Lance, climbed down a rough ladder to get to the bottom of the deepest mine around. While down there, he spied a large piece of copper close to the ground. He dug it out with his hands, and then the ground above it caved in. Soon he was in serious trouble. He grabbed at the ladder on the side but only succeeded in pulling it over on himself. Now the trench was filling with wet mud; there must have been a pocket of water there, it had become a well of water with Red Lance at the bottom. His cries for help brought men to the top of the trench but one side was rapidly caving in.

Oskeendi crawled on his stomach to equalize his weight over a larger area. With his head hanging well over the side, he called to the struggling boy, "Climb

Le Grand Lac – 1623

up the opposite wall as far as you can and I will pull you up." Other men braced themselves and held tight to Oskeendi's ankles as he wiggled into position. Meanwhile, the stronger side of the trench was also beginning to weaken from the water filling the hole.

Red Lance managed to get the ladder that had fallen into the muck and held it up to Oskeendi. It didn't reach. He tried climbing and kept slipping, but even a foot more was enough so that Oskeendi, by sliding over the side slightly, could catch hold of the top rung of the crude ladder. The boy held tight to the other end and was dragged to the surface before the ladder fell apart.

The miners didn't harbor any ill will against Red Lance for ruining the trench they had dug with such effort, and even said that it wasn't the first time such things had happened. The boy and Oskeendi went down to the lake to wash off several layers of dirt, and then rested on the beach while the sun partially dried their clothes. Meanwhile, Étienne walked around the village and engaged the older men in conversation. "Uncles, can you tell me anything about a great body of salt water toward the setting sun?"

"No. We have heard of a great body of salt water, but it is where the sun rises," said one.

"Is there a river that we could take to go toward the setting sun?"

"There are many rivers. None of them go far. After traveling several days' journey from the end of this lake, you will find a great river just beginning. We have not been down it, but have known people who did journey a long way. There is nothing there. Why go?"

Étienne stopped trying to find a waterway west

Le Grand Lac – 1623

from these people. They didn't know of one. He took out a pipe and a bag of tobacco. He lit the tobacco by using a piece of charcloth he kept in a tiny metal box. With a piece of flint he struck a spark that quickly ignited the charcloth. Everyone was interested in knowing how he did that, but since a small metal box was needed to hold either cotton or dried mushrooms. It was considered useless until Étienne suggested they make boxes of copper. The men sat and smoked, and like a good fur trader, Étienne talked about the possibility of them making up a flotilla and bringing furs and perhaps copper trinkets to the trade at Trois Rivières.

One of the older men said seriously, "I don't think there is anything anyone would want that would make us travel that far. I have heard of people doing it. I have never known any of them. We have everything right here."

Étienne said, "Oh I agree that it is a very long journey. You could just bring furs to the Huron people – either those at Manitoulin Island or those in Huronia. Our Bear Clan in Huronia goes to the trade and we will take your furs and bring you back a profit. Of course, we will keep some of your furs for our trouble, but it will be fair. You can either wait for our return in Huronia, or you can go home and get your profit the next season when you bring more furs. I can guess what the furs will bring and so, if you like, I could pay you immediately with French shirts like I am wearing, red caps, blankets, tools of many kinds."

"I think we might go down to Huronia in the spring if we could count on you paying us for the furs right there," a younger man said cautiously.

Le Grand Lac – 1623

"Good. Even if I am not in Huronia, my brother-in-law, Ahouyoche, can give you a reasonable price and pay you, so your trip wouldn't be wasted. I like to get to Trois Rivières by the time the ice goes off the River of Canada. A problem is that spring comes so late to this peninsula. But I could wait in Huronia if you told me you were going to arrive when the first leaves are on the trees in your country."

After a short discussion it was agreed that it would be good to make the trip as far as Toanché, and Étienne should expect them in Huronia in late spring. They finished the tobacco, and feeling like he had been smoked over a slow fire like a fish, Étienne went back to the rest of his crew, and decided he had learned all he could. The copper was abundant, but difficult to get out. There was no waterway to the west. *I have known that for years, but I continue to ask because both Champlain and de Caen keep hoping.*

The return trip seemed easier, as they knew some of the landmarks and they were even expected at Manitoulin. Grey Lynx was more hesitant about leaving his home to live there, but he was still in love and feeling romantic because he would always believe that fate had ordained his choice. Étienne said, "You know, Grenolle, for the first time I have a slight hint of how women must feel in France, always having to leave the only home they ever knew. Here it's the men."

"Étienne, the only way to avoid that sort of thing is to remain single like I am." There wasn't an answer to that, but Étienne smiled inwardly, thinking of his wife and how glad he would be to see her.

Peace Mission

"Sara, I'll be back in a little while. I'm going to see Père Le Caron."

"I hope you aren't going to upset him. You know how he is. Be patient."

"Oh, I'm not going to argue with him about anything, I just want to talk." With that, he went out the door. It would be good to speak with Le Caron. Unthinkable to mention to Sara what he intended. She would cry and become terribly depressed when she couldn't change his mind. He felt determined to try to make peace between Huron and Iroquois; the constant warfare was draining everyone's energy.

As he walked along toward the little bark shelter that the Recollect priest called both home and chapel, he thought about how eager that priest was to bring Christianity to the Huron, how he went west at his first chance, even before Champlain thought it was safe. He endured a miserable trip from Québec to Huronia in a crowded canoe where he was resented when his long brown skirts brought in water and sand. He was considered useless baggage because he could not paddle well enough to do his share in the canoe. His wide-brimmed black hat annoyed the men behind him. No one was delighted either about his insistence on bringing along wine and biscuit so he could say mass. His life as a simple priest in France had not trained him for long portages, incessant mosquitoes, dirty, half-raw food, and sleeping on bare, wet ground. He bore all with good will, and believed he could easily share the life of his little flock when he reached Huronia.

Unfortunately, there was no little flock because none of the natives were able to imagine that he had anything of value to impart. At Toanché the people didn't object to him, they just ignored him. Le Caron's life was so hard it made Étienne shake his head in sadness and in exasperation.

Not seeing the priest outdoors, Étienne called out, "Bonjour, mon père, je voudrais vous parler!"

The priest hurried out to meet him, while adjusting his worn-out cassock as best he could. "Bonjour, mon fils! I am so happy to see you. You say you want to talk to me! I cannot tell you how much I want to talk to you!"

"Nothing wrong, I hope?"

"Nothing wrong, but nothing seems right either. I get very lonely here and it is always a joy to have visitors. Sometimes I wonder why I am here. I try to learn the language – the man you hired to teach me has been helpful – when he actually comes to my cabin. But how can I possibly teach about the soul when they have no concept nor word for soul? Nor for grace, nor redemption, nor even for sin? The doctrine of eternal damnation just seems to make them disgusted."

"It makes me disgusted too, mon père." Étienne laughed.

"You shouldn't make jokes about it!"

"No, and you shouldn't try to teach Christianity by

Peace Mission

frightening people! Do you still have those awful pictures of the poor souls suffering in Purgatory or in Hell?"

"Certainly. I think that because the savages use fire to torture prisoners, they can more easily understand the pain of purgatory and hell."

"No doubt, but does it make people want to become Christians?"

"Not yet. First, I have to lift the weight of superstition off their backs."

"That is what I try to do, too."

"But, Étienne! I have heard that you made an offering to some god at a large rock on the river where all offer tobacco."

"Wrong of me. Yet, if we had any trouble on the water, guess who would be blamed for it if I hadn't thrown my tobacco on the rock along with theirs? We usually have serious problems on that stretch of water, and I always comment on how little good the sacrifice did, although it's no sacrifice for me since I only smoke it when to refuse would seem rude. I'm trying to do business here, and trades are made in a blanket of thick smoke. They know I don't believe in their superstitions. Lots of them don't either. The Huron are ripe for conversion. It doesn't seem like it most of the time, but they don't have any oki that they really trust and none they admire. The same is true of the Algonquins in all the tribes I've ever seen. You are probably doing more good than you know just by being here and being patient. The Huron are the most patient of people."

"I wish they were more honest."

Peace Mission

"Oh that. Have they been stealing from you?" Étienne looked around in amazement at the tiny bark cabin that had nothing but a rough cot built into the wall, a table with three books, pen, ink and a small supply of paper. There were three pegs for clothing and vestments, a little supply of dried fish and sagamite. "I don't think they even want anything they steal from you, it is more a game with them than anything else. You do know, don't you, that they are severely punished for getting caught? I'll suggest in council that they return any goods they've stolen from you – return anonymously, of course, so no one is hurt."

"Wouldn't it be better to let them be caught and punished?"

"No, because they would be punished for being clumsy and not for being thieves. First, they have to believe that theft is wrong. They don't steal in their own longhouse, you know," Étienne said.

Father Le Caron sighed. "The things they never thought about in the seminary are the things that plague me here. I'd like to train the children. I actually had two of them coming here now and then, but I had to punish them gently for laughing and chasing around during Holy Mass, and this made their parents furious with me. I wanted to train those little ones to respect their parents, too. I feel so shocked when children strike their fathers and mothers."

"I do too, but the savages, both Huron and Algonquin, are even more shocked when an adult strikes a child! I know what a difficult task you have. The suffering of the Spanish priests in Mexico seems

237

Peace Mission

mild compared to what you go through. But then, they have the Spanish crown helping them, we have nothing but merchant groups with monopolies that can be taken away at the King's whim. They have Spanish soldiers with arms and ammunition. We have six soldiers now, and they are in Québec, and sometimes those few have no ammunition. Spaniards have regular supply ships, and in the Spanish lands, the natives have stores of food, clothes and building supplies to trade. I shouldn't mention these things, they make me angry."

Father Le Caron looked happy just having someone to commiserate with him. He simply said, "I can tell that Champlain told you about his experiences with the Spaniards."

"He certainly did. I would like to see Peru and also that narrow peninsula that separates the Atlantic and Pacific. If we had peace we would have more settlers, more trade. We could go south from Québec instead of always north into even colder lands. The French are always dreaming about going west, but I am convinced there is no water route to the Pacific Ocean. Champlain told me about that narrow peninsula between the oceans and his idea of a canal joining them, but that is for Spain, not for France."

"Does Champlain really still think there is a waterway west from les Grands Lacs after that frightening trip into the northwest that you took with him?"

"I think he wants to believe in one. But he is far less sure than he was."

"What happened to the liar who told you he knew

of a way and kept leading the expedition farther and farther along?"

"When the chiefs convinced Champlain that Nicholas Vignau had never been farther north, he was left alone to find his way back, or to settle in with any tribe that would take him. I suppose he is dead."

"We should pray for him."

"Do that, but first pray that we can find something of value to offer the Iroquois to join in a peace treaty. I would like to go to the River of the Iroquois, the one we are starting to call the Richelieu after Cardinal Richelieu who probably has never even heard of that great river.

"From the River of the Iroquois, I'll send men of the Neutral Nation, or the Petuns – you know, the ones who raise all that tobacco, down to the Seneca village to see the old chief who helped me. Or, if he is dead, his son. I know there are people there anxious to find peace. It will be a very delicate mission. There is much to be gained for the people here who could stop that long detour and just go east to Québec. We are less safe in our villages every year. The Algonquins aren't living inside palisades so they are worse off than we are. Fields of corn get smaller and closer to the center of settlements all the time. Without a good supply of food, there is nothing for us to trade for the furs we need from nomadic tribes."

"Étienne, I long for peace. It would be wonderful to feel safer. I haven't converted anyone and the only baptisms were of children close to death. I don't want to die before I feel I have had a true purpose here. To be able to visit other missions and see my brother

Peace Mission

priests would be…" His voice trailed off, there was no way for the poor man to describe his desire for some companionship in his lonely life.

"I agree, and you deserve that. But what do we have to offer the Iroquois that they might understand? I am not going to promise them arms like the English do, or that miserable brandy that is the scourge of the savages. What can I offer? The Iroquois are closely allied with the English, the English are getting stronger and their colonies larger. If the French Huguenots ally with the English, our colony at Québec is finished. The French will be lucky to be allowed to stay there." Étienne shrugged his shoulders and sighed.

Father Le Caron thought for just a moment and then said sadly, "My son, all you can offer is a share in the fur trade."

"The Huron would kill me for that!"

"Don't tell it like that. Start with the Iroquois and their desire to trade farther west, and be free of Huron raids. The Huron will be better off, even with Iroquois competition, because they, too, will be able to travel far and wide without fear. If you had serious guarantees from the Iroquois that they would respect the peace, perhaps the Huron would also accept peace in return for the same thing the Iroquois would get, freedom from fear of attack and freedom to hunt, fish and trade."

"D'accord, mon père. I suppose that is the heart of the matter. I am completely helpless to stop the Huguenots from joining the English against us in Québec. Ma foi, I can't even stop the Catholics from annoying the Huguenots! By the way, did you hear

Peace Mission

about the minister and priest who couldn't get along?"

Father Le Caron was smiling, waiting for the joke, but Étienne said, "No, this is the truth! It happened in Québec. The Huguenots sent out a ship with many of their co-religionists on it. They sang heretical psalms at the top of their lungs to annoy the Catholics – even when they reached New France where it is against the law 'to bawl Huguenot psalms on the Saint Lawrence' as the law describes the offense. The minister and the priest battled incessantly and made the sailors disgusted with them both. When they finally landed, they actually came to fighting with their fists before others broke up the fight. Hunger and scurvy are not respecters of persons, and that winter, both died. The sailors insisted on burying them in the same grave so they could continue to battle." Étienne was amused, Father Le Caron was dumbfounded.

"So you see what I mean, mon père, it won't be easy to bring peace to Huron and Iroquois who have been fighting for centuries. Since both love war as much as the French and the English do, there had better be something in it for them to agree to peace."

"I can see what the Huron would gain, I can't think of anything special for the Iroquois who are stronger, other than what we just suggested. Perhaps Champlain knows something?"

"No. I think the only way is to ask them what they might want. Trade privileges, I suppose. Give me your blessing mon père. I'm going to take a short trip to the Tobacco Nation, pick up some men, and then we are going back to the Seneca village and hope to find the old chief or his son. I think I will dress like the natives

Peace Mission

and keep my mouth closed until I am sure of a good reception." He spread out his mangled fingers and said simply, "My hands can't take any more."

The priest gave Étienne a warm embrace and blessed him. "I will pray for you unceasingly until you return."

★

"Sara, I'm going to be gone about a month. I need to map the area between here and the Petuns and Neutrals better because Champlain would like a mission there. I'll do some trading too, of course."

"Can't you map that area in your sleep?"

"Some of it, I probably can. I need to talk to a few people down there, too. I wish you could come along. I want to show you off in Québec. When I go to the trade fair next spring, let's take P'ti Étienne over to your mother's longhouse. He has cousins to play with there, too."

Nothing could have made Sara more agreeable to his trip away from Toanché than the prospect of going with Étienne in the spring to see the French village on the River of Canada that she had heard so much about.

"Étienne, what shall I wear? I want to have French women's clothes. Can you bring any back on this trip?" Sara sounded so worried that Étienne had to laugh which didn't please his wife.

"When we get to Québec I will take you to Madame Hebert. I have spoken of the Heberts – they are fine people and have several daughters – all of them can sew. I will ask them to make you dresses and in return

I will have them send for any materials they want from France. They probably have some good cloth on hand to work with, after all, Madame de Champlain has been in Québec now through several seasons and she is always well dressed. The daughters of Hebert probably sew for her."

With Sara contented and happy thinking about her promised trip, it was easy to get together the maps and paper and pencils he would need, some trade goods and food. He did a thorough inspection of his canoe and was ready to depart. No one but his family was down to see him off, after all, it was just to be a short trip down to the Tobacco Nation, or so everyone thought.

★

"Ho, hho!" Étienne called and waited for someone to come help with his canoe. He was in the Tobacco Nation and knew full well that his arrival had been noted.

"Ho, Aderestouy!" called a young brave.

"Don't you know who I am that you have to call me 'Man of Iron'? I am not only a Frenchman, I am Étienne, a member of the Bear Clan!"

"Well, yes. I just forgot what you are called. Not easy to remember those strange French names, you know. I suppose you are here to trade?"

"That's true. But I want to see your chief first – still the same cranky old warrior you had last year?"

The young man helped him beach his canoe and then walked alongside him commenting freely on the

Peace Mission

chief's bad disposition. "I believe it is because he has two wives. It is driving him insane. Have you ever known anyone with two wives?"

"Oh certainly. Sometimes they are sisters and get along rather well, but most men find one wife enough. I like mine very much, but two of her would be enough to make me cranky, too. Bring me to him, if you please."

The chief lived slightly apart from the others, but close enough so everyone knew about his domestic problems. Fortunately for Étienne, both women were working in the tobacco fields and the chief was taking his ease outside the cabin with some dogs he was fattening up for the kettle.

He put down a pup he was playing with and greeted Étienne warmly. "I am glad to see you again, but we don't have much to sell at this time. The new tobacco crop isn't ready and we won't have extra corn this year. There are some men with furs that you can do business with, I think." The chief looked at him quizzically.

"Good," Étienne said as he sat down, took out the pipe he so detested and waited for the chief to offer him tobacco. He had some of his own, but these people got touchy about tobacco; if they didn't raise it, it wasn't fit to smoke. The chief penned up his dogs and motioned for the young brave to take his leave. Then he brought out a bag of tobacco and sat near his guest to have some private conversation.

Étienne got right to the heart of his visit, "I want to take some men from here and go down to the Seneca village where I was imprisoned years ago. While I was there, I met a few men who would like to have real peace with the Huron. It would be foolish to take Huron men in; we would all be killed. But the Petun go down there all the time. I will wear clothes just like the men wear here, I will shave my beard and my chest and grease my hair till it lies perfectly flat. Most of all, I will keep my mouth closed so there is no clue that I am French or Huron."

"But why?" asked the Chief in alarm. "What good could come of your talking about peace when the Iroquois are at war with everyone except the Neutral Nation and the Petuns! The Hurons hate the Iroquois so much that it hardly matters whether the Iroquois want peace or not!"

"Perhaps. But the last two years, Iroquois canoes went up to Québec to trade instead of going to the Dutch at Fort Orange. There is little game left in Iroquoia, and they need to travel west and north to get furs. The Huron themselves must buy furs from the Nipissings and other tribes, and we have to make great detours to avoid the Iroquois. No one is safe. It is foolish to have constant warfare that settles nothing. The Iroquois are stronger than we are, and every year they are getting more arms from the Dutch and the English. If we don't all want to be slaughtered or enslaved, we had better act together, and soon."

"So, you would go in with tobacco to sell? You would promise the important men of the tribe that they would be welcomed again at the trade fairs? And you would tell them that if they agreed to peace they would be allowed into Huronia and into the cold country around Lake Nipissing, and in the lands toward the setting sun?"

Peace Mission

"Yes."

"What will the Huron get out of this?"

"Life. Without peace, we will be destroyed. With it, we can trade wherever we want to go, we can raise fields of corn and squash far from our villages if we wish. The men can hunt and fish anywhere. We can send our women and children out to work without fear that we will never see them again. We can fish any river and not fear death at the snapping of every twig."

"I can see that you have given this serious thought, Étienne. What good would come of it for the Tobacco Nation if we sent men on a mission that risks our neutrality with both Huron and Iroquois?"

"The honor of helping to make peace between people who have been at war during the lifetime of your father, and his father, and his father, and his father. But what will most impress your people, is that you will not have to buy your way through Huronia. You can take your own goods to Trois Rivières or Québec, without paying the Huron anything. The more trade there is, the better off your people will be. Will you help me get a crew of four men to go to Iroquoia?"

The chief laughed and said, "Why not! There are more than four idle young men around here whom we would all like to send on a long trip."

"That's not the kind of man I am looking for. I want intelligent men who can keep their own counsel. I will see that they are well paid. The rest of the village must consider it a trading trip and not be told anything else, even when we return. There are Algonquin villages here and there where we can stop. We don't have to

Peace Mission

tell everything we know. It would not be safe for me, nor perhaps even for the Iroqouis I talk to while down there. Certainly not if the men I take along are inclined to talk freely. In a few years the truth can be known."

"I have men who are good in a canoe, very serious men who can be trusted. We would hate to lose them, Étienne." The chief looked at him darkly.

"I can't guarantee anything. But if they commonly trade in Iroquois country, that should protect them. I hope you have plenty of good tobacco to sell?"

"Certainly, last year's crop, of course."

Two days later he embarked again, this time with four men to help paddle. The canoe was better suited to five men than to Étienne alone and it seemed to leap over the quiet green-blue waters. The chief was right. These were serious men. They rarely spoke, never smiled, and never broke into song. Étienne reflected that it would have been more enjoyable with Ahouyoche and a couple of his Huron friends, but he didn't want to involve any Huron in this. He asked himself if any peace mission, ever in history, had to be done like this. Could he keep it a secret? Probably not, but if he succeeded, there would be no need for secrecy. If he failed... best not to think of that.

★

Instead of trying to skirt Iroquoia, they plunged right into it. They stopped at one small village, sold tobacco for pounded corn, and continued down to the very village Étienne had been in seven years before. It had not been moved in the meantime, not even the usual

Peace Mission

few yards to keep down bad smells. The torture post was where it had always been.

The old chief lived in the same cabin. "Ho, Étienne! I never expected to see you again. You are a brave man, indeed. I think you are safe here, but I can't always count on the young braves anymore. Well, I never could. Nowadays my son is really the chief, I am old and tired and he is young like you. He lives here with me and his wife. We were glad to receive the five knives you sent. We made sure that Oneida, Onondaga, Mohawk, Cayuga and Seneca each have one knife. In every case, it belongs to a strong man in the tribe who is in favor of peace. My son has the Seneca knife. Here, there are several of us known to be in favor of peace and the people just accept that. But what would happen to us if we actually made peace gestures openly?"

"I don't know. You heard that Iroquois canoes went to Québec to trade? We thought that would be a first step."

"That is what encouraged me to come down to your village. There is much to be gained for both Huron and Iroquois with peace, and the Algonquin suffer because of our wars."

In the evening, the chief invited all the men of the village to his cooking fire where a feast would be given. Étienne and the chief had a conversation about the dangers of telling all the men instead of just those whom they knew agreed with them. But a sure way to turn the Seneca against peace would be to have some of the men feel left out, they would instantly think of treason, and not of a reasoned and thoughtful attempt at peace to improve the lives of the Iroquois.

The already overly-serious men who arrived with Étienne were by now almost frozen with fear. From being simple tobacco traders, they were now put in the position of being allies of the Huron... but perhaps no one recognized their French leader.

The ever-provident Iroquois had plenty of food on hand for the feast; and no one had been told that one of the visitors was a man they had tortured years ago.

Étienne was with the old chief all day, and finally said, "Uncle, I am afraid that there will be many women standing around just behind the men. They might also cause trouble. In the Bear Clan, they often speak at the council meetings and the older women usually choose the chief."

"Many women may be around our fire tonight too. But they think you are all tobacco traders. I will give a speech of welcome, one of the Petun can give a speech. If the tobacco smoke gets thick enough, and the speeches boring enough, the women will probably go back to the longhouses. Of course, some of the men will talk to their wives about it all anyway. Étienne, you have done a brave deed. Far braver than attacking an enemy. Let us not worry, just act as though the most normal thing to help trade is peace."

"And of course it is!" added Étienne.

★

The chief had women serve dried fish in sagamite soup, a whole deer which was a great and unusual treat. There were a few roasted porcupines and some

Peace Mission

cooked roots. Dried berries and baked corn bread completed the meal. Étienne ate like everyone else did, heartily, his head practically in his wooden bowl, and then burped pleasantly and wiped his hands on his clothing so that the grease would make them more waterproof. He didn't want to cause comment of any kind.

But there was no way to hide his mangled hands, and he heard some of the women whispering about them as they served food to the men. In that instant, he guessed that they all knew he was Étienne, the one they had tortured twelve years before. Still, no one said or did anything to indicate that they knew who he was. After the meal, the chief stood to address the crowd. He was full of praise for the Neutral Nation, for the Petuns who had just arrived, and for anyone who wanted to walk the way of peace with their Iroquois friends. This didn't cause any overt comment, and Étienne didn't hear any muttering, but then, he himself had often heard both Huguenots and Catholics tell how they longed for peace in the horrible religious war that had long engulfed France. Still, if the Huguenot city of La Rochelle could finally cede to the French crown, as he heard it recently did, perhaps there was hope for peace here.

One of the men from the Tobacco Nation said a few words. It was evident that he was not used to public speech making like both Iroquois and Huron were. He told the crowd that their chief was wise and his words good, and then he sat down, contented that he had done his duty. There was a general murmur of approbation from the Iroqouis gathered in front of him.

Peace Mission

Étienne was sweating profusely. Should he speak or wait? If he admitted to being a member of the Huron Bear Clan, or a Frenchman, he could be killed instantly, or worse, slowly. The Seneca seemed pleasant, relaxed, well-fed and well-disposed to the idea of peace. He found himself on his feet and heard his own voice coming from somewhere – surely not himself. His ears were ringing, the crowd seemed to phase in and out in front of him. The Petun who were with him looked at him in shock. No one had expected him to speak. Yet, not speaking could be even more dangerous if they already knew who he was.

"People of the Seneca, I have long wanted to return to your village. I remember with pleasure the friends whom I made here after the Great God rescued me from the torture pole by sending a tremendous sudden storm. Praise to God! I was well cared for here after that. I was invited to many feasts, accompanied you on many hunts and showed you some French games – remember boules?" He looked around and several of the men were smiling or laughing. "Warriors of this village saw me safely out of Iroquoia when I was able to leave. When I heard that some of you had shown the courage to go to Québec to trade, I determined to show courage myself and return to you with ideas for peace. The Petun who brought me here did not know I was going to speak. But if Huron and Iroquois want trade and freedom to go anywhere they wish, they must have peace. I cannot speak for the clans of the Huron, you cannot speak for all the clans of the Iroquois, but the great Dekanawidah of the Mohawk people has spoken of a code of laws for the nations that

251

Peace Mission

would bring peace. Seneca, consider the wisdom of that great Iroquois! The French people want peace with everyone. What pleasure it would be to trade and travel anywhere! To hunt and fish and work anywhere! Greater men than I am will make the peace, but let it be said that it started here in this village."

Étienne sat, crossed his legs ceremoniously, drew deeply on a pipe of tobacco that was handed him by one of the Petun, and waited for response. None seemed to be forthcoming. Everyone sat as still as stone. There were a few women behind the men, although most had gone home. Whatever else he had learned in his years in New France, one of the lessons was that women must never be ignored. He looked over the crowd and let his eyes fall on each woman at a time, he tried to communicate with each at a deep level just with his eyes. One of the women smiled slightly and nodded. He smiled, looked at another who turned her face angrily from him. All the others were either non-committal or looked at him with approval.

A Seneca warrior stood. Quiet reigned. He thanked the Frenchman, member of the Bear Clan, for his words of friendship, and assured him he was safe in the village, as the Petun always were. An almost audible sigh came from the man on Étienne's right who was half-expecting Iroquois wrath. Étienne tried not to show any relief. It would be considered weakness.

The Seneca continued, "We will talk with our brothers, the Mohawks, small steps are suited to infants learning to walk. We have been at war very long. I am a warrior, not a peacemaker. But I will take

Peace Mission

the small steps that I can take to bring peace."

Étienne looked at the Seneca with admiration. What a strong and brave man he was.

The feast broke up soon after that, with loud "Ho's" of appreciation to the host for the feast. The chief then took his bowl, filled it, and began to eat, now that all his guests had been fed. Everyone found a place to rest and the day was over. Étienne did not expect to sleep well, but sleep he did, wondering if possibly he could be included in, "Blessed are the Peacemakers, they shall be called the children of God."

He felt such relief and pleasure in the successful mission that he took the knives and adzes that he'd brought along, and stopped at cooking fires in the early morning to ceremoniously give gifts to the women. There was no doubt in his mind that all of them knew what had been said the night before. "With peace, my sister, life will be easier for you and you will know less fear." He was soon out of trade goods, but he hoped his words would catch fire among the women, too.

Many people came to see them off. The Seneca chief insisted they take the remains of the feast with them, so they were well provisioned. The chief looked very old to Étienne, but his weathered and battle-scarred face was now wreathed in smiles. "I have done a great deed for my people. I saved your life many harvests ago, now many lives will be saved with the peace I hope will come."

Étienne's previously silent companions were barely out of hearing distance when everyone wanted to talk at once. They were excited and each wanted to tell his own version of what had happened. Étienne sat in the

Peace Mission

back of the canoe to steer, and listened intently to what they had to say. Every one of them thought that they had been part of a historic moment. Their excitement was not a good sign. They absolutely must keep still about the peace mission – at least for a few months.

Finally, when each of the men had said what he thought, and then repeated it at least once, Étienne said, "The five of us know. Many Seneca know. It will be best for us if we just don't mention it. I know you are safe enough in the Tobacco Nation, but if someone from there talks to Hurons before the peace is agreed upon, it will be very bad for me. I have to trust you." The Petuns hastened to reassure him. They would only mention their part in it when the peace was agreed upon.

"Good. I have a pain in my head and I want to lie down and cover my eyes."

As he said that, he gave his paddle to one of the Petuns, who then took up the task of steering. Étienne stretched out the best he could on the bottom of the canoe with a piece of deerskin soaked in the waters of the Lake of the Iroqouis covering his eyes. This wasn't the first time he'd had a terrible headache after the danger was over. From time to time he leaned over the side of the canoe and vomited. He lay down again in the canoe. He felt happy and sick at the same time.

His companions went back to their normal ways, saying nothing but plying the paddles in quiet rhythm, Finally he fell asleep. When he awoke, the other men were bringing the boat up on the beach. He was better, but weak. One of the men built a fire, another cleaned the fish, a third prepared the sagamite and the fourth put the remains of the venison on a paddle for them to serve themselves. Étienne found the leftover corn cakes because that was all he wanted to eat. Tomorrow he knew he would be as strong as ever. The Petun were treating him with something like deference. It certainly wasn't because he had been sick. None of the savages did much for the sick, unless it was for a child. Food was always set out for all members of the tribe, even when they could not eat it – as long as there was anything to share, the sick person was served. The treatment Étienne received seemed strange to him, and he finally asked why.

"You are brave," said one.

"No, it is more than that," said another. "You have shown us how brave we can be ourselves."

Étienne laughed, and ate his corn cake.

"We should go first to Toanché, so I can pay you. I will stay there. I will ask my brother-in-law and his sons if they want to go down to the Tobacco Nation with you. They can bring the canoe back to me, or if they are busy, there will be someone else to go down with you and bring the canoe back. Remember, you are to tell no one much of anything. Simply say that you sold tobacco, I encouraged people to go to the trade fair in the spring. All of that is true. Speak of other things. Ahouyoche likes to sing, you will enjoy his company. I must stay in Toanché and prepare to go to Québec, and I need to re-draw some maps."

Étienne was happily anticipating seeing Sara and his children again when he realized he had nothing for them. "What can I bring my little ones?" he asked in alarm, making the serious Petun look at him as though he'd lost his mind.

Peace Mission

One of them said he himself made tiny canoes that would float on puddles.

Étienne was satisfied, "We must find you some wood, and you carve away while we paddle." Pitying glances were exchanged. But in a few hours, Étienne had something for the children and could safely go home.

The Petun spent the night on the beach where Étienne brought them their wages in the form of French shirts and kettles. Ahouyoche and his sons left with them the next morning and Étienne realized his peace mission was over. Whether he would suffer for it or not, he couldn't guess.

★

In July of 1623, William (Guillaume) de Caen, who now had the fur trade monopoly, went with Champlain across the Saint Lawrence and then to the River of the Iroquois. Brulé met them there with three hundred Hurons. With the permission of the Iroquois themselves, the French and the Hurons were now meeting and doing business in Iroquoia. Not all the Huron were in favor of peace, but it proved easier than Étienne had ever dreamed to gather together so many Hurons to go into Iroquoia to trade. The Iroquois seemed tentative and concerned that something might go wrong. Champlain was delighted. Brulé's gamble seemed to have paid off.

Champlain accepted Guillaume de Caen and his nephew Emery in the best possible fashion. Both de Caens were respectful to Champlain and realized that the monopoly of the fur trade that had been taken from Champlain and given to them must have been a harsh blow. Neither of the de Caens cared much about the tiny village of Québec. Their interests lay solely in the fur trade. It was necessary for them to have the translators and coureurs des bois working for them if they were to succeed. And since the de Caens were the only legal source of ships in and out of New France, the Frenchmen already working in New France had no choice but to accept their new employers.

Champlain wanted to build up New France and to find a way through the continent to China. The fur trade provided the money Champlain needed for everything.

Neither Québec nor voyages of discovery mattered much to the de Caens, and they were not interested in the conversion of the native people. Étienne must now work only for the de Caens. The disappointed Champlain returned to France.

Fall of Québec

In the spring of 1627, Étienne and Sara, Ahouyoche and Speaks Loudly paddled into the harbor at Québec. Sara asked anxiously, "Étienne, how do I look? Speaks Loudly braided my hair last night, but it has been so windy on the water. Does it seem well-combed to you?"

"Oui, mon amour, you are always beautiful." She smiled, so he guessed he'd said the right thing. Étienne was shocked at the state of the village of Québec, and horrified when he saw the Habitation where everyone had worked so hard. One of the guard towers had fallen down, windows were broken or completely missing, and shutters swung clumsily on rusting hinges. Sara walked along at his side, enchanted by the place, while Étienne looked for familiar faces. He spied Guillaume Couillard, the son-in-law of Louis Hebert.

"Bonjour, Guillaume!" The men embraced warmly.

"Ah, mon ami! Have you just arrived?" Guillaume asked, pounding Étienne's back and grinning.

"Oui, just stepped out of the canoe. Sara, I want you to meet Guillaume, he is the son-in-law of Hebert, of whom I have spoken so often."

The courtly Guillaume took Sara's hand and raised it to his lips. She had been practicing this with Étienne and was as graceful as any French lady. "This is your wife, I presume? Mes compliments, mon ami."

Fall of Québec

"Merci! Sara and I were married in Toanché, we have a son, too. We left him there with my nephews and her mother. My brother-in-law, Ahouyoche, and his wife are with us. They have gone off in the other direction to see the church. When his wife learned that mine was coming to what she calls this great French village, she wanted to come too. What happened to this place? It is in ruins!"

"Champlain is in France trying to get help for the colony. Without him, there doesn't seem to be a true center. The de Caens don't worry about Québec. The best trading area for them is Tadoussac, or perhaps Trois Rivières. They don't care about anything but the fur trade. They certainly aren't going to spend any money or time keeping up our little church! Ma foi! They are Huguenots. The Habitation and fortifications should be kept up, but... by the way, do you remember when my father-in-law, may he rest in peace, tried to buy a plow?"

"Yes, but did Louis Hebert die?"

"Oui, with his whole family around him and in the odor of sanctity. A wonderful man."

"I am sorry to learn of his death. He always said that you were the wonderful one, and that he relied on you for many things."

Guillaume wiped a tear from his eye and said, "Louis felt such disgust when Emery de Caen wouldn't even let him send for a plow from France. Our produce has to be sold at a price de Caen sets, but nothing was ever done to help us raise crops. Louis wasn't even allowed to buy a plow. I know that you tried to lend him money without interest. Remember how annoyed de Caen was? He wouldn't lend it to him even with interest! You gave Louis money when he needed it, too. De Caen would gladly have lost the only farm family in New France! As it is, most food still has to be imported. Champlain understands the importance of a colony here, and you do too, and always tried to help us. We never forgot your kindness."

Étienne waved his arm in a gesture showing that he considered it of no importance.

"You are keeping up the farm?"

"Mais certainement! It's the only farm in New France. Well, that's not strictly true, now. The Jesuits have planted a fine garden and tend it carefully. They'd better, because the de Caens won't even let Jesuits buy food. Emery de Caen did sell them a barrel of biscuit from the storehouse when they landed or they'd have starved. Then he'd surely have lost the monopoly of the fur trade." He looked wonderingly at Étienne and asked seriously, "How can you work for the de Caens?"

"The same way Champlain can. In truth, they pay me the same as Champlain did. They also give me a lot of room for voyages of discovery, and I avoid religious discussions with them. Not that either of them has ever suggested philosophical argument with me!" Étienne laughed, imagining the insanity of it.

Guillaume had to laugh, too. "Going from the ridiculous to the sublime, how do you like Père Brébeuf?"

"I am as impressed with him as the savages are, and that is all anyone could hope. They call him 'Eschon', a term of respect, and the Hurons are very proud to have him live with them."

Sara was trying, but failing, to follow all this rapid French. She occupied herself by looking wonderingly at the few cabins she saw, and what she later described as "the flock of walking birds" that a little girl was trying to lead down the street. Chickens were unknown in Huronia.

Guillaume asked, "See those hens, Étienne? You would do well to buy a couple right away if you plan to stay here. There is nothing left in the storehouse. Nothing at all. Champlain will be back soon, and he will be so discouraged. The lazy Frenchmen who are holed up in the Habitation have not used the lumber he left for them. They just left it outside to rot. Instead of building with it, they all live in one room! The grapes he planted died for lack of water. I could go on, but what's the use? How are we to train the savages when the French set a bad example?"

"Usually when people talk about the French setting a bad example, they are talking about me!" Étienne said, and shrugged his shoulders.

"People who really know you don't talk like that. You, Grenolle, Marsolet, and Nicolet have done what no one else could! Mon ami, you must bring your wife to our house to visit our family."

"We had planned to visit them. Do any of the women sew for others?" Étienne asked hopefully.

"My wife is very skilled with a needle. She will make you something – well, not you, Étienne, your wife. I suppose Sara wants French dresses?"

"You can tell all that by looking at her!"

Fall of Québec

"No, but Pierre Le Noir was here last month with a Nipissing wife, and believe me, she wanted as many dresses as a French bride."

Étienne hurriedly translated this exchange for Sara who was amused. Then he asked, "Pierre's wife is quite beautiful? They have a son?"

"Very beautiful, very demanding. Smart little son, too. Pierre is going to be as rich as you, my friend!"

"And money does exactly what in New France?"

"At the very least, it always provides you with passage home."

"Unless, of course, home is really in Huronia, and then it is back to the canoes and you paddle your own. I'll see you before dark at your house."

"D'accord!"

Sara was pleased that she was going to have a dress made, and asked where they would spend the night.

"Oh, I think we will simply bring along some blankets and spread them on the floor at the Hebert home. Everyone else does. There ought to be an inn here by now, but unless farmers and tradespeople come to Québec to settle, that isn't likely. De Caen promised to bring out many farmers and keep them supplied for two years, but he didn't bring any at all. One of these days, the King and the Church are going to realize that he hasn't kept his promises."

This information seemed strange to Sara, and she asked, "Bring them out? Keep them supplied for two years? What does all that mean? And why do it?"

Étienne laughed. He was going too fast. Those were not concepts familiar to the Huron.

In the meantime, Ahouyoche and Speaks Loudly

met another Huron convert to Christianity when they visited the little church. The man lived all year round at Québec, and helped the Franciscans fathers when they were in New France, and now was working for the Jesuits. He was pleased to meet other Huron Christians, and invited them to stay with him and his wife during their visit to Québec, which Ahouyoche and Speaks Loudly were glad to do.

Ahouyoche knew the village from previous visits; he enjoyed taking his wife to see how people lived in Québec. But it worried him to hear his Huron host say that the Dutch at Albany had asked the Montagnais to join with them and the Mohicans to annihilate the Iroquois. They expected the French to join in with enthusiasm, and were surprised when Champlain said the French didn't want anything to do with it! A chance to destroy the Iroquois sounded to Ahouyoche and to his new-found friend, the Christian Huron, like a chance to destroy Satan. Why would anyone pass it by?

★

The Hebert-Couillard family welcomed them warmly, and thoroughly charmed Sara who desperately wanted to learn to sew like the women in the family did. They taught her a few things, but it was soon too dark to do much sewing.

Strangely disparate people lived with the family. One was a little black boy from Madagascar whom someone had picked up on a trip and then didn't know what to do with; a Montagnais orphan, and the

Fall of Québec

abandoned wife of a fur trader who was either dead or unwilling to return to Québec. All worked and prayed together and made up an exemplary family. They were determined to stay in New France, and believed that somehow Champlain would manage to convince Cardinal Richelieu that New France deserved help, and that it couldn't come from the fur trade alone.

On the trip back to Toanché, Ahouyoche told Étienne of the Dutch idea of annihilating the Iroquois, and of Champlain's refusal to even consider the "wonderful plan".

Étienne said, "I'm not surprised. How often have the French joined in the wars against the Iroquois? Sometimes our allies fail to show up, and even when they do, they never follow Champlain's orders. If he tells them to set fires to burn down the palisades, they set them up with the flames going in the wrong direction and the fire bothers us, and not the Iroquois. When the Huron feel like charging the enemy, they do sometimes, one at a time. They aren't cowardly, they just won't obey orders."

"The Huron is always free, Étienne," Ahouyoche intoned piously.

"I believe you have mentioned that before on thousands of occasions," Étienne answered.

"It is still true. This time you would be helped by the Dutch, and they are heavily armed and have supplies."

"Wonderful. Then the Dutch would be a problem for us if we annihilated the Iroquois. Isn't it enough that the French are already fighting the English? Do we need to worry about the Dutch as well?"

Fall of Québec

"I don't like your reasons."

"I'm not pleased with them either, but there is sense in what seems senseless, to you. And please remember that we do have a treaty of sorts with the Iroquois at this very moment. I don't know exactly how it came about, but we are all safer because of it, and the longer it lasts, the firmer it will become – if we don't do anything foolish."

"I don't trust them."

"No. And I don't trust them, the Dutch, the English and sometimes I wonder about the French. France is involved in a religious war with the Huguenots."

"But they are French, too, aren't they?"

"The Huguenots are French and they encourage the fur trade, but they take no interest in settling New France. It is all quick profit to them, and they are allies of the English."

Now it was Ahouyoche's turn to sigh deeply as he said, "It's very difficult for me to think like a Frenchman, even though I am a Christian."

"Don't bother to try. Thinking like a Huron will be plenty for le bon Dieu; if not, He would have made all the world French, and He didn't."

Ahouyoche said it was a wonderful blessing that the furs they brought along had all been sold at Trois Rivières where there were representatives of de Caen ready and willing to buy them. If they had brought them to Québec, they would have had to wait for ships from France. This in itself was very strange, and made Étienne think some long, dark thoughts in spite of recognizing that of course Trois Rivières is closer to Huronia.

265

Fall of Québec

"Let us stop at that cabin outside Trois Rivières that Grenolle and Marsolet built. We can rest there and maybe even see my two old friends." He didn't add that he also wanted to let some time elapse before they returned to Toanché. It was important to him to know that none of them were carrying any disease. He didn't find any sickness in Québec, but one of Guillaume's children had a very unpleasant cough which sounded like it might be coqueluche, the much dreaded cough the French brought that caused fearful whooping sounds and often many deaths in the longhouses of the Huron.

Marsolet was chopping wood outside the sturdy cabin he and Grenolle had built as a good stopping place on trips farther west. When they weren't there, often some other fur trader was. But it was Marsolet whom Étienne most wanted to see. It seemed like a piece of unusually good fortune to have him there when they arrived. "Bien venus, mes amis! You could not have come at a better time! The hearty welcome from the short, sturdy Marsolet was like balm to Étienne's spirit, he couldn't help but be depressed at all the work they had done, coming apart in Québec.

When Ahouyoche went down to the water to fish, the two women took small kettles and went off to look for berries. If there was something useful to do, the Huron always found it. This left Étienne and Nicholas Marsolet alone. Étienne couldn't seem to stop talking; he wanted his old friend to know everything that he knew about the hoped-for peace with the Iroquois, and the bad situation in Québec. Nicholas was carefully piling the chopped wood against the cabin for winter use.

Fall of Québec

Finally, he went inside and emerged with a bottle of wine. "Join me, Étienne. I have had this for a long time. You need encouragement, because I must tell you that the agreement not to break the peace has already been broken. I was in Trois Rivières when a voyageur came in and told everyone there this story: A few of our native allies ran into a small party of Iroquois whom they captured and brought back to a Montagnais settlement near Québec for leisurely torture. Champlain heard of their plan and managed to talk them out of it. Since some of the Iroquois had escaped when the others were caught, it was decided that Frenchmen should take them back to Iroquoia. That way, it would be clear that the French were going to do what they could to keep the treaty in force by personally returning the captives. Unfortunately, the Frenchmen who volunteered to go down to Iroquoia with them were not very good specimens. One of them had killed an Iroquois some years ago and he was easily recognized. Another member of the group was wanted for murder in France. Well, you can just about guess what happened?"

"So who came back alive to tell the story?"

"No one. The Iroquois didn't hide anything about it. They told the story in many places. When the Frenchmen and the former captives arrived in an Iroquois village, they were asked, "Are you hungry?" The party had walked for hours without food, and they gladly said they were.

"At that, the Iroquois host took out a knife and cut slices off his guests' arms and threw them into the boiling pot. They were forced to eat the half-cooked

Fall of Québec

flesh. This went on until they died. As you can imagine, there is no peace now, and no one seems to be grateful that the captives were returned."

"We have seen such nightmarish things, Nicholas. There doesn't seem to be any end to human cruelty. What do you think about the plan to join the Dutch, the Mohicans and the Hurons to annihilate the Iroquois?"

"No, Étienne, Champlain is right. For one thing, I don't think we could. For another, none of the savages like the Dutch. They all like the French best. Perhaps we are the most charming?" Marsolet allowed himself a small laugh.

"Possibly, Nicholas. But more likely it is because we have always recognized that we can't do a thing here without the goodwill of the natives. The English are down there with the intent of settling in and never leaving. They are farming, and do not rely on others. But we have a short growing season in much of New France, and can raise nothing on uncleared land. Around Québec, the natives are primitive. If anyone but Champlain had been in charge, there would be no goodwill there. Remember how he fed the starving Montagnais when we ourselves were short of supplies?"

"Mais oui, Étienne! Have you often wondered why only eight of us survived? Twenty-eight strong men and only eight of us in the spring."

"Nicholas, God has to have a reason for us living on. I can understand his sparing Champlain, but I often wonder about myself. I thought it was to make peace with the Iroquois." Étienne seemed almost to be thinking aloud. He sounded desperately sad.

Marsolet said, "I have heard soldiers talk like that. Perhaps all of us think that way, there must be a reason for our work. Whatever we did in New France, we had to rely on help from Algonquins or Hurons. Impossible to get goodwill from the Iroquois." Marsolet finished his wine and sat next to his friend in silence for several minutes.

Étienne continued voicing his thoughts with, "And yet, Nicholas, I will never forget the interest in peace I found two years ago down in that Seneca village where I was tortured. I am glad I went down there and tried. Now that the truce is broken, I suppose I am in danger. I think I am safe in Toanché at least, and perhaps with the Petuns and the Neutral Nation. Oh well, nothing I can do about it."

During the few days they stayed at the cabin, neither Nicholas nor Étienne spoke further of the dangers to him, to the French at Québec, or to New France in general. Marsolet was charmed by Sara and told her in halting Huron that he planned to find himself a native wife. Sara asked if he would not prefer a French woman, and Nicholas said truthfully that he would, but seeing his old friend so happy and well married to a Huron woman encouraged him. Besides which, where would he find a French woman in New France? If by chance he found one who wanted to marry him, could she really cope with his way of life as well as a native woman could?

★

Fall of Québec

The next months at Toanché were uneventful except for the arrival in the village of the Huron convert from Québec and his wife. The couple moved into the longhouse of Speaks Loudly's mother and told anyone who cared to listen about the great famine that was afflicting the French at Québec. The supply ships had not come in, and there was nothing to eat except what could be found in the woods. The game was gone and the people were living on edible plants and roots. The food the Jesuits had so carefully stored was eaten and winter looked bleak. The converts had returned to Huronia knowing that the Bear Clan would have something to share.

When Étienne heard this story second-hand from Ahouyoche, he hurried over to the longhouse to talk to the man personally.

"Did anyone go down to Tadoussac, or to the Basques at the cod fisheries to see if ships were coming in?"

The convert said reproachfully, "We aren't stupid, Étienne. Of course men were sent out to see if there were ships there!"

"Did anyone know anything about the supply ships?"

"They were sunk by French heretics. They are trying to starve the French out of the country. The Jesuits say they work for the English."

"Was de Caen one of them?"

"No. It was not that name. I know that one, and that was not it."

Étienne returned to his cabin feeling downcast and helpless. He knew firsthand how bad it was to be hungry all the time. They would probably have to contend with scurvy as well as hunger and the blockade. He wished he could help, but it was too late in the year to take canoes to Québec. Perhaps Nicolet, up there with the people on the Île des Allumettes, had known in time to get some food to Québec? Maybe by spring the English blockade would be broken by the French?

There was nothing at all he could do about it. He spent his time teaching his son, visiting with the Jesuit priest who had replaced Father Le Caron, mending nets, and going out with Ahouyoche looking for just the right birchbark to make canoes. It was too cold to work on much of anything. The cabin was warm and Sara was happy to do all the cooking inside the cabin now that the winds howled continuously and the snow piled up against the door.

Not many canoes from Huronia would go to the trade fairs, since most of the villages already knew that the French supply ships had either been pillaged or sunk. Étienne warned some of the people off, but to a few it seemed totally unbelievable that Québec would have no fur trade, and neither would Trois Rivières nor Tadoussac. Thinking of Tadoussac, Étienne wondered if Marsolet was there. He probably went to Tadoussac to see what he could do for Québec, or at the very least, to help them to live through the winter.

★

"Saraaa, the ice is off the Ottawa. I think I will go to the Nipissings."

Fall of Québec

"You know, Étienne, I can tell by the way you say my name when you are planning to go somewhere." Sara was laughing, so he knew she wasn't angry. The years had taught her that he always came home, and if he was just going up to the Nipissings, she wouldn't worry.

"Ahouyoche and a couple others can take some of the goods, too. I will buy Nipissing furs for myself, since there are no trade fairs this year. I'll have to store them here, but I already have to store all the kettles, knives and shirts, so it won't be much trouble." He had built a large storeroom onto the cabin where he kept goods for times when the hunters couldn't go to Trois Rivières or Québec. The natives blamed him if they didn't get good prices for the furs, so he could imagine how furious they would be if they paddled all the way to Québec for nothing.

There was a trader already at Lake Nipissing when Étienne and the Hurons arrived. He didn't have a lot of goods, but he was doing a brisk business with the people who had just returned from their winter wanderings farther north. They had beautiful furs to sell. Étienne strode across the beach to the Frenchman and greeted him with a warm embrace, "Bonjour, vous êtes Pierre Le Noir?"

"Oui – et vous êtes le bien connu Étienne Brulé?" Pierre asked, sounding amused to finally meet the man responsible for uniting him with his Nipissing woman and child.

"I'm Étienne, and I suppose I am well known, as you say. I have been living with the Hurons and trading for almost twenty years. I should have guessed

Fall of Québec

that having a Nipissing wife you would have come here yourself to tell people not to bother going to the fairs this year. Do you know anything more about Québec?"

"I know that the Huguenots, sailing for England, captured a Basque fishing boat and forced the Basque captain to take a message up the river to Champlain. The message was couched in elegant terms, but what it said was basically, "surrender or starve". Champlain told them in equally flowery terms that he had a good store of food in the warehouse and had no intention of surrendering. But he doesn't have anything there."

"I know. But Champlain doesn't give up easily."

"He has Guillaume Couillard making a pinnace to try and run the blockade, everyone is helping – well, everyone who isn't out hunting for roots in the woods. Some of the people have gone to live with the Montagnais! Champlain sent two men to the Abenaki people to see if they would take anyone in; I don't know if they ever came back. The Abenaki raise corn and squash, and probably beans, too, so they eat better than the Montagnais. If the pinnace Guillaume and his helpers are building won't float, or can't be steered, then the plan is to take the forty or fifty pounds of gunpowder they have left, and go down to Iroquoia in canoes, attack one of the smaller villages, and raid their stores."

"That sounds insane," Étienne said, thoroughly shocked.

"Certainement! But things are very bad at Québec. Well, perhaps Eustache Boullé, Champlain's young brother-in-law, will be able to run the English

273

Fall of Québec

blockade in the homemade vessel. I didn't stay to find out. I left what food I had. Marsolet was there for a day or two, he left a cask of corn and disappeared. Have you seen him?"

"Not since last year." Pierre Le Noir's news depressed Étienne who immediately started trading French goods for sagamite instead of furs. The Nipissings didn't have much of it to spare, but they had some pumpkin to trade and some dried fish. He loaded one of the canoes with it and made two of the Hurons from Toanché a good offer. "If you take this down to Champlain at Québec, I will give you more French goods than you have ever earned in a year of hunting. Then go back to Toanché. We don't need that canoe here now, and people are starving in Québec. Neither of the Huron said a word; they got into the canoe and paddled off.

Étienne had no desire to go personally to Québec, there wasn't a thing he could do there, and one more mouth to feed wouldn't help. Supplies were needed more than his company.

During the next year, he made several successful trading trips to the west. De Caen was intelligent and realized that his monopoly of the fur trade wasn't going to last. He had not done any of the things he had promised to do, other than helping six missionaries get settled. Then he washed his hands of them and went back to the fur trade. Although his interests didn't lie with exploration, he always found Étienne's voyages of discovery fascinating. He didn't care to take credit for them, and was content to have Étienne give maps of newly explored land and water to Champlain.

Fall of Québec

Étienne finally went to Tadoussac looking for Marsolet. It was a hive of activity. English ships, Basque fishing boats with their captured crews, French Huguenots and a handful of genuine Englishmen, mingled with Abenakis, Montagnais, Mohicans and even a few Hurons. It was easy to spot Marsolet, because he seemed to move at a different pace than other men, at least twice as fast and so purposefully that people always seemed to be moving aside for him.

"Nicholas! I am so glad to see you! I was sure you would be here. What shall we do about Québec?"

"I was expecting to see you and I want to ask you the same question. Did you stop there?"

"No. I have seen starving people before. I saw the state Québec was in two years ago, I must be getting soft, I spare myself the sight of things I cannot help."

"Moi aussi! David Kirke sent a message to Champlain last year telling him to surrender or starve. This year his brothers, Thomas and Louis, are here and they are tired of waiting. In a way, I suppose we have to be grateful that they tried blockade instead of charging the fort. Champlain, Guillaume, Eustache, and God knows how many others would all have been killed. The Kirkes aren't so bad, their mother was French and they were raised in Dieppe where their father was an English merchant. They are in the service of England. Now they are looking for someone to pilot an English ship to Québec. They want us to do it, and have been expecting you because I said I thought you'd be here in early spring. What do you say to that?"

"What is the alternative? Eustache Boullé was taking

275

Fall of Québec

a pinnace down to run the blockade, he hoped to find a French ship to take him to France to get help. Did he make it, do you know?"

"No. It was a joke of a vessel, a brave and gallant joke. It foundered. Eustache is here somewhere, I think. The English will want to send him back to France. He's alive, at least."

"Did you hear that Champlain was planning to storm an Iroquois village and raid its stores if Eustache didn't get through for help?"

"Bon Dieu! We can't have that. It wouldn't work. Remember how weak we all were by the spring of 1609? We couldn't have stormed a bunch of schoolboys after that winter of sickness and hunger. Québec has gone two years with real starvation."

"I think we must pilot the Huguenots and see if Québec can be taken without further loss of life." They started at once walking to where the larger ships were anchored. Marsolet knew which one was to be used to take their beloved Québec. "Nicholas," continued Étienne, "have you seen Emery de Caen?"

"No. But I don't think he went back to France. I suppose you have heard that he has lost his monopoly? It now belongs to a group called The Company of New France. Champlain is a member. But, of course, now everything will belong to the English. I suspect they will have to employ the de Caens and people like us. Who do they have who speaks any native language? No. This is New France, no matter what they re-name it. The Hurons love the French and distrust the English. The Algonquins whom Nicollet has been living with also are firm French supporters. Which of

Fall of Québec

the tribes support the English?"

"Well, the Iroquois," admitted Étienne.

"They deserve each other," Marsolet said with a laugh.

They were now standing in front of the ship. Thomas Kirke spied them from the deck and motioned for them to come aboard.

"I'm glad you are here, Étienne Brulé. Marsolet told us you are a better river pilot than he is, and we thought the two of you could also help in any needed pacification of the French at the Habitation, or in the village. Le Bailiff and Pierre Raye are going to join us, too. Do you know them?"

Marsolet said, "We know who they are, that's about all. We will pilot you to Québec and expect you to immediately feed the people there. If you insist on taking people to the Huguenot areas of France, or to England, we expect you to treat them well."

Étienne added, "I would greatly prefer it if you wouldn't deport anyone. The Hebert-Couillard family are the only farmers in New France. They harm no one. The French have never helped them, the English don't need to hurt them! The others are workers who have hopes of a better life here. There are a few missionaries. It would be a pity to be afraid of them."

"We don't want to hurt anyone, but we must bring back Champlain and the priests."

Étienne asked, "When do you want to leave? Can I put my canoe on deck?"

"We can leave in a few hours. Bring your canoe, you won't be returning with us so when we need that space for Champlain and the Jesuits, you will be paddling

Fall of Québec

back to Toanché, I suppose. This will be the lead vessel. There will be two others behind us to bring out the goods in the warehouse and other things of value. We need you because these are the largest ships to go up to Québec since the time of Cartier – in, I suppose, 1535?"

"Probably. We will do our best to get you there safely. I can show you any problem areas that you should watch for on your way back, although you will have Champlain with you then, and he is a wonderful captain." Étienne sighed.

Thomas Kirke said, more in answer to the sigh than anything else, "I take no pleasure in removing him from a place he built. I feel it is my duty as an Englishman."

This made Marsolet laugh derisively and ask, "An Englishman?"

Thomas Kirke, defending himself, said, "My father was English, and I am a Protestant. Would you prefer an Englishman like Sir Frances Drake?"

"No. Don't be offended. It might as well be you. At least you speak French."

"I'm not going upriver with you. You just pilot the ships for the English captains. I must stay here and keep French vessels out of the Gulf of Saint Lawrence." He added darkly, "If there are any left."

When they were sailing up the river to Québec, Marsolet said, "It is much easier sailing along like a king in this comfortable ship than paddling hard from dawn to nightfall. How easy life can be!"

"You have not seen my comfortable cabin and warehouse in Toanché! There I live like a king, warm and dry and always well fed. I have the company of a wife and child, both of them even speak some French. Business is good, and to tell you the truth, Nicholas, it will be much the same for us with the English as with the French. Just not as enjoyable."

The English captain was obviously nervous. He kept muttering stories he'd heard about the great Champlain who never gives up, and the fearless old Pontgrave, who was said to be bedridden, but was that just a French lie, and were they sailing into a trap?

Marsolet knew only a few words of English but enough to know that the mutterings about Pontgravé and Champlain meant the captain was frightened. "Du courage, mon capitaine!"

Étienne laughed and said, "With or without courage, Québec will fall into their hands like a ripe apple. I don't like piloting them, they don't deserve Québec, and Champlain does. I can't see how the poor village will be much worse off, the French crown never helped it. I'll be glad to get the people there fed. Then, as for me, it's back to the fur trade. If the de Caens aren't around, I'll buy and sell furs myself and send them back with the Basques or the English, or even the Dutch. How about you, mon frère?"

"I will either stay at Québec or go to Tadoussac. There will be trading there for a long time. I plan to see you often. D'accord?"

They embraced warmly and Étienne said sincerely, "D'accord, mon vieux." This show of affection and agreement between his two pilots made the English captain nervous again. Were they leading him into a trap of some kind?

When the Habitation and Fort were clearly in view,

Fall of Québec

Étienne said, "If I were you, I'd anchor beyond cannon range." The captain of the ship and the two ships following them did just that. The Englishman nervously adjusted his clothing to make it look proper in every way, he combed his hair and his moustache, cleared his voice several times and practiced his speech.

A small boat was let down with the captain in it. As it pulled away from the ship, a white flag could be seen above Fort Saint Louis. The Englishman climbed the steep path to the fort where Champlain was waiting, well-dressed and wearing his plumed hat. Both men bowed ceremoniously and made several pleasant remarks, but since they were basically unintelligible to each other, they might as well have been speaking Chinese.

The Englishman only intended to present Champlain with the letter from Louis and Thomas Kirke, but Champlain needed to know further details. Father de la Roche d'Aillon conducted the questioning of the Englishman in Latin. Satisfied that he understood the terms, Champlain withdrew and wrote a polite reply.

Although he knew they had starved for two winters because the Kirkes had sunk all supply ships, Champlain suggested in the letter of capitulation that their suffering had been due to weather and the perils of the sea which prevented ships from arriving.

When Champlain was finally embarked on one of the ships going to Tadoussac, Étienne changed his mind about returning to Huronia from Québec, and continued on to Tadoussac with Marsolet. When they arrived there, Marsolet tried to get Champlain's oldest

Fall of Québec

Montagnais ward to stay behind and marry him. The Kirkes wouldn't allow her to go to France with Champlain anyway. He told Champlain he would be a good husband to her, and that France would prove too different for the girl. But Champlain refused and left them in the care of the always hospitable Hebert family. Marsolet protested, and even tried to seduce the girl into staying with him. She was horrified and insulted him publicly, so he gave up. Both girls eventually returned to the wandering Montagnais and they were never again heard from.

But it was Brulé who received the worst of Champlain's scorn. Champlain was furious with him for piloting the English ships to Québec. He knew, certainly, that the English could have found others to do the job, or they could have come in fishing boats. Québec was lost, but not because of Étienne. Even as Champlain called him a traitor, Étienne questioned the insult. Traitor to what? Not to Champlain and Québec. He didn't respond to any insult. It seemed silly, and he knew Champlain would realize he had been unjust, and would know the reason why Étienne had not answered him back was because he understood Champlain's pain. It was years since Étienne worked for Champlain, but whenever Étienne had information about New France, he made a map of the area for Champlain. Their visits were always enjoyable to both. Marsolet stayed in Tadoussac. Several members of the Corde and Bear Clans were returning to Huronia, so Brulé put his canoe in the water with theirs and returned to Toanché. He carefully averted his eyes as they paddled past Québec.

His Death

All of his senses seemed too sharp. He didn't mind feeling hungry and thirsty; those were familiar sensations to him. It was pleasant to feel the softness of the beaver furs beneath him on the sleeping bench, but the smell of the smoldering fire in the center of the cabin seemed more acrid than ever, and the flickering shadow of every child and dog who ran in and out set his heart pounding.

He knew the men were meeting outside the village in the clearing next to the cornfield – it was the logical place to gather. Fifteen years ago his wedding feast was held in that clearing.

He could hear the sounds of the kettles being filled for the evening meal. Some of the mothers had started feeding the younger children. The women would be told everything, but not until it was all over. This was not going to be an ordinary Huron execution, and many women were numbered among his best friends. Goes Softly, for one, would never agree to anything that would hurt him. He felt gratitude that his daughter, Water Song, and her husband were at a fishing camp. He smiled thinking of how close he was to Water Song who looked like a French woman in Huron clothing. Catherine always wanted to see her half-Huron niece. Perhaps they would meet some day. Life was full of wonders.

His Death

He could distinguish the voices of women he knew and of children, but no man's voice – proof that all the men were together, and that he was not called to be with them. So, they were deciding whether or not to kill him. He wasn't surprised. He felt sad, misunderstood, ill-treated, but not surprised. Ahouyoche and his closest friends must be tired of saying the same things over and over in an attempt to save him.

His canoe was in the water, but in full view of the field where the men were gathered. He might outrun them, he had certainly done that often enough on bets, but there were so many of them and he was tired. It would be just a matter of a few days living as a fugitive, even if he managed to get clear of Toanché. A few more days without enough food, with no shelter. There was sagamite in the cabin, he could take that and... He sighed and shifted his position a little, but made no move to leave.

Ah, P'ti Étienne and Sara. What would become of them? He told himself that they would probably go back to the Habitation with Marsolet. What a lucky turn of events it had been when they were simply too tired to go on, so he had left them at a cabin he and Grenolle had often shared. Marsolet and Grenolle would see to it that his wife and son were cared for. The Heberts would help them, too.

The return to the Bear Clan had been a mistake. But he knew it was now or never if the Huron were to have peace with the Iroquois. Soon it would be too late; there would be no Huron. The love of hatred was stronger than common sense. The Iroquois were so

His Death

powerful, their delight in war and their desire to finish off the Huron would wipe out his tribe and many of the Algonquins. He should have known that even talking about peace here would be considered treason. Well, he had known, but he did it anyway.

The Huron were as finished as he was, but just didn't know it. Adieu to the Bear Clan, the Tortoise, and the Corde, and probably to all their allies as well. Why must they disappear? Behind the loss of the fur trade there was always the great unremitting savage hatred that bubbled up from hell and answered no human need for either Iroquois or Huron.

It was fully dark now. If Aenons came in smiling, and told him about the meeting, they weren't going to kill him. The other men knew he would be wondering. Why did he feel embarrassment at being left out? Why didn't they ask to hear his side of the story. He shrugged his shoulders. They knew his side. He knew theirs. Perhaps they would consider him more of an asset dead than alive. If so, he would die.

Aenons pushed aside the deerskin covering the door and entered the cabin looking weary and discouraged. He sighed, came over to the place where Étienne lay and sat next to him.

"Uncle, will it be swift?"

"Yes, if a friend does it, and you have friends in spite of the vote."

"What was the reason for deciding against me?"

"The old men say it is to protect us against the anger of the French now that Champlain is back and the French rule again. They fear the loss of the fur trade. The young men say it is because you were trying

His Death

to make peace with the Iroquois – treason." Aenons went silent for a moment – "and that Champlain hates you."

"Champlain doesn't hate me. He was angry that I piloted the Huguenots, who are allied with the English, into Québec. But it is not only Marsolet and I who knew the way! Others would have taken them if we had not. There were only sixty people at Québec when we arrived and they were all starving! Some had already gone off to find wandering Montagnais who might feed them. Many died of hunger long before."

"But why did Louis Amantacha say that Champlain was angry with your deeds?"

"As you yourself say, "When there are no deer, the hunter kills porcupine." Champlain was hungry and discouraged. He was far more angry with me than he was with the Kirkes, even though they were the enemy who took his beloved Québec. But you see, he never expected me, his friend, to be with the English. I am glad he has that village again. How we suffered for it! I understood Champlain's anger, so I didn't even defend myself. He couldn't strike out against the English or the Huguenots. But he's scolded me ever since I was a lad. Uncle, Champlain knows that we must have peace with the Iroquois or we will have no fur trade. All of us here should realize that by now."

Aenons spoke slowly, "There is so much of this that I don't understand. The only part I can see, is that you asked us to send a peace delegation to the Iroquois. You should not have done that. You were able to sell our furs with de Caen at Tadoussac even when the English were in command. It was not as good for us as when the French were there, but at least we had trade and could buy things from the English that we used to buy from the French."

"Yes. But now that the English are gone and the French are back, you are worried about what Champlain will do."

"That is what the young men said, that Champlain would be angry at us for trading with the English through you, so you must die."

"Such nonsense! Champlain himself often worked with the Huguenots. The Huron still has to make the Grand Détour, we all live in fear of the Iroquois who are stronger every year and so are their English allies. What value is there in just fighting and losing all the time? But I explained all that to the council. They all know. They don't want to go to war with the Iroquois any more because they know they will lose, but this is not peace!"

"Oh Étienne, I have known you so long. I spoke for you."

"I know, Uncle. Champlain will miss me, too. What Frenchman speaks Huron and Algonquin better than I do? Who knows the rivers, the streams and the Sweetwater Sea of the Huron and the Lake of the Puants with its great green bay? What Frenchman but Grenolle and I have seen the Grand Lac and the people who make copper? Who knows the trails and the portages, who can map it for Champlain and the fur traders?"

Aenons sat silent. He may have said much of this himself out in the clearing. Others surely would have spoken for Étienne who had lived as a member of the Bear Clan for twenty-two years.

His Death

Étienne spoke gently to his old friend, "Thank you, Uncle. You have always been good to me. Now, see that my children are cared for. Water Song, her babies and her husband will live here in Toanché. I don't know if Sara will ever come back to Huronia. I think she will not. She has Petit Étienne with her, they will be protected by Marsolet, and our son is big and strong himself now. Ahouyoche will sell my goods and get the money to Sara. I have provided much trade, many kettles, axes, knives and blankets – I have shown the path to so many. If they return, Petit Étienne and my wife deserve to be well-treated, Uncle." He paused a long time and then added, "I will expect the blow soon – and let it be quick." He smiled his old smile and added, "With an axe I brought the people."

★

The grandchildren of Aenons came into the cabin then, and seeing the two men, came up and asked for a story. Étienne said he would tell them one. What kind did they want?

"Tell us about your poor country, and why you left to come dwell with us."

He told this story, which was retold by those children to their children for many years.

"In that land far beyond the sea, I lived with my uncle and my sister. We worked in fields much bigger than any we see here. The work was hard, but we had a huge animal called a horse to help us make our crops. Some fine day we will have horses here, too. We had no corn."

His Death

The children gasped. "How did you live on just pumpkins and game?"

"My little brothers, we had many kinds of food."

"Did you have enemies trying to take your food away?"

"No. The wars were not over food. People in France go to war with those who have different ideas of religion than they do. A fine chief, called Henry the Good, ended the terrible wars and we lived in peace. I wanted to find the path of peace, too, and end the wars with the Iroquois so we could all put our canoes on any waters, hunt in any woods, send our children and our wives to work in fields anywhere and not be afraid they would be captured. I have said that many times."

"Are the Iroquois afraid of us too, Uncle?"

"Yes, they are. But they are feared far more by us than we are by them."

"When I grow up, I will make them fear the Huron more and we will not be afraid of them at all."

Étienne sighed. "Did you know, my little nephews, that the Huron and the Iroquois were once one people? We were, a long time ago."

"Uncle, you seem so sad. Do you miss your family in that land you came from?"

"No, not now. The Bear Clan became my people. Sometimes I have wanted to see my sister, my uncle, our friends – our fields. I always intended to go and visit, and I think I would have gone three years ago but the war broke out again, the religious war that I spoke of. It was also between two different tribes, France and England. Usually there was one more river to chart in this land and one more path to find. And always more

His Death

people to send to Tadoussac with furs. But I did intend to visit my sister."

"If you are not sad, Uncle, then maybe you are hungry – the sagamite is cooked and there is porcupine in it and Mother has cooked a large fish in the coals. Come and eat!"

"A waste of food, little nephews. I will go out when all have eaten. I will walk to the water alone tonight."

Aenons groaned, got up from where he sat near Étienne, and taking his two grandsons with him, went out to eat the evening meal and leave Étienne alone. It was quiet in the cabin and not as noisy outside as usual. This was the time allotted the condemned man to make peace with God, he told himself.

"I lived the way I thought I should," he said by way of prayer. "Except I should have struggled harder to keep brandy and wine from the natives. I couldn't have done it anyway. I am sorry I didn't at least try. I am not sorry about the Algonquin girls along the Ottawa, nor about Goes Softly and Water Song. I thank you, Lord, for Sara and Petit Étienne. I love them all. Bless them, Lord, and bring them to heaven where I trust I will be.

"My life has not been much like Saint Peter's, but he didn't live among the Huron either. Henry IV had two wives, two mistresses and eleven children by three of them, but you will forgive him because he was a peacemaker. I did not make peace between Iroquois and Huron, but it was not for lack of trying. Now I will die because I wanted peace, and because of the French and their wars of religion.

"Don't blame Champlain, Lord. He was tired and hungry, the scolding would have been forgotten if

His Death

Louis Amantacha had not told the Hurons about it. Ah well. Even when I explained why I wanted peace, they could not comprehend."

Étienne realized he was not afraid. Not of the Huron, and certainly not of le bon Dieu. Not frightened, but tired. Tired of years of poor food and smoke-filled lodges, the plagues of mosquitoes in summer and frostbite in winter, and of an aching back from days and sometimes nights of paddling endless waters.

"Still, I loved those waters, the beauty of the forests, my fine companions. I hope to see my brother-in-law again in Heaven. How good Ahouyoche is, how brave and faithful. Oh Lord, my wife and Petit Étienne – will they die soon, too? Please, Lord, not of hunger or Iroquois torture. Will they be all right?"

No spoken answer came, but the dark of the lodge seemed calm and peaceful and he knew that Marsolet and Grenolle would help his family, too. They would be taken to Québec to live.

He stood up then, feeling clean and free and ready for the blow he knew awaited him just outside the door.

Marsolet's Letter

Ma chère Catherine,

I beg to present myself. I am Nicholas Marsolet, a companion of Étienne on many a long journey. It is my painful duty to inform you that his voyages are over. He is with le bon Dieu where he is happy and warm, safe from all harm. He awaits us in heaven.

I write this through a veil of tears, but I must tell you everything, so that when news reaches you, as it surely will since you are near Paris, you will know as much of the truth as can be known at this time. There is now a French ship at Tadoussac with a sailor on board who has been a good friend to Étienne ever since his voyage to New France in 1608. I think you may have met him because it was probably Jean Girodet who brought you letters from Étienne on other occasions. He will be sure that you receive this letter.

You will wonder how your brother died, and why. I will tell you first that he was killed by the blow of an axe and that it was one of his Huron companions who did it. He was certainly killed instantly. He knew the blow was coming and had time to review his life and ask pardon for any sins he committed.

Now I must tell you why he was killed. As is always the case here in New France, everything is paid for by the fur trade: exploration, missionaries, flour, oil, needles. The war between France and England was just one more struggle to control trade, as far as we here are concerned. As you may know, the English were allied with the Huguenot French, both here and in France. All of us, Champlain included, have worked with the Huguenots for a long time. They had the enthusiasm and the means to develop the fur trade. They allowed Champlain to bring in first Franciscan and later Jesuit missionaries. Neither Étienne nor I had any particular trouble working for and with the Huguenots.

When the brothers Kirke, French Huguenots working for the English, tried to get Champlain to surrender the fortress at Québec in 1628, he refused. They did not know how easy it would be to take the Habitation, and they thought it best to retire.

It is important to remember that during all of the years your brother was in this land, there were never more than one hundred French people at any time. There were only twelve soldiers to defend the fortress at Québec, and they were starving. The Kirkes intercepted a supply ship coming in with desperately needed supplies. They plundered the ship and then sank it.

When the Kirkes returned a year later, there were no more than sixty people remaining with Champlain, and they were reduced to searching the woods for edible roots. Some had taken refuge with the Montagnais, hoping thus to avoid death by starvation. I do not know what became of them and no one else does either.

So it was, that in 1629 the Kirkes needed a guide to sail up the river to Québec. They sought out Étienne as an experienced pilot, and asked Pierre Raye, Le Bailiff and me to accompany them. We were all glad to go because we were anxious to relieve the suffering at Québec. Remember, we knew most of those people well.

Marsolet's Letter

Étienne, Champlain and I were among the eight men who survived the first winter in Québec. Our other twenty companions died and were buried in the snow. I think it is possible that you were never told about the worst of our hardships. That was certainly one of them. Étienne always admired Champlain. I still do.

Naturally, fur traders among the Huron and Algonquin and among the French had paddled down to the Kirkes' ship at Tadoussac and told of the misery at Québec. If we had not arrived when we did, most of those at the Habitation would have died.

The sick and weak inhabitants greeted us with joy, and the Huguenots immediately fed all the people there. Champlain alone was not glad to see us. He believed that somehow the English would be defeated and that France could keep this land. As it happened, we later found that the Kirkes had taken the Habitation a month after the signing of the peace treaty that left New France in French Catholic hands. But none of us knew. No matter who ruled in New France, the people at the Habitation had to have food immediately.

When Champlain was embarked on their ship by the Kirkes for a return voyage to England, he saw fit to give a long harangue, blaming Étienne for the loss of the Habitation, and therefore, for the loss of New France! This was so manifestly unjust that your brother didn't even bother to answer Champlain's charges of "Treason and irreligion".

Remember always, Catherine, that your brother was the first white man to see each of the five Great Lakes. He not only saw them, he canoed around them and mapped two of them. No one knew the rivers better than he, and Champlain always accepted that. We could see how distressed that great man was at the loss of the Habitation that had taken so much work. Étienne and I believed he was most sickened by the belief that he would never find the Northwest Passage now. Hunger, loss and failure had not improved his disposition. I am sure that if Étienne had lived, he and Champlain would have continued their close relationship, exploring and mapping the wilderness and always looking for the Northwest Passage.

It was a common thing for Champlain to accuse Étienne of irreligion because he often ate meat on Fridays and days of fast and abstinence. But your brother rarely knew what day of the week it was!

The scolding was a carry-over from the days when we were boys and Champlain a mature man and our employer. He paid Étienne one hundred pistoles a year, which I understand, he always had sent to you. Your brother made a good living in the fur trade, and he was as intensely interested in exploration as Champlain. They were a good pair, complemented and needed each other.

The sad part of all of Champlain's ranting is that it was heard by Louis Amantacha, a Huron boy who went to France one year with Champlain. He became a Christian there and learned French. Louis Amantacha returned to the Huron lands with Étienne and he gave the account of Champlain's anger because we had taken the Kirkes' English ship to Québec. But the Huron see everything through the eyes of people terrorized by the Iroquois. Treason is to go over to that hated enemy; they would not have given any thought to the French war

Marsolet's Letter

with England when the Iroquois are so near.

I am sure you have heard of Étienne's capture and torture by the Iroquois in 1616. From that time forward, one of his dreams was to bring peace to the Huron and their greatest enemy. A kindly chief of the Iroquois confided to your brother that he, too, wanted to find the path of peace, and between them, and later the chief's son, they did make several small steps in that direction. It would have been suicide to openly espouse peace.

You can compare these wars to the civil wars in France. Nothing of lasting value could be achieved without finding a way to stop the enmity. Both Huron and Iroquois will cheerfully kill anyone in the other group, or anyone allied with their enemy. It is very possible that the Bear Clan suspected Étienne of consorting with the Iroquois. It was known that he was captured and tortured by them, but made friends there, as he always did, wherever he was. Four of their warriors accompanied him out of Iroquoia to protect him!

The Huron are great orators and never give speeches without seriously considering every word. They naturally supposed that the great Champlain did the same. In this instance, they were mistaken. It is well known that the Iroquois are allies of the English as the Huron are of the French. So when a man living among them was called a traitor by the great white chief, the idea festered and grew.

After returning to Huronia, your brother did not stay long at the village in Toanché but left on his usual trading expeditions and had only recently returned to

Toanché. During his trial he stayed with the Huron captain, Aenons, and his family. Aenons remained his friend and insists to this day that he had nothing to do with Étienne's murder. But he could do nothing to stop it once it was agreed upon in council by the Bear Clan. Étienne's friend, Grenolle, with whom he traveled to the Grand Lac, believes that Étienne was killed from behind with one blow of the hatchet a form of execution.

Now that Champlain is back at the Habitation, and the French are in command again, the Huron feared they would be punished for their continued close relationship with your brother. There is reason to suppose that they were immediately sorry for their wicked deed and it is obvious to me that Champlain was saddened.

Étienne is buried near the village of Toanché, and now the missionaries will return and will give your dear brother Christian burial as they take up their missions again in New France.

I will remain at the Habitation and at Tadoussac except for trading expeditions. Champlain doesn't seem to remember how severely he scolded us, and I would not remember either if it were not for the unexpected and tragic result.

Write to me here and send the letter with Jean Girodet and perhaps I can tell you later where Étienne's wife and children are and what they plan to do. I believe they are in one of the Huron villages, perhaps even Toanché, and they are safe there.

With affection,
Nicholas Marsolet

Printed in the United States
20316LVS00001B/50